AMERICAN LEGENDS COLLECTION,
BOOK 5

CHARLIE RED

MICHAEL ZIMMER

FIVE STAR

A part of Gale, Cengage Learning

GALE
CENGAGE Learning®

Farmington Hills, Mich • San Francisco • New York • Waterville, Maine
Meriden, Conn • Mason, Ohio • Chicago

GALE
CENGAGE Learning®

LIBRARY OF CONGRESS CATALOGING-IN-PUBLICATION DATA

Names: Zimmer, Michael, 1955– author.
Title: Charlie Red / Michael Zimmer.
Description: First edition. | Waterville, Maine : Five Star Publishing, a part of Cengage Learning, Inc. [2016] | Series: American Legends Collection ; Book 5
Identifiers: LCCN 2015047691| ISBN 9781432832292 (hardcover) | ISBN 1432832298 (hardcover)
Subjects: LCSH: Stagecoach robberies—Fiction. | Outlaws—Fiction. | BISAC: FICTION / Historical. | FICTION / Westerns. | GSAFD: Western stories.
Classification: LCC PS3576.I467 C48 2016 | DDC 813/.54—dc23
LC record available at http://lccn.loc.gov/2015047691

First Edition. First Printing: June 2016
Find us on Facebook– https://www.facebook.com/FiveStarCengage
Visit our website– http://www.gale.cengage.com/fivestar/
Contact Five Star™ Publishing at FiveStar@cengage.com

Printed in the United States of America
1 2 3 4 5 6 7 20 19 18 17 16

FOREWORD:
THE AMERICAN LEGENDS
COLLECTIONS

During the Great Depression of the 1930s, nearly one quarter of the American workforce was unemployed. Facing the possibility of economic and government collapse, President Franklin Roosevelt initiated the New Deal program, a desperate bid to get the country back on its feet.

The largest of these programs was the Works Progress Administration (WPA), which focused primarily on manual labor with the construction of bridges, highways, schools, and parks across the country. But the WPA also included a provision for the nation's unemployed artists, called the Federal Arts Project, and within its umbrella, the Federal Writers Project (FWP). At its peak, the FWP put to work approximately 6,500 men and women.

During the FWP's earliest years, the focus was on a series of state guidebooks, but in the late 1930s, the project created what has been called a "hidden legacy" of America's past—more than 10,000 life stories gleaned from men and women across the nation.

Although these life histories, a part of the Folklore Project within the FWP, were meant to eventually be published in a series of anthologies, that goal was effectively halted by the United States' entry into World War II. Most of these histories are currently located within the Library of Congress in Washington, DC.

As the Federal Writers Project was an arm of the larger Arts Project, so too was the Folklore Project a subsidiary of the FWP. An even lesser-known branch of the Folklore Project was the American Legends Collection (ALC), created in 1936, and managed from 1936 to 1941 by a small staff from the University of Indiana. The ALC was officially closed in early 1942, another casualty of the war effort.

While the Folklore Project's goal was to capture everyday life in America, the ALC's purpose was the acquisition of as many "incidental" histories from our nation's past as possible. Unfortunately, the bulk of the American Legends Collection was lost due to manpower shortages caused by the war.

The only remaining interviews known to exist from the ALC are those located within the A. C. Thorpe Papers at the Bryerton Library in Indiana. These are carbons only, as the original transcripts were turned in to the offices of the FWP in November 1941.

Andrew Charles Thorpe was unique among those scribes put into employment by the FWP-ALC in that he recorded his interviews with an Edison Dictaphone. These discs, a precursor to the LP records of a later generation, were found sealed in a vault shortly after Thorpe's death in 2006. Of the eighty-some interviews discovered therein, most were conducted between the years 1936 and 1939. They offer an unparalleled view of both a time (1864 to 1916) and place (Florida to Nevada, Montana to Texas) within the United States' singular history.

The editor of this volume is grateful to the current executor of the A. C. Thorpe Estate for his assistance in reviewing these papers, and to the descendants of Mr. Thorpe for their co-operation in allowing these transcripts to be brought into public view.

An explanation should be made at this point that, although minor additions to the text were made to enhance its readability, no facts were altered. Any mistakes or misrepresentations resulting from these changes are solely the responsibility of the editor.

Leon Michaels
January 21, 2014

Revenge is a curious thing. So is love, for that matter. Both figure prominently in the story of Charlie Red.

A lot of people, when they first hear about Charlie, they'll look at me like I'm either crazy or lying. Eventually, if they know me, they'll believe me, as I'm not a man to spin a windy on a whim. And on those rare occasions when I do fib, you can bet your bankroll it'll be outlandish enough that folks will know I'm joshing them. Crazy is a matter of opinion that I'll leave up to you to decide.

As far as outlandish, what I'm going to tell you about Charlie Red ranks right up there, which is why I haven't told this story to anyone in more years than I care to count. I suppose I got tired of the looks on the faces of the people who didn't know me. People who would walk away shaking their heads as if pitying a senile old man's attempt at humor. And I guess, when you get right down to it, that's why I reacted the way I did when you phoned last week, telling me you wanted to record the story for that government writers' project you're working on. Even after I cooled down and told you I'd do the interview, I almost called you back later to say I'd changed my mind. It was only after I thought about it for a while that I decided I wanted to tell the story one last time. I wanted to get it down on paper, or at least onto one of your recording disks. The truth of what happened out there ought to survive after I'm gone, along with the memory of Charlie Red. I don't think that's too much to ask, considering all the hell we tore loose across western Arizona in his name.

Before I can tell you about Charlie Red, though, I need to tell you about the circumstances that threw me into his story at such a critical point. You already know this happened in the summer of 1882, when I was riding shotgun for the Colorado and Prescott Stagecoach Company, out of Ehrenberg. I say "riding shotgun" because that's what most people call it today, but those of us who were in the business preferred the title of "express messenger," or "messenger," although I suppose when you slice it open and look inside, it amounts to the same thing—a heavily armed guard riding atop a rocking stagecoach next to the driver, constantly scanning the land in every direction for signs of an ambush. Robbing stagecoaches was a popular occupation for a lot of Arizona hard cases in those early territorial days, and the Colorado and Prescott attracted its fair share of stickup artists over the years.

For me, this all started in early June, a Friday if I recall correctly. I'd gotten down to the C&P offices before sunup that day, and I still remember how pleasantly cool the morning had been, although there was a stiff breeze out of the southwest that promised soaring temperatures before we got too far down the pike. Ira Tucker managed the Ehrenberg office in those years. He was a middle-aged man with thick black hair, brooding eyes, and a mustache chewed ragged and thin from the anxieties of his job. He was standing above his desk, shuffling through stacks of papers when I walked in. His glance was brief, his greeting curt—just my name.

"Slade."

My reply was equally laconic. "Ira," I said, then walked over to the little railed-off alcove in the far corner where Coltrane kept a desk, a file cabinet, and a locked gun rack bolted to the adobe wall. It might surprise you to know that, although I rode shotgun for the Colorado and Prescott, my employer was Coltrane Brothers, Limited, out of San Francisco.

Coltrane was an express company, like Wells Fargo before they started stagecoaching, or American Express before they got into banking and traveler's checks. The way it worked was, when a company or government entity wanted to transport any kind of commodity that needed to be insured against theft or damage, their simplest and usually best option was to go through an express company. It was the express company's job to deliver the merchandise on time and without damage. Or in the case of gold shipments, bank transfers, and company payrolls, without losing the money to road agents. That's where I came in. Well, me and a double-barreled Parker 12-gauge, shortened to twenty-four inches by the firm of A. J. Plate, out of San Francisco.

Coltrane issued its largest contracts from either the home office in San Francisco or from one of their district offices scattered throughout the Intermountain West. The Ehrenberg office was a regional bureau, one of the company's smaller ones, under the jurisdiction of a district office in Prescott. Although Martin Coltrane—the oldest of the three Coltrane boys who'd taken over after the old man retired—had kept a superintendent at Ehrenberg for a while, he eventually contracted the position to Colorado and Prescott, which had then dumped the responsibility directly onto Ira Tucker's already harried shoulders. Now Ira worked for both C&P and Coltrane, but got his paycheck from C&P, while mine came monthly from Coltrane, out of California.

That probably sounds a lot more confusing than it really is, and it needn't be. As far as the Charlie Red story is concerned, all you need to remember is that I was riding shotgun on the Friday, June 2nd stage out of Ehrenberg, bound for Prescott, Arizona Territory, two hard days' drive to the northeast.

The key to the Coltrane gun rack was in the top right-hand drawer of the alcove desk. It took only a second to free the Parker from its assigned notch alongside two other shotguns and a '73 Winchester. After relocking the gate, I tossed the key back into the drawer, slapped that closed with my knee, then pulled a box of double-ought buckshot from a shelf under the rack.

"Who's driving today?" I asked as I opened the Parker's breech.

Ira didn't even look up. "Driscoll."

I nodded to myself as I dropped a couple of brass shells down the 12-gauge's twin tubes. Pete Driscoll was an experienced linesman who'd started his career driving for the old Hockaday Line out of Independence, Missouri, in the late '50s, although since then he'd driven for companies all across the West. I liked Pete. He was a keen-eyed old codger and fun to have a drink with of an evening after work, although he didn't talk much once he had his team in motion. Most drivers didn't, I'd learned. They liked to keep their focus on the hitch, and the road in front of them, and let the passengers do the conversing.

After closing the breech and setting the Parker's hammers to half cock for safety, I strode back outside. The sky was still dove-wing gray with dawn, although growing brighter by the minute. I paused at the edge of the boardwalk to have a look around. I could make out my reflection in the window of the old Goldwater mercantile across the street. In that old-time glass, my profile was wavy and out of proportion—a four-foot chest balanced atop stumps for legs. In reality I was twenty-six years old that summer, just a shade under six feet tall and generally quick on my feet, if I hadn't spent too much time at Molly Herriman's Saloon, down on the river. My hair was sandy-colored and close-cropped for the times, my eyes light green beneath thin brows. My nose hadn't been broken then, and jutted out straight and slim above a neatly trimmed mustache of the same tawny hue as on my head.

My dress was proper for the position. A plain suit of dark broadcloth—trousers, vest, and jacket—a white linen shirt, and a gray silk ascot that I'd shove into my warbag as soon as we were out of town. Or out of Ira Tucker's view, whichever came first. My hat was black with a flat crown and a broad, pencil-curled brim, my boots low-heeled and comfortable under a pale coating of Ehrenberg dust. I was wearing a sidearm, of course—we all did in those days—and I had a second, shorter-barreled revolver tucked into a shoulder holster under my left arm. Both handguns were Smith and Wessons, chambered in .45 Schofield.

The dark suit and ascot—especially the ascot—were Coltrane hallmarks, and not something I would have worn of my own accord. The ascot included a solid gold stickpin embossed with a stylized "C" as a kind of company logo that they added to all their property, which I suppose is what they considered me. You'd see it on the tops of strongboxes and letterheads, and they even had it burned into the Parker's walnut stock, beside its inventory number.

I didn't mind the suit, even though it was hot for that Southwestern climate, but the ascot was an altogether different animal. I think I speak for most of the company's messengers when I say wearing a tie was about as painful as wearing a brand. In all the years I rode for Coltrane Brothers Limited, I didn't know a single messenger who kept his in place once they were in the field. I know I sure didn't.

Despite the early hour, there were quite a few people out and about, trying to complete as many chores as possible before it got too hot. Ehrenberg was a bustling little town in those days, although largely unimpressive except for the sprawling, riverside warehouses just south of town. Those low-ceilinged adobe structures were usually crammed to the rafters with merchandise—both civilian and military—bound for Arizona's interior. Ehrenberg was a port city on the Colorado River, the first dump north of Yuma, and, in 1882, the quickest and most direct route to the territorial capital at Prescott. [*Editor's Note:* A dump is an antiquated Western definition for an off-loading location for steamship companies; as used by Slade, it has its roots in military nomenclature.]

There wasn't a tree in sight in Ehrenberg, not even along the river, and precious little grass for the town's livestock. Most of the feed had to be hauled in from elsewhere. The buildings were either flat-roofed adobe or flat-roofed brush and mud *jacales,* and local businesses catered more to the wayfarer passing through than the town's five hundred or so permanent residents. An intense desert heat was a fact of life in Ehrenberg. So was dust, which often ran ankle-deep in the middle of the street, where wheeled traffic kept it ground to a fine powder. Missus Aretha Holmes, who ran the boarding house where I lived and did my laundry for a small additional charge, complained that you couldn't hang a wet shirt on the line without mud collecting in the creases before it dried.

Some of Ehrenberg's more profitable businesses featured verandahs across the front of their buildings, which helped keep some of the grit outside, and also discouraged sidewinders from crawling indoors, seeking shelter from the sun. The C&P office had one, the walk constructed of pine planks freighted down out of the northern mountains, the roof from the springy ribs of saguaro cactus that provided only an illusion of shade. I moved to one of the verandah's outer posts and leaned into it with my shoulder, the Parker's muzzles sloped casually toward the ground.

We were waiting for the *Barbara Kay,* due in that morning from Yuma. The *Barbara Kay* was a sternwheeler, capable of shipping fifty tons of cargo during the high-water season. On this particular upstream voyage, she was also carrying $45,000 in payroll for the Bradshaw Mountain mines, south of Prescott. She had been due in the night before, but got hung up on a sandbar about ten miles downriver, and lost a couple of hours prying herself back into deep water; this according to a Papago runner the *Barbara Kay*'s skipper had sent ahead after the ship tied up for the night rather than risk coming on in after dark. I could see the smoke from the *Barbara Kay*'s stacks even as I stepped outside, and had barely made myself comfortable against the post when the clear, piercing screech of her whistle cleaved the quiet morning air, bringing heads up and to the south all along the street.

Ira Tucker's boots thumped across the floor behind me as he came to the door for a look. He didn't say anything, and I didn't turn around or acknowledge his presence. He went back inside, and a few seconds later I heard the rear door open. Ira's voice, calling for the tenders to get the teams hitched and the stagecoach ready to roll, and for Robles to bring the small wagon around front, sounded miles-distant as it echoed back through the C&P office. He returned a few minutes later, but again stopped at the door.

"You got plenty of shells?" he asked.

"Twenty rounds on me and a full box in my warbag," I replied.

After a pause, he said: "Better take along some extra."

I turned partway around, giving him a questioning look.

"That Papago that came in last night brought some correspondence with him, including a letter from the Yuma office. There's talk the Apaches are stirring again."

"The Apaches are always stirring," I reminded him.

"These might be Tontos, closer to home than Geronimo's bunch down on the border. Sanders ought to have better information, if better is available."

Sanders was Captain Jared Sanders, skipper of the *Barbara Kay,* and Ira was probably right about him having the latest information. If anyone had reliable news on the rumors that were always floating up and down the Lower Colorado River, it would be him.

Ira went back inside, and I soon heard the rattle of the chain on the C&P gun rack behind the ticket counter—another example of two companies operating out of the same office. Both furnished long guns for their employees. The C&P rack held an assortment of rifles and shotguns, most of the latter being sawed-off coach guns with barrels under sixteen inches, but Coltrane insisted its messengers be armed with longer weapons. I preferred the Parker's twenty-four-inch barrels myself, mostly for the added range, although I also appreciated its better balance.

Ira came back outside a few minutes later, snugging a gun-belt around his waist, a stubby coach gun tucked inside the crook of his left arm. We could see the *Barbara Kay* by then, its single wheel churning the already-muddy waters of the Colorado to a deep umber. Black smoke coiled from her stacks like curly pigtails, and her forward deck was lined with passengers eager to escape the ship's cargo-cramped decks.

A couple of soldiers from a small bivouac near the dump were already standing at the river's edge, ready to catch the wrist-thick hawsers the *Barbara Kay*'s crew would toss to them when the vessel drew close. A whiskered sergeant was overseeing the preparations, ready to accept the army's share of the *Barbara Kay*'s freight. After off-loading a portion of her lading at Ehrenberg, the *Barbara Kay* would continue on upriver to its northernmost port at Hardyville, while the sergeant escorted his small train of half a dozen blue-painted military wagons northeast over the Prescott Road to Fort Whipple.

Ira and I waited on the verandah until Antonio Robles

brought the small wagon around. I'm calling it a wagon because that's what Ira called it, but it was really a rubber-tired carriage, a twin-seater with a black leather top that could be pivoted up from the rear to provide shade for its passengers. I think it annoyed Ira more than he'd ever admit to have such a vehicle in his fleet, a conveyance he considered much too natty for frontier use. I noticed when Robles drove the carriage out of the alley between the C&P's main office and a feed and grain importer to our west, its top was down, in accordance with Ira's instructions that it always remain hidden behind the rear seat unless one of its passengers was female. That may sound illogical in a land where summer temperatures could climb above a hundred twenty degrees, but it was a decree Ira remained adamant about for as long as he managed the Ehrenberg office.

Robles hauled up in front of the C&P, and Ira and I climbed in. It was a five-minute ride to the levee. We made the drive in silence, Robles handling the lines. The *Barbara Kay* was just starting its back-paddle when we got there, the pilot bringing the bulky craft gently alongside the bank. The ship's captain stood atop the hurricane deck as the stern began its inward swing, calling commands to the crew below through a megaphone, now and again offering advice to the helmsman through the open window of the pilothouse. Ira and I climbed down from the wagon, but remained well back from the landing until the ship was secured and the gangplank lowered. One of the soldiers immediately started up the plank toward the main deck, until an angry bellow from the ship's captain drove him back.

"McMurphy, get yer tail over here," the sergeant shouted, and the chastised trooper quickly jumped to the muddy ground at the river's edge.

At my side, Ira chuckled in approval of the captain's strict command of his vessel. Jared Sanders ran a tight ship and would tolerate no breach of protocol, which included allowing anyone to board his craft without permission.

After a brief moment spent glaring daggers after the retreating trooper, Sanders motioned for Ira and me to come aboard. Meanwhile, the *Barbara Kay*'s first mate was making his way down the gangplank to meet the Fort Whipple sergeant. They'd off-load the army's cargo at midship, using block and tackle for the heavier crates.

Sanders met us at the head of the stairs to the boiler deck, smiling graciously as he shook Ira's hand, then tossing me a quick nod. I knew from past encounters that, in the captain's eyes, a messenger didn't rate the same level of courtesy as a head of a regional office, although his aloofness never bothered me. I've dealt with men like Jared Sanders all my life and learned to let their arrogance roll off my shoulders like a summer rain.

While Ira and Sanders spoke quietly between themselves, I stood at the railing, staring down at the passengers gathered near the head of the gangplank. I was looking for anything out of the ordinary, but saw nothing that concerned me.

"Slade," Ira said after a moment, and I turned away from the rail. Farther up the deck, a tall man in a simple black suit nearly identical to my own was standing in the open door of the forward-most cabin, gray ascot and gold stickpin neatly in place. He was holding a shotgun in both hands, and looked mean enough to use it without discretion.

Stepping past Ira, I moved cautiously forward. Harlan Price was tall and scarecrow-thin, with a face that might have been molded out of lava. His hair was jet black, his eyes dark and dead-looking. I noticed a fresh scar under his left eye, the skin still tender against the weathered darkness of his cheek, and found myself wondering who had put it there and what Harlan's opponent looked like afterward. Although Harlan and I were supposed to be on the same team, I was never quite sure of my standing with the lanky messenger. He was one of those men who always seemed vaguely put out with the world, and in all the time I knew him, I never saw him smile. Not once.

I probably ought to explain that the money I was escorting to Prescott had originated out of San Francisco, most of it coming from the Granite Lady herself, which is what we used to call the US Treasury building before the federal government moved her to its new location last year. [*Editor's Note:* One of only a handful of buildings to survive the infamous 1906 San Francisco earthquake, the Granite Lady served as a branch of the United States Mint from 1874 to 1937; the original San Francisco mint was opened in 1854, in response to the Gold Rush of 1849.]

A Coltrane messenger had picked up the payroll at the Lady several days before, then escorted it south to San Diego aboard a coastline clipper. In San Diego, he'd turned the money over to the Southern California regional office, where a manager had assigned another messenger to take it inland over the Southern Pacific Railroad as far as Yuma. From Yuma, Harlan Price had brought it north to Ehrenberg, where Ira would accept delivery. Ira would then turn it over to me to take it on into Prescott, where it would be delivered to the payroll superintendents of the various mining companies that were waiting there for it. From that point on, it would be out of Coltrane hands.

As I made my way forward, Harlan was watching me real close, making no effort to hide his distrust. When I look back on the guy now, I sometimes wonder if he wasn't half a bubble off plumb. He was a good man for the job, though. I believe I'd rather try to wrestle supper away from a grizzly bear than attempt to lift a nickel off of some payroll Harlan Price was guarding.

"Howdy, Harlan," I said when I drew near.

19

He made a motion with his shotgun. "That's close enough, Slade."

I nodded and stopped and glanced behind me to where the *Barbara Kay*'s second mate had appeared with a clipboard and fountain pen. Sanders slid a sheet of paper from the top of the stack and signed his name to the bottom. Ira signed a second sheet that he and Sanders exchanged, then the captain and the second mate moved off. Ira came over with a pair of documents clutched in one hand, the Coltrane Brothers Limited name and logo emblazoned across the top.

"Got your slips, Price?" Ira asked gruffly, a lot less tolerant of the guard's surly attitude than I was.

Reaching inside his jacket, the dark-eyed messenger brought out yet another form, and he and Ira quickly completed the transfer. After stepping forward to sign my own John Hancock to a fourth document, the deed was done. Harlan backed out of the doorway and Ira and I entered. The strongbox sat on the floor beside an unmade bed, its solid oak construction reinforced with twin iron straps. A heavy lock was inlaid in the front panel, its surface etched with the same ornate letter "C" as our stickpins. Empty, that box weighed twenty pounds or more. It would be quite a bit heavier with $45,000 in coin and paper bundled inside.

"Give me a hand, Price," Ira said over his shoulder, and Harlan shifted his shotgun to his left hand so that he could pick up one end of the chest with his right.

I moved outside, my nerves taut as I surveyed the crowd below. No one seemed to be paying us any mind, but I still had that antsy feeling I always got when moving something valuable from one secure location to another. I led the little party along the hurricane deck to the companionway, and was reaching for the top step when a shout from below sent a jolt of alarm slamming up my spine. I swayed back, instinctively shoving Ira,

Harlan, and the strongbox against a stateroom wall even as I brought the Parker partway to my shoulder.

"Easy, Slade," Ira said. "It's just Granger."

"I can see that," I replied irritably.

Ed Granger lived on the Colorado River's shore, in a grass wickiup similar to what the Yavapais and Mohaves used. He owned a small skiff that he'd brought in from God-knows-where and regularly fished the waters around Ehrenberg, netting an assortment of chub, razorback, squawfish, and other species that he sold to the town's three restaurants and most of its permanent residents. Hunting along that section of the Colorado was a poor proposition, and unless you could develop a taste for rattlesnake or grasshoppers, it was generally cheaper to eat fish. Cattle hadn't yet come into the valley in any substantial numbers, and I doubted that they ever would, as skimpy as the graze was.

Ed was standing on the bank, shouting and waving his arms to attract Sanders's attention.

"What does that old coot want?" Harlan demanded, peering over my shoulder.

"His boat pulled loose a couple of days ago," Ira explained. "He's been looking for it ever since. I guess he's hoping someone spotted it downstream."

"He says it was stolen," I added.

Ira snorted dismissively. "Ed Granger spends too much time in the sun. Nobody's going to steal a sieve like that old bucket of his unless they have plans to drown themselves."

I shrugged but didn't argue. A lot of people shared Ira's opinion of Ed Granger, but I wasn't one of them. I considered the man eccentric, rather than daft, although I suppose there's often a fine line between the two.

"Let's go," I said, moving back to the companionway, then down to the boiler deck. Ira and Harlan stayed close behind all the way, the sluggish sway of the strongbox revealing its weight. Although the sun had just risen above the Dome Rock Mountains in the east, sweat was already glistening on Ira's face, and the tendons in Harlan's neck were standing out like bones on a starving hound. We paused briefly on the lower deck while Sanders had some of his crew clear the gangplank for us, then crossed to solid ground. Robles was waiting in the front seat of the company wagon at the end of the plank, the lines to his team in one hand, his own scattergun in the other. Ed Granger stood nearby, looking distraught. I suspect his conversation with the *Barbara Kay*'s skipper had been short and unproductive.

It took only moments to slide the strongbox onto the floor of the rear seat. Harlan and I climbed in after it, flanking the box on either side, while Ira moved up front with Robles—four heavily armed men without a hint of lenity among us. The crowd, already thinning, didn't waste time getting out of our path, and we rolled into town at a swift trot.

The C&P tenders had brought the stagecoach around while Ira and I were collecting the strongbox, and were already stowing the passengers' luggage inside the rear boot. Robles brought his rig to a stop next to the coach and I quickly jumped down, then scrambled into the driver's box to raise the lid on the journey chest.

If you've never heard of a journey chest, don't fret, and don't waste time looking for a description in any of Daniel Webster's dictionaries, because I doubt you'd find reference to it there or anywhere else.

The journey chest was my own creation, and one I was mighty proud of. I'd gotten the idea some years earlier of building a solidly mounted trunk under the driver's seat to replace the smaller jockey box already there, but with a lock and keys only the regional managers would have copies of. The box would be just large enough to accommodate an average-sized Coltrane strongbox, yet incapable of being "thrown down" at some road agent's command, since it would be bolted solidly to the rear panel of the front boot. Like the strongbox itself, iron straps were added for reinforcement, and to prevent some determined highwayman from trying to open the heavy oak chest with an ax.

Even the normally unimpressionable Ira Tucker had perked up when I introduced the idea to him. He'd immediately sent word to the district office in Prescott, requesting permission to install them on both of the C&P coaches under his jurisdiction. Approval had come down the pike on the next southbound stage, and the company eventually added them to all of its coaches. [*Editor's Note:* In 1882, the Colorado and Prescott Stagecoach Company owned eight coaches, and maintained a twice-weekly run between Ehrenberg and Prescott, Hardyville and Prescott, and Phoenix and Prescott; it also ran a once-per-week stage over the newly opened road to Flagstaff; a jockey box is similar to the glove box in a modern automobile, a place to store gloves or small tools for repairing harness, etc.; no data could be found on the dimensions of an "average-sized Coltrane strongbox," but its construction was probably similar to those used by other express companies, approximately twenty by twelve by eight inches; it is interesting to note that Slade describes a wooden strongbox; by the 1880s, most were made of iron.]

With the strongbox tucked safely inside the journey chest, I snapped the lock closed and handed the key to Ira. I think we all breathed a little easier after that. With a brief salute, Harlan Price turned up the street, probably in search of breakfast—he would stay with the *Barbara Kay* all the way to Hardyville, then back to Yuma—while Ira went inside to secure the key in a small safe behind the ticket counter. I'd left my warbag on the verandah outside the office earlier, and one of the tenders was kind enough to hand it up to me. I stowed the flat-bottomed portmanteau under the seat, wedging it between the outside wall of the front box and the journey chest. Then I settled back with one foot braced against the footboard, the Parker resting across my lap where it would be handy in case of trouble.

Pete Driscoll had been out front with his team all this time, talking to the more fractious of the six animals in an effort to keep them calm, checking the harness for small tears or weak seams, adjusting a bit here, a headstall there. Like I said earlier, Pete was an old-time linesmen; very little got past his keen eye.

Ira returned a few minutes later. While the tenders rolled the leather cover down over the rear boot to strap it in place and Pete continued talking to his mules, Ira climbed partway up the side of the coach, standing with one foot on the hub, the other dangling in midair.

"A light load," Ira observed.

I glanced toward the knot of passengers waiting in the shade of the verandah. There were six—three men, a woman, and two small children—one of those a boy of eight or so, the other a girl a year or two younger. I've been on runs with as many as a dozen passengers riding along, including the more adventurous types who would perch among the baggage on top like whiskered nestlings, so a light load suited me fine. It was less strain on the team, and made it easier for me to keep an eye on everyone.

"The woman is Missus Emma Rhodes," Ira went on. "She's joining her husband in Phoenix, with a connection through Prescott. The kids are hers. The two men standing off to the side are officials with one of the Bradshaw mines, a Mister Brown and Mister Trepan. They came in on the *Barbara Kay*, but if they know about the payroll, they haven't mentioned it to me. You know Garrett."

Dan Garrett was a drummer representing some of the bigger clothing companies along the East Coast. He made this run three or four times a year, a gregarious man of ample proportions, with a fondness for food and whiskey, although he was good about honoring the C&P's policy of not drinking inside a coach.

Brown and Trepan looked like mine officials, lean, rugged men in durable business suits, each of them toting a sturdy cloth valise. Both wore revolvers with an ease that suggested they knew how to use them, not all that surprising when you consider a lot of those managers started out grubbing in the dirt as common tinpans.

Missus Rhodes looked to be in her late twenties, attractive but nervous in a way that made me suspect this might be her first time traveling alone, and that she would be glad to get to wherever it was she was going.

"What did Sanders have to say about Indian trouble?" I asked Ira.

"Nothing more than we already knew. He'll talk to the commander at Fort Mohave, and take a report back to the military at Fort Yuma, but he seemed to think that if there was any real trouble, the Mohave commander would have sent a dispatch rider south with a warning."

Pete gave his near wheeler an affectionate slap on the hip, then moved back along the coach in his rolling, bow-legged gait. He was a short, knobby man with gray hair, a sparse beard, and work-scarred hands that looked large in comparison to his frame. Drawing his wages from C&P instead of Coltrane Brothers Limited, Pete wasn't hampered by any arbitrary mandate regarding dress, and wore comfortable range clothes instead of dark broadcloth—sturdy trousers, a cotton shirt under a light canvas vest, and a sweat-stained hat with a wide, soft brim.

"Best be getting inside, folks," he told his passengers. "We'll be pulling out in a couple of minutes."

Ira gave me a measured look before jumping down. "Keep an eye on the horizon, Slade. The thought of a bunch of Apaches running loose out there worries me about as much as all that money tucked inside the journey chest."

I didn't reply. Staying sharp until my cargo was safely delivered was my job. I didn't need a desk wrangler telling me how to do it.

Pete helped the woman inside, then saw that the kids were settled next to her. Leaving the men to find their own way aboard, he came around the coach and climbed into the driver's box, one cheek bulging around a fresh wad of tobacco.

"They about ready?" Pete asked as he accepted his lines from a tender.

I leaned over the side as the door was being slammed shut behind the last man. Watching from the verandah, Ira called: "All set down here."

"Looks like we're ready to roll," I told Pete.

The older man nodded, took a moment to thread the lines between his callused fingers—a single rein to each of the six snaffle bits—then used his foot to release the brake that sloped up along the right-hand side of the coach.

"Pulling out!" he shouted, and the tender who had been standing between the two leaders quickly jumped out of the way. Pete yelled sharp and the mules dug in. The stage lurched and rocked, and I bit back the grin that always wanted to spread across my face whenever we got underway. I'll tell you right now, I never got tired of riding the coaches. Even that same brutal route between Ehrenberg and Prescott—once a week for three years straight—would always bring a smile to my face, make my pulse surge a little stronger.

Pete swung the rig into the middle of the street and shook out the lines, and the mules settled into one of those swift, walking trots that really eat up the miles without being overly taxing on either the team or the coach. You'll notice I didn't mention the passengers. That's because, as far as the C&P was concerned, the comfort of the company's human cargo was well down on its list of priorities. The livestock came first and foremost. Then the coaches and harness, followed only then by the drivers and tenders. Being a Coltrane employee, I fell in somewhere below the tenders but still above the passengers, for without a government mail contract, the C&P depended heavily upon its association with the various express companies. Passenger service alone never paid enough to keep a staging company afloat.

It doesn't take long to leave a town like Ehrenberg, its main street not much more than a small-bore rifle shot from one end to the other. We'd barely gotten underway—in fact, I'd hardly gotten my ascot off—when Pete nudged me with his elbow and nodded toward a livery on the south side of the street.

"See 'em?" he asked.

"Those two jaspers standing inside the entryway?"

"Uh-huh. New faces, I'd allow."

I gave Pete a questioning look as I slipped the folded piece of gray silk with its accompanying stickpin under the flap of my warbag. New faces were hardly a novelty in Ehrenberg, the town being a major jumping-off point for a lot of those small mining camps that dotted western Arizona. "What was it about those two that caught your eye?" I asked curiously.

"Saw 'em earlier. They was walking up from the *Barbara Kay*, both of 'em looking as hound-eyed as a Bible thumper in a deserted saloon. They was around while we was loadin' up, too."

"Doing what?"

"Watching." He shrugged, then leaned to the side to arch a brown stream of tobacco spit over the thin fan of dust kicked up by the coach's iron-rimmed front wheel. "Just watchin'," he added, then leaned back in his seat and braced the worn heel of his boot against the brake lever.

Taking a final, rearward gander, I'll admit to a twinge of uneasiness when I spotted those same two gents, standing at the edge of the street now, free of the livery's shadow as they watched us roll out of town.

SESSION TWO

It was just shy of twenty miles from Ehrenberg to our first stop at Tyson's Well. Twenty miles is an easy, four-hour run on a good road, but for us it was closer to six because of that long, arduous climb to the top of the Dome Rock Mountains. Traveling west to east, it isn't a steep ascent, but it is a hard, steady pull, with very few flat stretches over a road that was rutted and rock-strewn. That's why the C&P used mules going both ways over the Dome, and didn't switch to horses until east of Desert Wells.

Pete pulled up on top like he always did to give his team a chance to catch its wind. After locking the brake, he sat there staring out over the valley far below. There hadn't been a breath of air coming up the Dome, but a nice breeze was stirring at the pass, and the mules were tossing their heads in appreciation of the cooling zephyrs. After taking a moment to enjoy the view, Pete splattered a nearby rock with tobacco spit, then climbed down from his seat and pulled the coach door open.

"We'll be stoppin' here a few minutes to let the animals rest," he informed his passengers. "Might be a good time to get out and stretch your limbs, if you're of a notion."

"How far until our next official stop, Mister Driscoll?" Emma Rhodes asked.

"I'm afraid that'll be a few hours yet, ma'am. I'm sorry for the inconvenience, but we have to build our stations where there's water, and that won't be until Tyson's Well, on down to the bottom of these here hills."

"Yes, I understand. Thank you." Extending a gloved hand, she allowed the old linesman to help her to the ground. The kids came next. The girl looked tired and grumpy and sleep-rumpled, but the boy piled out like a bronc from its chute, scampering toward a jumble of nearby rocks.

"Hey, get back here," one of the mine managers shouted, leaping from the coach to race after the kid.

Emma Rhodes gasped, but Pete assured her that it was all right.

"Mister Trepan is only thinking of your son's safety, ma'am. There's rattlesnakes and Gila monsters and such in a lot of these rocks, and it wouldn't do for the lad to run into one."

Pete's description of the terrain's less-obvious dangers brought another anxious gasp from the woman, and she rushed forward to grab the boy's hand as Trepan returned with the youth in tow. "Jeffrey, you stay near me, and don't go bolting off like that," she scolded.

Trepan smiled consolingly. "I didn't mean to startle you, Missus Rhodes, but I've been stung by whiptails, and it is painful. A Gila monster or rattler could prove fatal to one so young as your son." [*Editor's Note:* Whiptail is regional slang for scorpions.]

"That is quite all right, Mister Trepan, and I thank you for your swift action. Are . . . are there such creatures near Phoenix, as well?"

"I'm afraid so," he replied. "You'll need to be watchful."

"It ain't nothing folks out here don't deal with regular," Pete amended, giving the mine manager a chiding glance. "Just takes getting used to. Matter of fact, if you and your young ones'd like to step off behind those boulders yonder for any reason, I suspect you'd be safe enough. Just watch where you step or put your hands."

"Yes, thank you, Mister Driscoll. I believe we will seek a moment's privacy, if there's time."

"Plenty of time, ma'am," Pete replied, then doffed his hat and moved forward to check on his mules.

With the coach stopped, Trepan, Brown, and Garrett wandered into the rocks on the other side of the rig. I stayed up top, my gaze roaming. Messengers generally didn't like unscheduled stops, and I was no exception, especially with so many hiding places within easy rifle range. But we all understood the importance of a strong team, too, and Pete's mules needed a few minutes to recover after their strenuous climb.

Even with young Jeffrey Rhodes's brief distraction, we were rolling again in under ten minutes. Pete's foot worked the brake with a delicate skill as we began our descent. The grade was steeper going down, the road just as treacherous, littered with small boulders that had rolled down from the surrounding slopes and deep ruts that ran like shallow streams in rainy weather. Making matters worse was that it was coming onto midday, and it was really starting to warm up. It would be a lot worse before summer's end, of course, but even in early June, the temperature in that part of Arizona will often flirt with the century mark.

We were two hours coming down the east side of the Dome in the Concord. [*Editor's Note:* The Concord stagecoach was produced by the firm of Abbot and Downing (later Abbot, Downing & Company), of Concord, New Hampshire; famed most for the smoothness of its ride, the Concord was sold throughout North America, as well as in such far-flung locations as New Zealand, Australia, and South Africa.] A more reckless driver could have shaved thirty minutes off of that time, but Pete wasn't reckless and kept a firm hand on his team until we leveled out again at the bottom. That was when he gave his mules their heads, and the chains really started to jangle.

Even with our early morning start, the sun was past its apex before we spotted the squat, adobe structures of Tyson's Well, way off in the distance. If you didn't know what you were looking at, you might at first mistake the handful of buildings— there was a main station house and nearby stable, a blacksmith's lean-to, a tiny one-holer out back, some corrals, and a Colorado and Prescott grain shed, where the local hostler kept the oats and corn that Tucker sent him every few weeks—as just another clump of brown dirt, but the mules knew what it was, and started pulling harder.

As stations go, Tyson's Well never ranked very high on my list. Isolated and dry save for what water could be bucketed up from a well dug back in the '60s, it was little more than a wind-scoured layover for stagecoaches and freighters bound for elsewhere. Even as miserable as the place appeared, it was an improvement over the surrounding countryside. There was shade from the elements, and the water wasn't bad if you were thirsty enough. The food . . . well, it filled the belly, and generally didn't set up too bad. I'd have hated to have to eat it every day, though.

Tyson's Well offered another bonus for me, and that was a chance to climb down off the box to ease the pain in my backside. It was a twenty-minute stop, just enough time for the tenders to switch out the exhausted teams for fresh stock, and for the passengers to grab a bite to eat or visit the privy—or both, if you were quick enough. I never dismounted on top of the Dome, but always looked forward to stretching my legs at Tyson's.

You know that feeling you get when you sense something's not right? Kind of a tightening of the muscles across your stomach or the back of your skull? That's what I was feeling as we rolled into the yard. Pete didn't say anything, but he must have felt it, and eased the coach to a halt about forty yards shy of the station.

"Looks kinda empty, don't it?" the linesman observed. He kept his boot resting lightly on the brake lever, ready to trip the latch at the first sign of trouble. Those C&P mules were smart animals. They sensed as well as Pete and I that something was out of whack, and it wouldn't have taken much to send them into a gallop if we had to get out of there in a hurry.

I rose with the backs of my legs pressed against the front of the seat for balance, my thumb stretched tautly across the Parker's twin hammers. The coach was still rocking gently on its leather thoroughbraces, and the mules were high-headed and skittish, the off-side leader snorting loudly in apprehension. Over at the station, no one was in sight, and the corrals were empty.

Prying a wad of tobacco from his cheek with a stained finger, Pete tossed it into a patch of prickly pear, spit once to clear his mouth, then shouted: "McGinnis! Angus McGinnis!"

After a long pause, the front door cracked open and a shiny bald head above a thick, iron-gray beard poked hesitantly out of the dark interior. "That you, Driscoll?"

"Who do you think it'd be?"

"Watch yourself," the station keeper warned. "They's Injuns about."

"Indians," Pete repeated softly, his head swiveling.

I looked, too, but didn't see anything, and that's some pretty open country out there. A few shallow washes and plenty of greasewood and cactus to hide behind, but I reasoned that if there were Apaches nearby, they'd have showed themselves by then.

Glancing my way, Pete said: "What do you think?"

"I think we'd have been swallowing lead by now if there were Indians around."

"That's the way I track it, too." Raising his voice for the station keeper, he called: "Get out here and help me with these mules, McGinnis."

"Mister Driscoll." Emma Rhodes's voice sounded quavery in the hot stillness of the yard.

"It's all right, driver," Trepan called from inside the coach. I could hear him and Brown speaking gently to the woman and children, assuring them that everything would be fine, and that Pete and I needed a few minutes to sort out what was going on.

Shaking his lines above the mules' backs, Pete turned them toward the station at a leisurely walk. I remained standing, swaying with the motion of the coach, my eyes prowling the outbuildings like a hunting cat. As if taking courage from the lack of gunfire, Angus McGinnis leaned a little farther out the door, took a quick peek around, then slid into the sunlight with an old Springfield needle gun gripped tightly in both dirt-encrusted fists.

"I'm tellin' ya, Driscoll, they was some lively doin's here this morning," he called.

"Well, it's quiet now. Where's your tenders?"

"Harley, Eddie, get out here and take care of Mister Driscoll's mules."

"Hold on, McGinnis," Pete said, bringing his rig to a stop. "Where's the relay team?"

"Dangit, Driscoll, I tolt you we was raided this morning. 'Paches got 'em all, company mules and both my saddle horses. Damned near got ol' Harley here, too." He inclined his head toward one of the station's two assistant hostlers, a lean-shanked kid with red hair and a nose that always seemed to be peeling from sunburn. As if cued, Harley held a splintered arrow up where we could see it.

"Gimme that thing," Pete said gruffly, leaning from his seat to snatch the projectile out of the kid's hand.

Pete studied the arrow thoughtfully for a minute, then

grunted and handed it to me. Balancing the shotgun across my left arm, I ran my hand reflectively up and down the bent shaft. The tip was iron, still shaded with dirt from where it had been embedded in the station's adobe wall, the fletching slim and black.

"Apache, you say?" Pete queried the station keeper. "Did you see 'em?"

"Nope, but we surefire heard 'em. Howlin' and screechin' like they was bein' spit straight outta hell, they was. Me'n Harley was headin' for the barn to look after the stock when they opened up on us." He nodded toward the broken arrow still in my hand. "Came near about skewering ol' Harley in the breadbasket, it did."

Pete and I exchanged glances, but didn't say anything. Then Pete started to climb down, and I tossed Harley the arrow that he'd likely keep until he died of old age, a souvenir from his Wild West days. I followed Pete down the side of the coach, then moved away from the vehicle while the driver and hostlers helped the passengers to solid ground. Angus's old one-eyed redbone hound, named Soap, nosed the newcomers' legs speculatively, but thankfully didn't lift a leg, which he'd been known to do. I heard McGinnis telling Missus Rhodes that there was a meal laid out inside if she was hungry, and that a pail of water could be brought in from the well if she wanted to freshen up. He kept on talking, but I was moving out of earshot by then and didn't hear the rest. Keeping my thumb over the shotgun's hammers, I moved slowly through the low scrub fronting the station. Pete found me there about ten minutes later, down on one knee studying a set of prints in the flinty soil.

"Moccasins?" he asked, coming up beside me.

"Boots, although I don't suppose that means much." I stood and looked around. "What do you think?"

Pete held a handful of arrows that he'd collected from around the station. Plucking one from the bunch like a rose from a bouquet, he shoved it into my hand. I eyed it a moment, then handed it back. "About the same as the one Harley showed us." I gave the old man a calculating look. "This isn't Apache work, Pete."

"Hell, I know that. Them arrows ain't Apache, either. Besides, when was the last time you heard of an Apache using a bow? Most of 'em are better armed nowadays than the soldiers they got chasin' 'em."

I nodded toward the clutch of arrows in the old driver's hand. "Those were made by river Indians, maybe Mohaves or Yavapais. That shank's Mule's Fat, if I'm not mistaken, and I'm pretty sure the fletching is off some kind of water bird." [*Editor's Note:* Mule's Fat (*Baccharis salicifolia*) is a large, native shrub of the Southwest desert, usually found near sources of water or along the banks of rivers; its limbs were commonly used in the construction of wickiups, baskets, and for arrow shafts.]

"Someone wanted this to look like an Indian raid, but it weren't." Pete threw his collection of arrows to the ground, as if in disgust. "What I think is, somebody wanted those mules, but it don't make sense to blame it on redskins. That's too much work for any thief I ever knew."

"Maybe they wanted to distract our attention. Or else misplace the blame."

Pete turned a narrowed gaze on me, waiting for me to go on.

"Apaches have their own kind of magic out here," I said. "Even just the rumor of a raiding party can set people into a stampede. They'll abandon a whole country and hightail it somewhere safe until the army tells them they can go home. That'd make it a lot easier to drive a herd of stolen mules to wherever they wanted to take them."

Pete shook his head with the vigor of a dog working a bone.

"It don't track straight, Slade. It's still too damned much work for a mule rustler, and you know it." He fixed me with a challenging glare. "Something don't add up here, boy."

I glanced toward the station. Trepan and Brown were standing outside the front door keeping a close eye on Pete and me, but the others had gone on inside. All except for McGinnis's tenders, who were watering the exhausted mules, still in their sweat-darkened harness.

"What are you going to do without a fresh team?" I asked.

"I reckon I got two choices. One is forward, the other's back. Either way, it'll be a hard pull. It's twenty miles to Ehrenberg, closer to twenty-five to Desert Wells."

"Well, you already know where I stand."

Pete growled like he was still working on that bone. Then he shook his head. "All right, we go forward."

"Suits me. The sooner I get that strongbox to Prescott, the better I'm going to feel."

"We'll have to take our good ol' sweet time about it, though. Them mules is tuckered. They won't have much left to give if we have to make a run for it."

We walked back to the station, where Harley was watering the off-side wheeler and Eddie was rubbing down one of the swing mules with a piece of coarse sacking, rearranging the harness as he went along to allow some fresh air to slide beneath the leather. Pete went over to supervise, while I stopped at the door where I could take advantage of the shade, yet still keep an eye on the coach.

A lot of those early stage stations were pretty dismal when it came to hygiene, and others could remind you of home, assuming you hadn't grown up in a pigsty. I'd say Tyson's Well, at least during the time Angus McGinnis was manager there, slanted closer to hog pen than home. I'm not criticizing dirt floors and exposed rafters—a lot of adobe buildings had those—

but at Tyson's there were spider webs everywhere, bugs, thick dust on the floor, and dirty dishes stacked on top of what were supposed to be cleaned ones, so that you constantly had to eat off a film of someone else's last meal—or several meals, depending on who was in charge of the kitchen that week.

Emma Rhodes was sitting on a bench at a long table cluttered with unwashed utensils from earlier meals. Her children were seated on either side of her, all three of them staring at plates of cold bacon, burned beans, and hard biscuits with the kind of revulsion that no amount of good manners could veil. Being more familiar with the perils of roadhouse grub, Trepan, Brown, and Garrett had taken positions at a small bar at the rear of the room, where they were softening the impact of their midday fare with shots of Old Overholt. McGinnis stood opposite them, clutching the bottle's neck with a grimy paw, waiting eagerly to rake in another ten cents as soon as one of the men motioned him forward.

Glancing over her shoulder, Missus Rhodes said: "Mister McGinnis, are these plates clean?"

Guffawing, McGinnis replied: "Just as clean as Soap can make 'em, ma'am."

I gave the station keeper a hard look, but kept my mouth shut. The truth would have only upset her further, and not changed anything. Pete came inside a couple of minutes later, and didn't waste any time getting to the meat of the matter.

"Ma'am," he said to the woman, then raised his eyes to include the trio at the bar. "We're going on, as I reckon that's our best option, but if anyone here thinks differently, they're free to stay put until the next stage comes through from the east. They can catch a ride back to Ehrenberg without additional charge."

"Is there danger on the road ahead, Mister Driscoll?" Emma asked.

"Ain't no way of knowin', ma'am, which is why I'm making the offer of free passage back to Ehrenberg."

The men at the bar stirred, and Garrett said: "Those Apaches could have gone that way, too."

"Could've, but I doubt it," Pete replied. "I figure whoever stole those mules are long gone by now."

McGinnis scowled until his brows nearly met above the bridge of his nose. "You sayin' they weren't 'Paches, Driscoll?"

"I ain't saying nothing about nothing, except that whoever did take 'em is probably a long ways off by now, and still running."

Emma Rhodes spoke tentatively. "What is your suggestion, Mister Driscoll?"

"Ma'am, I wish I could make one certain-sure, but I can't. All I can say is that me and Mister Slade here are going on, and we'll keep to the C and P schedule as close as those bone-weary mules will allow."

"We'll be going with you," Trepan said, then glanced at Brown, who voiced his own intention of proceeding. Garrett made it unanimous among the men.

After a lengthy pause, Missus Rhodes said: "I must confess that my primary concern is for my children, but I am also eager to reach Phoenix and home. Mister McGinnis informs me that the next stage due here from Prescott isn't to arrive until the day after tomorrow, assuming there are no delays along the road east of here."

"Mister McGinnis is correct, ma'am," Pete replied. "That'd be Frank Travis's run, due into Ehrenberg Sunday evening. There's supposed to be a steamboat leaving there Monday morning that'd take you back to Yuma, if that's your wish. The *Cocopah*, if I ain't mistook."

"Is there another route to Phoenix?"

"There are several," Trepan said with a chuckle, "but none

that are any safer or quicker than the Colorado and Prescott."

Emma gave her children a worried look, but you could see that her resolution was wavering. "Very well, then. We shall continue on with you, Mister Driscoll, and pray we suffer no further delays."

"We'll do our best, ma'am," Pete said, then tipped his hat to the woman and went outside to help with the mules.

With Pete watching the coach, I walked over to the bar. "What have you got to eat that isn't moldy or rancid, McGinnis?" I asked, leaning my shotgun against the facing.

The station manager's face reddened, but he went to the stove at the far side of the room without a reply and began putting a plate together. Trepan chuckled at the station keeper's silent ire. "You're a reckless man, Slade. I'd watch close that he doesn't spit in your food."

"He does, and I'll club his ears," I said loud enough for McGinnis to hear. But I watched him anyway, and felt reasonably confident that my meal was returned unsullied.

I ate quickly, the same cold beans and bacon and biscuits as the others were choking down, then ordered a slug of Old Overholt that I'd swear was thinned with . . . well, I don't know what a man like McGinnis would use to dilute his whiskey, and I'm not sure I want to. Although drinking on the job was against C&P rules, I didn't consider it any more of a sin than what the company was trying to pass off as food. As soon as I finished, I walked outside to where Pete was examining the teeth of his near wheeler.

"Trouble?" I asked.

"No, just checkin'. I'd say we ought to be all right as long as I don't gotta push 'em none."

"When do we pull out?"

"As soon as Missus Rhodes and them kids are done eatin'. I want to keep these mules movin', before they stiffen up."

"She was just about finished when I left."

"Good. I'm gonna grab a bite myself, then I'll roust everyone out. I'd like to make Desert Wells before dark."

I gave him a surprised look, but didn't say anything. As a general rule, we would have made the next station well before nightfall, so I knew he was serious about babying his mules over the next leg of our journey.

Pete went inside, and I walked over to the well to refill the canteens, one for the passengers inside the coach and a second one that Pete and I would share, although the old linesman seldom irrigated his gullet between stations. It went against his grain to drink when his mules had to go without.

McGinnis came outside with the passengers, kicking at his old dog when it got underfoot. "Get outta the way, Soap," he shouted. Missus Rhodes's eyes widened as the dog yelped and scooted around the corner, its tail tucked between bone-thin legs. I crawled into my seat with the Parker cradled across my left arm, while Pete herded his passengers inside the coach.

"You tell 'em when you get to Prescott, Driscoll," McGinnis said.

"Tell 'em what?" Pete snapped. "That some lowdown skunk ran off with a bunch of C and P stock? Dangnation, McGinnis, I'm glad you reminded me. I likely would've clean forgot to mention it if you hadn't."

"You drivers . . . ," McGinnis started to reply, then abruptly shut up.

Pete gave him a withering look, then climbed aboard. Taking the lines between his fingers, he "hupped" his team into motion, and off we went.

"That damned fool ought to be fired," Pete grumbled to me when we were back on the road.

I chuckled. "The company probably figures it's lucky to have someone out here who'll stay for more than a couple of months at a time. Before McGinnis, they probably went through half a dozen station managers every year."

"Angus McGinnis can kiss ol' Sally's ass," Pete said, nodding toward the hindquarters of his favorite wheeler. "With any luck, she'd kick his damn' fool head off for liftin' her tail, and save the company the bother of cuttin' his pin for him."

Pete Driscoll didn't like McGinnis, but then, not many people did. Angus was abrasive to just about everyone, company man or not, although you couldn't fault him for the care he gave to the horses and mules that were left in his charge. At least not until someone ran off with the whole bunch, leaving behind a fistful of broken arrows and a couple of shaken tenders.

The stage began to pick up speed as the mules settled into that mile-eating walking trot that so many drivers were fond of. After leaving Tyson's Well, we crossed a long, flat plain surrounded by saw-toothed mountains that looked like the broken teeth of ancient predators. Everything was brown, or some variation of it. Barren and brittle-dry, it was an intimidating land in both its vastness and desolation. By midafternoon, the sky looked more white than blue, and the heat shimmered off the granite-like soil. Sweat darkened our shirts despite the breeze created by the moving coach. I could feel it soaking through the soft beaver felt of my hat, trickling across my scalp like running lice. Neither Pete nor I spoke as the miles ticked past, but after a while I noticed he was starting to ever so gently haul in on his lines, the mules slowing gradually and without their usual head-tossing protest at being reined in.

The Plomosas were the next low mountain range we had to cross. Pete brought his mules to a walk as we started up their western slope. We were both aware of how vulnerable we were to an Indian attack on that long climb, and held no illusions regarding the deadliness of a Mohave's arrow compared with a bullet from an Apache's rifle. Dead was dead, no matter what kind of weapon was used.

Crossing the Plomosas was a lot easier than crossing the Dome. We reached the top in under two hours, and immediately started down the far side. I gave Pete a curious glance when he didn't stop in the middle of the pass like he normally did, but he shook his head and kept his eyes on the road, his foot expertly feathering the brake on the steeper sections. At the bottom he shook out his lines, and the mules settled into their now-familiar walking jog, although I noticed they'd lost a lot of their alacrity. Their long ears were beginning to droop in the heat, and their gait became more jarring as the day wore on. At the rate they were beginning to flag, I figured we would be lucky if we didn't end up crawling into Desert Wells at a stagger, the passengers trudging along on foot behind the coach.

Desert Wells was a larger and more efficiently run operation than the Tyson's Well station, in part because there was more water from a better-producing well, but mostly on account of the station manager. Noah Hoffman was a stocky German with ruddy cheeks and a full, gray beard, but no mustache. He was smart, industrious, and well-liked by just about everyone, although I always thought Noah's greatest asset was his wife, who ran the domestic side of the business.

At Desert Wells, the accommodations were cleaner, the food better. So much better, in fact, that it was claimed by drivers and freighters alike that Elizabeth Hoffman was the best damned cook on the C&P line. And they weren't just talking about that Ehrenberg to Prescott run, either. They meant all of northwest Arizona.

Elizabeth was short and plump and so plushy soft in appearance you'd almost wish you were a kid again, just to be encased by those warm, beefy arms of hers for a goodnight hug. Pete insisted Noah's ample belly was a testament to both the quality and quantity of his wife's cooking, and never failed to sing her praises. If he didn't think much of the Tyson's Well crew, he sure liked Noah, and he adored Elizabeth to a degree that bordered on embarrassing. Pete stated regularly that if Elizabeth would promise to marry him, he'd personally haul Noah across the Pacific until he found a volcano to toss the station manager into. His offer always brought a flustered giggle from Elizabeth, and, more often than not, an irritated glower from Noah.

Besides the Hoffmans, there was a full-time hostler at Desert Wells, a tall, gangly stick of a man named Jethro Hanks, who maybe wasn't the brightest star in the night sky, but who knew horses and mules about as well as any man I've ever met. I liked Jethro, and so did Pete, mostly, I think, because Jethro liked animals so much. It's always been my contention that a man or woman who liked critters, and was liked by them in return, was probably a pretty good person to know.

It was late that afternoon when we came in sight of Desert Wells. The main station and outbuildings sat on the far side of a shallow wash, within a low forest of cholla, saguaro, and manzanita. Mesquite trees offered a semblance of shade close to the house, which served as both a way stop for passengers and other travelers, and as the Hoffmans' private residence.

Pete brought his mules to a walk to negotiate the wash, but didn't jingle them back into a trot like he usually did. He didn't say anything and neither did I, but I was already cursing under my breath as I took in the empty corrals and the lack of smoke from either the station's chimney or the little beehive oven out back where Elizabeth baked her famous biscuits.

Softly, so that he wouldn't be overheard by the passengers, Driscoll said: "If they've been raided here, too, we're in a heap of trouble, Slade."

Pete wasn't telling me anything I didn't already know. My eyes were probing every little nook and cranny as we approached the station, in case whoever had hit the place hadn't already pushed on like they had that morning at Tyson's.

We rolled to a stop about sixty yards out, and Pete, as if offering his opinion of the situation, spat a glob of tobacco juice into the scrub along the road, then fingered the wad out of the pocket of his cheek and flung it at a stubby barrel cactus beside his front wheel. He cursed quietly, out of respect for the woman and children inside the coach, then he looked at me and sucked in a deep breath.

"What do you want to do, Slade?"

"Go on in, I guess." What choice did we have, with our mules wrung out like they were?

"You could sneak in on foot, see what's about."

"Uh-uh. My job is to stay within shotgun range of the strongbox. That's what I intend to do."

Pete didn't argue the point. He already knew I wouldn't venture that far away from my responsibilities as a messenger, any more than he would have abandoned his coach or mules if the shoe had been on the other foot. But he did say something that really caught me off guard.

"I reckon we're carryin' a peck of money, huh?"

"Is that right?" I kept my response purposely vague, as I considered the contents of the strongbox to be privileged information, no one's business but mine until it was safely delivered to its destination in Prescott.

"Yeah, I figure so. You could tell Ira was about to spit up his liver this morning, worryin' about whatever it is you've got locked inside that box under our butts."

"You got a point to this conversation, Pete?" I asked evenly.

He shrugged. "Just thinkin' about them arrows we found back to Tyson's, and how it don't add up for it to be Apache. Been recallin' them two fellas we saw inside the livery at Ehrenberg, too, and wondering how they fit into ever'thing."

45

"Maybe they don't fit in at all."

"Maybe," he replied, but he didn't act like he believed it. Taking another deep breath, as if screwing up his resolve, he said: "I reckon we'd best get on in there, see what the damages is."

"Go slow," I instructed, cocking the Parker's right-hand hammer.

Pete shook his lines, and the weary team leaned into their collars. I felt sympathy for those mules. They'd covered close to forty-five miles that day, much of it under a blazing sun with temperatures well into the nineties. They were exhausted, and had every right to be. It made me wonder what Pete would do if we got into the station and discovered that Hoffman's relays had also been taken.

My gaze was shuttling steadily between the station house, the entrance to the flat-roofed stable where Jethro Hanks would have normally been waiting with a team of stout wheelers already in harness, and the other structures. The quiet was so eerie that the flesh across the back of my neck began to crawl. I've seen the bodies of men and woman caught by wild tribes, and in my mind were images of Noah and Elizabeth similarly butchered. It made me feel cold inside, half sick with the possibilities of what we might find.

As he'd done at Tyson's Well, Pete stopped the coach some distance away. Leaning forward with his elbows on his knees, he stared hard toward the stables. "Noah," he bellowed.

My eyes narrowed when I thought I spotted movement at one of the windows in the station house. "Did you see that?" I asked.

"Someone's in the barn."

I glanced in that direction. "No, I thought I saw someone at the window. The one to the left of the front door. I didn't see anything at the barn."

"Might be our eyes is playin' tricks on us after a full day in the sun," he remarked after a pause.

"What do you think?"

"I think one of us is gonna have to climb down and take a look, and I need to stay up here where I can set these mules to runnin' if anything goes wrong."

Pete had me there. I'd refused to leave the coach out on the desert, but now that we were up close, I didn't see where I had much choice.

"Wait here," I said grimly, my foot already reaching for the top of the left-front wheel.

"I ain't going nowhere unless somebody starts shootin' at me. If that happens, you can catch up with that strongbox of yours in Prescott."

Standing there with one foot atop the coach's iron-rimmed front wheel, I almost smiled at Pete's dry declaration. Then a rifle boomed from the station, and the near-side wheeler screamed and reared in its traces, before collapsing limply across the tongue, splintering the wood close to the hounds. [*Editor's Note:* The hounds are the two support pieces that tie into the tongue, just in front of the frame and front axle.]

The entire team jumped, and the coach lurched forward, the front wheel rolling neatly out from under my foot. I did a partial midair flip before striking the ground with enough force to bounce the Parker out of my hand. The air in my lungs kind of whooshed out after the shotgun, leaving me lying there gasping like a fish in the middle of a dusty corral. My fingers, which only a half second earlier had been firmly grasping the Parker's stock, were opening and closing like gills, and I can still hear the raw wheezing of my lungs as they struggled for oxygen. Then I looked up to see the coach heaving forward as the surviving mules attempted to bolt, the Concord's big rear wheel churning grit as it rolled toward my midsection like an oversized pie cutter.

Excerpt from:
Minutes of Military Inquest
Reedcatcher Insurrection
28 May 1882–8 June 1882
Major Leandro Marcus, Presiding
13 July 1882, Fort Yuma, A.T.

"Would you please state your name and occupation for the record?"

"My name is Mel Alvins. I'm a sub agent for the Fort Mohave Indian Reservation, at Bosque Wash."

"Bosque Wash?"

"On the reservation's southern border."

"Tell us what your responsibilities are at Bosque Wash, Mister Alvins, and what authority you possess there."

"My responsibilities are varied, but mostly I just keep an eye on things, then report back to the main agency every week or so. It's a big reservation, and me being at the Bosque Wash village just makes things simpler. I don't have any real authority, although I try to keep a lid on trouble when I can. The Mohaves at Bosque Wash consider me an extension of the main agency. They also look at me as a representative of the government at large."

"The United States government?"

"Well, the army, which is about all they know on the subject. Sometimes you'll hear speeches where they talk about the Great White Father in Washington, but the Mohaves, at least those at Bosque Wash, consider that a bunch of . . . well, they don't take it as serious as they do a troop of armed soldiers."

"Were you acquainted with the Mohave Indian known as Ben Reedcatcher, Mister Alvins?"

"Yeah, I knew him, but he wasn't Mohave. Not all the way through. His daddy was a Pima out of California. His mother was old Bean Tree's daughter. She was Mohave. Bean Tree was a big chief at Bosque Wash, although Ben never amounted to much. His real name was Big Reedcatcher, but somehow he got known as Ben, and that's what everybody called him."

"Thank you for that clarification, Mister Alvins. It will be noted in the final draft of my report. Could you tell us now of your knowledge regarding the Reedcatcher insurrection of twenty-eight May of this year?"

"Well, like Mister Hughes already told you, we'd been hearing about rumors along the reservation's southern boundary for two or three weeks by the time Reedcatcher made his jump. There was talk of whiskey peddlers and gunrunners, and people saying the army was coming in to arrest a bunch of Bosque Wash men for stealing horses from the mines up around Eldorado Canyon . . ."

"Excuse me, Mister Alvins, but are you saying the Mohaves at Bosque Wash stole horses from the mining camps along Eldorado Canyon?"

"No, but there were rumors that they did, which is why everyone down there was so jumpy."

"Surely they understood that if they didn't do anything wrong, they wouldn't have anything to worry about."

"Uh . . ."

"Is there some confusion, Mister Alvins?"

"Well, I don't really know how to answer that, Major."

"You answer it truthfully, sir. This court of inquiry will demand nothing less."

"Then, begging your pardon, but that's a bunch of hogwash. I doubt there's an Indian anywhere in Arizona that hasn't been blamed one time or another for something he didn't do."

"I would caution you, Mister Alvins, to encase your responses with respect for this court of inquiry."

"All right, but that doesn't change the fact that rumors were circulating around Bosque Wash that the army was going to retaliate for someone stealing a bunch of horses up around Eldorado Canyon. The Mohaves, based on earlier incidences, believed these rumors to be true, which added to the unrest."

"Could you substantiate the full names of the insurgents, Mister Alvins?"

"I thought you wanted to hear my opinion on why Big Reedcatcher jumped the reservation?"

"What I'd like at this moment is a substantiation of the full names of the individuals involved in the Reedcatcher insurrection, as compared with those already compiled by other sources."

"All right. There were nineteen Indians who made the jump with Reedcatcher. Bear's Tongue was one, Louis Tall Eagle was another . . ."

SESSION THREE

Are you recording again? All right, well, before we stopped for you to change disks on your Dictaphone, I was telling about how all hell seemed to bust loose there at Desert Wells. How the stagecoach's front wheel spun out from under me when someone opened fire from the station with a rifle, and then me lying there like a turtle on its back, staring at the Concord's rear wheel as it rolled forward like the whining teeth of a sawmill's giant blade.

Pete Driscoll was hauling back on the lines with everything he had, just about standing on the brake's tall lever to keep his team from taking their bits and running. Between those two measures and one of the lead mules taking time to rear in its harness, he managed to slow the coach long enough for me to scramble clear, although just barely. Had I taken another moment to catch my breath, they likely could have buried me in a half-sized coffin.

Gunfire continued to pour out of the house and barn, and Pete's mules were going crazy from all the noise and excitement, not to mention that dead near-side wheeler draped across the coach's splintered tongue. The scent of warm blood was pungent on the hot air, and Pete told me afterward he thought the mules were more terrified at the sudden death of their teammate than they were of the thunder and chaos going on around them.

All of this happened really quick, and I was still pretty foggy-headed from my tumble from the front wheel, although not so much that I didn't know I needed to keep moving. Spotting the Parker a few feet away, I scuttled toward it on my elbows and knees. I was only vaguely aware of the coach door popping open behind me, and of Trepan and Brown leaping clear of the violently rocking coach. I croaked a warning for them to get down, but I doubt they heard me.

Trepan was the first one to dart past, racing bent over for a stone water trough sitting next to the corral. Brown was right behind him. I grabbed for Trepan and missed, but managed to snag a handful of Brown's trouser leg as he attempted to swerve around me. I was still trying to tell him to get down when he spun toward me with the snarl of a cornered wildcat. Caught off guard by the fierceness of the man's expression, I dropped his cuff and swayed away. Then something white-hot and as loud as a locomotive exploded against the side of my head, and my whole body convulsed in a spasm of pain.

I sprawled belly-flat to the ground, my left arm launching out straight in reaction to the blow, levering me partway up on my right side even as the world spun a crazy dance around me. For a while, all I could do was lie there with the fingers of my left hand splayed wide, my palm braced against the flinty soil as the din of the battle—braying mules and peppering gunfire and Pete Driscoll's frantic cursing—filled my ears until I thought surely my skull would pop. Then, in what seemed to take minutes but probably didn't last for more than a few seconds, my arm relaxed and I sagged to the ground, my cheek flopping limp as a rag in the dirt.

After a bit I was able to push up on both elbows and have a look around. There was a hell of a commotion at the barn, filtered by roiling dust like images viewed through smudged glasses. Horses lunged as they tried to break free of the desperate men hanging onto them, the men shouting and swearing; a haze of gray powder smoke drifted like fog through the mesquites, adding a surreal quality to the scene.

Behind me, the coach had finally come to a stop, the mules standing motionless in a tangle of harness leather and chain that was going to take quite a bit of diligence to straighten out, at least without resorting to knives and bolt cutters. Pete was perched low in the front boot, firing methodically toward the stables. I could see the barrel of his Spencer carbine leaning muzzle-up against the kickboard, shot dry and dribbling smoke. He'd switched to his Colt by then, and was spacing his shots to make them last.

Drawing a ragged breath, I slid the Parker out from under me and brought it to my shoulder. The tiny brass bead of the front sight wavered and reeled before it finally settled on the knot of pandemonium at the barn. I thumbed the right-hand hammer all the way back, then tightened my finger on the rear trigger, but at the last instant a sharp contraction of muscle yanked the twin muzzles skyward, so that my load of double-ought flew high, peppering the front of the barn above the door but missing the ambushers.

I shook my head in frustration, but that only worsened the problem. Lowering my head, I closed my eyes and took a series of deep breaths. When I looked up a few seconds later, the world had ceased its spasmodic jumping around, but the yard was empty. Way out beyond the station to the west, their horses' hooves kicking up little whirlwinds of dust, the raiders fled.

"Shoot, damnit," Pete hollered.

I struggled to my knees, the Parker's muzzles sloped toward the ground. "They're too far away," I replied, then pushed to my feet and eased over to the coach. Pete had climbed down from the box and was sitting with his back to the front wheel, both hands clutching his right leg, just above the knee. Blood seeped from between his fingers, advancing slowly across the canvas ducking of his trousers.

"The son of a bitch shot me," he announced through clenched teeth.

"Who shot you?"

"I don't know, but someone sure as hell did." He jerked his head toward the coach's side door. "You'd best go check on the others, Slade. I ain't optimistic."

Instead I glanced toward the station, my brows furrowing. "Where's Trepan and Brown? I thought they were making a run for the water trough."

Pete guffawed dryly. "Just how big of a dent did that gun barrel put in your brainpan, boy? Them two was in on it. They took off with those jaspers holed up inside the station."

My scowl deepened, and I reached for the top of the front wheel.

"You okay, Slade?"

"Yeah, I'm fine." I looked down at the driver. "You sure they were in on it?"

"As sure as there's dirt in McGinnis's stew. Hell, don't look so glum. Ain't no way you could've known what they was up to." He tipped his head toward the coach. "Go on now. Take a peek and see how bad it is."

The Concord's door had been slammed open when Trepan and Brown jumped out, but the force of their exit had slapped it closed again. My muscles tightened as I reached for the latch. Gritting my teeth against whatever awaited me inside, I gave the handle a twist and a yank, then grunted loudly as the interior popped into view.

The passengers were alive. They'd been bound hand and foot, then gagged with bandannas shoved so deep into their mouths that all they could manage were frightened little mewling sounds. The woman whimpered and cowed back when I leaned into the coach for a closer look. Tears streaked her cheeks and the little girl's, and the boy's expression registered fear, but Garrett just looked red-faced and angry. He kept thrusting his chin toward me, grunting urgently.

"What is it, Slade?" Pete called. "I hear something."

"They're all right," I replied, then climbed inside to release their bonds.

Trepan and Brown had been thorough with their knots, snugging the passengers up tight enough to hold them immobile, yet not so constricting as to cause injury. Dan Garrett, who had been riding Arizona stagecoaches for a good many years by then, had been down this pike before, and confided to me on his next trip through Ehrenberg that the Desert Wells stickup was the smoothest he'd ever endured, and the most professional.

"They were very concerned with our safety and comfort," was how he put it. "Like we were being held up by gentlemen."

It being Missus Rhodes's first, she didn't take the encounter nearly as well. As hard as she was breathing when I crawled inside, it's a wonder she didn't suck the gag down her throat. Some years later, she would write an article about her ordeal for a Phoenix newspaper and do a pretty good job getting the facts straight, at least from her perspective. Her criticism of the Colorado and Prescott Stagecoach Company seemed a little unfair to me, although I suppose it could be expected under the circumstances. [*Editor's Note:* Emma Rhodes's piece was published in the August 1886 edition of the *Arizona Topic,* which was a monthly publication for Maricopa County that ran from September 1884 to March 1889.]

I pulled their gags first, then slid a folding knife from my vest pocket and severed the cotton rope holding Missus Rhodes's wrists behind her back. After freeing Garrett's hands next, I handed him my knife and told him to cut the others loose. Emma immediately started protesting the impropriety of anyone other than her husband seeing or fondling her ankles, but I didn't go back. Bringing a couple of bandannas with me from the coach, I knelt at Pete's side, intending to wrap his injured leg before further exploration, but he wouldn't have it.

"Check the station, Slade. I gotta know what happened to Noah and Elizabeth."

I nodded and pushed to my feet, dropping the bandannas on Pete's lap. "Tie off that wound before you bleed to death," I ordered, then headed for the house.

My heart was thumping a wicked beat as I eased inside the adobe station. Even knowing the bandits had already fled, I'd drawn my strong-side Smith and Wesson, and didn't bother trying to rationalize why I might need it. I wasn't sure what I'd find, but I was hoping like hell it wouldn't be a pool of blood and a trio of flyblown carcasses.

Desert Wells had started out similar to Tyson's Well—a simple, one-room station house with a hand-dug well and a low-roofed barn for the horses and mules—but Noah Hoffman had more ambition than any of the Tyson's Well managers. He'd added on to the original building to expand it to four rooms, all with wooden floors, then planted mesquite trees on the west and south sides for shade. The first room was the original building, where C&P passengers and other travelers could get a bite to eat or take a brief rest from the unrelenting heat in summer. It had a long harvest table lined with benches, a short bar on the north side, and a pair of horsehide chairs flanking a small lamp table against the rear wall.

Although the front room was empty, I didn't feel a whole lot of relief. I stared bleakly toward the opening at the north side of the far wall. I'd never been back there, but I knew it was where Noah had added a kitchen for Elizabeth, plus a bedroom for the two of them and a combination storeroom and bedroom where their daughters had slept until they married a few years earlier and moved away—one to Prescott, the other to Phoenix.

I could see partway down the narrow hall from where I stood. A small window placed high in the wall—its position and size a precaution against Indian attack—offered only a dim illumination of the passage, filtered as it was by the dusty green of mesquite limbs outside. Taking a deep breath, I slipped into the hall, the Smith and Wesson pointing the way. The first entry opened on my left. There was no door, and when I peeked inside, I discovered a tidy, functional kitchen. The pots and pans looked freshly scrubbed, and braided rugs covered all but the corners of the planed oak floor.

I moved on to the next room, my nerves ratcheting up several notches as I approached a closed door made of knotty pine. I paused with my left hand on a simple hand-forged Suffolk latch that Noah had fashioned from his own forge. My right hand was gripping the Smith so tight my palms were starting to sweat. Then I lifted the latch and shoved the door open, and that's where I found them. I couldn't stop a sharply exhaled breath when I realized they were alive.

Both Noah and Elizabeth were sitting on plain, ladder-back chairs, their wrists bound behind them, ankles lashed to the front legs. Bandannas had also been crammed into their mouths, as if the raiders had rehearsed the operation beforehand, right down to the kinds of knots they would use. Holstering the Smith, I stepped into the room and removed their gags. Elizabeth's peeled free with a small gasp; Noah's came away with an angry curse.

"We heard shooting, Slade," were the stationmaster's first words. "What happened?"

"They robbed the coach," I explained, fumbling with the older man's knots. My knife was still outside with Garrett. "What happened here?"

"The sons of bitches . . ."

"Noah!" Elizabeth interrupted testily.

"Dangit, woman," he protested, then went on. "They rode in late yesterday and threw down on us with their pistols before we were done welcoming them into our home."

There was bitterness in Noah's words, and regret, I thought, for so quickly lowering his guard. Or maybe I'm just remembering my own early trust of Trepan and Brown, and the betrayal I felt when the full impact of what they'd done sank in.

"They tied us up," Noah continued. "Then one of them stayed behind while the others ran off all the livestock. I don't know where they took them, or what they wanted with a bunch of harness stock . . ."

"They wanted to leave us stranded," I interrupted, freeing the man's wrists, then moving on to his wife while he flexed feeling back into his fingers and arms. "Did they keep you tied up all night?"

"No. The man they left behind untied us about sundown, but kept us locked in the storeroom. They didn't bring out the ropes again until a few hours ago, when the others returned. You were late, which they seemed to expect."

I nodded grimly, then filled him in on what had happened that morning at Tyson's Well.

"We limped into Desert Wells with worn-out mules," I added.

"So we're stuck here until Driscoll's team is rested, or Frank Travis rolls in late tomorrow afternoon?"

I didn't reply, although I didn't see where they'd have much choice, especially with a bullet hole drilled through Pete's leg. For the first time, I began to comprehend the careful planning of the raid, its thoroughness in manipulating our every move. And was it a coincidence, I wondered, that they'd struck while we were carrying one of the biggest payrolls we'd ever contracted for, money not just for one mine, but for several of them?

I stood back as the bonds fell from Elizabeth's wrists. Noah kicked the rope away from his right ankle at the same time, and quickly went to work on the other leg.

"Will you be all right?" I asked Elizabeth, anxious to return to the yard and let Pete know that the Hoffmans were unharmed.

"Yes, of course. Was anyone on the coach hurt?"

I told her about Pete's wound, and how frightened Missus Rhodes and her children were.

"Bring them inside," Elizabeth said matter-of-factly. "I'll look after Pete's injury, then see about fixing something calming for the woman and children."

I nodded gratefully, knowing that Pete and the passengers would be well taken care of, then started for the door.

"Hold on, Slade," Noah called as I entered the hall. He was already down on one knee, loosening the ropes on his wife's legs. I stepped past the door to allow them a moment of privacy. Noah came out a few seconds later, toting a long-barreled Colt revolver in his right hand, his eyes ablaze with Germanic fury. "Let's go see what they left us," he stated resolutely.

"Where's Jethro?" I asked, following the older man into the front room.

"They said they locked him in the tack shed. I'll check there first. You take a look around the corrals, see if those whores' sons overlooked anything. That damned stage is already three hours behind schedule. It'll be a lot later if we can't round up a fresh team." His expression was glum as he exited the station. "It's going to chap my hind end royally if we can't get that coach running again until tomorrow," he added over his shoulder.

Noah Hoffman was a company man to the core, but I didn't have any intention of looking for livestock the bandits might have missed. Getting Pete inside where Elizabeth could tend to his wound was my first priority. After that, I wanted a better look at the Concord's interior. I'd noticed sawdust all over the front seat while freeing Garrett and Missus Rhodes, but hadn't taken time to examine its source.

You said when we began this interview that you wanted to hear every detail I could remember, but I doubt if you've got enough disks to record it all, so I'm going to skim over some of those things that don't really add anything to the story of Charlie Red. Like me carrying Pete Driscoll inside so that Elizabeth could tend to his injury, while Noah flitted and fumed over his missing livestock—thirty-two head of some of the best horses and mules in that part of the territory, by his reckoning.

I will mention Jethro Hanks. Noah found him in the tack shed as expected, the door braced shut from the outside with mesquite posts the station kept on hand for fence repair. After freeing his young tender, Noah sent him out to do the job I'd ignored, which was to look for any livestock the bandits might have missed or lost along the way. Jethro made it about halfway across the yard when his knees suddenly buckled and he collapsed. After Noah and Garrett carried him inside, they discovered a deep gash on the top of his head, hidden by his hat, surrounded by a wad of blood-matted hair and a slab of puffy flesh the size of a man's palm. Elizabeth immediately put him to bed in the storeroom, where he remained for the rest of the night. He was up and about the next day, but complained of dizziness. Two days later, while walking back to his own quarters in the stables, he went down again. He was still unconscious when they loaded him onto a Prescott-bound stagecoach to see a doctor, but passed away before he got there. Elizabeth was with him at the time, and said he never woke up.

So, despite the bandits' apparent efforts not to seriously injure anyone, they ended up killing an eighteen-year-old stock tender. Of course, I didn't know that when I saddled up and went after them, but it didn't take long to discover just how deadly that bunch could be.

With Pete and Jethro laid up, it was left to Noah and me to care for the bone-weary mules. It was no small chore untangling them from their harness. We used the swing team to drag the dead wheeler into the desert, downwind from the station, then turned them all loose in the nearest corral, where Noah finally began to work off steam seeing to their care, giving them grain and water in small increments to prevent them from overdrinking or colicking, and walking them to stave off cramps.

That was my chance to examine the Concord's interior, and I didn't waste any time getting over there. Having spotted the sawdust earlier, then having nearly an hour to contemplate it while I helped Noah with the team, I can't say I was surprised by what I found. I'd been so proud of that journey chest, bolted inside the front boot under the seat, then strapped down with heavy iron bands. No one was going to lift a strongbox out of there without a key or a stick of dynamite, and only the managers had keys, and explosives would have destroyed the paper inside, not to mention scattering any gold or hard coin in a hundred different directions. But no one—not me or Ira or the district manager in Prescott, not even the mechanics who'd installed the chests on the C&P's coaches—had anticipated the journey chest's vulnerability from the inside.

Brown and Trepan had used a six-inch hole saw to drill through the front of the coach, then on into the journey chest from the rear, where there hadn't been any iron straps to stop them. [*Editor's Note:* A hole saw is a ring-shaped saw used primarily for drilling circular openings through wood or metal, such as for doorknobs.]

The hand-crank drill with the blade still attached had been dropped to the floor, the oak core from the strongbox still wedged inside the steel bit. Extra rope and bandannas were dumped loosely on the rear seat, affirmation of the robbers' intentions, no matter how many passengers got on in Ehrenberg. The heavy valises both men had carried were missing, no doubt filled with the contents of the strongbox. Although certain that the mine payrolls were missing, I stuck my hand through the opening into the journey chest anyway. My fingers played briefly over the tight-fitting strongbox, then slipped inside. All I got for my efforts was a handful of sawdust and a sinking sensation in the pit of my stomach.

With my jaw clenched in frustration, I dropped from the coach and returned to the station. Emma Rhodes and her two kids were sitting at the big table, sipping on cups of warm tea. Dan Garrett stood at the bar with a bottle of something considerably stronger perched close to his elbow. Pete slouched in one of the horsehide chairs in the far corner, a tumbler of whiskey atop the small table at his side, although I noticed when I walked over that he hadn't taken more than a swallow or two.

"How are you feeling, old man?" I inquired, hunkering down on my calves at his side.

"Strong enough to kick your butt if you ever call me an old man again."

I grinned in relief. "How bad's the wound?"

"It punched a hole through the meat a couple inches above my knee, but missed the bone. Missus Hoffman fixed it up real nice."

"Hurt much?"

"Probably no worse than that goose egg you're sportin', although I doubt mine's affected my thinkin' any."

Pete was squinting at me in the station's dim light, eyeing the oblong lump across the side of my head, just above my ear. And yeah, if you're wondering, it hurt like the dickens, although I doubt that it was anywhere near as bad as what Pete was pretending he didn't feel. I'd left my hat by the door, though, and wasn't looking forward to putting it back on.

Keeping it short, I told Pete about the missing payroll and the stolen livestock.

"They were pretty slick about it," I added afterward. "They knew we might not've gone on if we'd suspected road agents had taken the relay mules at Tyson's Well, but Indians, hell, you just naturally assume they'd hit fast, then move on."

"They slickered us good, for a fact," the old man agreed. "Might as well've put blinders on the both of us." [*Editor's Note:* Blinders are square leather patches fastened to the side straps on headstalls worn by harness stock, allowing the animal to see only what is in front of it, and to go only where the driver guides it.]

"Noah figures you're stuck here until tomorrow, at least. With that hole in your leg, I figure it'll be longer than that."

"Naw, I'll be fine by morning. Soon as the sun comes up, I'm gonna pull outta here with five tired mules. I might have to walk 'em all the way to the next station, but I need to get these passengers into Prescott, then get word to the sheriff."

I pushed to my feet, anticipating a fight. "You're going to have to make that run with four mules, Pete. I'm taking your off-side leader."

Driscoll's head jerked up. "Like hell you are."

"I'm going after the payroll, and I'll need a mount to do it. That jenny you've got on the right lead is small and quick and sharp as a tack."

"That's a C and P mule, Slade. It don't belong to you or Marty Coltrane."

"I've already talked this over with Noah. He said to bring the rest of the herd back when I caught up with the thieves."

Pete laughed harshly. "That pointer's frazzled, boy. She won't catch up, and even if by some crazy damn miracle she did, there's still four of them against one of you. They'd make short work outta your hide, and not lose more'n a few minutes doin' it."

My muscles grew taut and my voice hardened. "I'm going after them, Pete, and I'm taking that jenny for my saddle. If you've got a problem with that, take it up with the district manager in Prescott . . . or Ira Tucker, when you get back to Ehrenberg."

Pete tried to shove up out of his chair, but the wound in his leg quickly clubbed him back. His face paled and his voice drew down into a shallow wheeze as he cursed me for my bullheadedness. At the big table, Emma Rhodes grabbed her daughter's head and pulled it against her breast, smothering the child's other ear with her hand.

"Please!" she cried, almost in tears. "For the love of God, give my children some peace."

A stricken look came over Pete's face, and he immediately reached for his hat, as if to pull it off in contrition. But Elizabeth Hoffman had already removed the sweat-stained lid and hung it on a rack beside the front door. While Pete sputtered an apology for forgetting his manners, I turned on my heel and walked outside.

It had been late afternoon when we rolled into Desert Wells. I reckoned it close to seven p.m. when I exited the main house that last time. I walked over to where Noah was pouring grain into a trough for the mules.

"How's that jenny?"

"She can handle it. You still intend to go after them whores' sons?"

I nodded stiffly.

Noah shook the last few grains from his bucket into the trough and stepped away from the corral. "What do you need from me?"

"A saddle with breeching, water, and enough food to last . . .

64

say three days. That ought to either get me where I'm going, or it won't matter anymore."

"What about a rifle? That scattergun of yours might be good for close-up work, but it could leave you stranded if you were bushwhacked from a distance."

"I wouldn't turn down a long gun, if you've got one to spare."

Noah jerked his head toward the corral. "Go get your mule, Slade. There's tack in the barn. I'll fetch a rifle and ammunition from the house, and have Lizzie put together some grub for the trail." He glanced at the sky. "Not much daylight left. You sure you don't want to wait until morning? It'd give that jenny a chance to rest."

"It'd give Trepan and Brown a bigger lead, too."

Noah nodded approvingly. "That's the way I'd see it. Go on and saddle up. I'll be back by the time you're finished."

A lot of people think the only animal we ever rode in those days were horses, but the fact is, a lot of men preferred mules, and I've known some who would rather ride a burro than a $200 thoroughbred—mostly prospector types and others who wandered the more remote regions of the territory. Although burros were never the mount of choice for most of us, a mule . . . yeah, a lot of folks rode them, which is probably why Hoffman already had breeching fixed to one of the saddles in his tack shed. [*Editor's Note:* A breeching strap, in its simplest form, is a leather band that rides loosely behind an animal's thighs, then fastens to the saddle on either side; it's normally used on mules and low withered horses to keep either a riding saddle or a pack saddle from slipping forward, while a breast band performs the same function from the front; the withers are that peaked ridge above the shoulders of an equine, just behind the mane.]

As tired as she was, the jenny wasn't hard to catch. I led her into the barn and quickly saddled and bridled her. I was snugging up the breeching when Noah returned with a set of saddlebags, a bedroll, and two oversized canteens. He had a rifle in a scabbard clamped under one arm, and allowed me to take it from him so he could set the rest of it out of the way. I slipped the rifle out for a closer look. It was a .40-caliber Marlin according to the stamp on top of the slim octagon barrel, and I grunted in satisfaction. [*Editor's Note:* Based on the year of the Desert Wells robbery, the rifle was probably a Model 1881 lever action, chambered in the popular Marlin .40-60-260 caliber.] Taking the rifle and one of the canteens around to the jenny's off side, I began strapping everything in place. Noah stood opposite me, arranging the saddlebags and bedroll behind the cantle.

"What do you know about these men, Noah?"

"Probably not as much as you do."

"Those fellows on the stage called themselves Trepan and Brown, although I never heard their first names."

"They might not have even used their real names." He paused, looking at me across the saddle's hard leather seat. "If you catch up with them, Slade, don't lower your guard. They acted real friendly to Lizzie and me, but I was watching them, and they're an ugly bunch underneath. You could see it in their eyes. Those kind, they're easygoing only as long as you do what you're told and they get what they want, but if you corner them, they'll turn as mean as a sack full of rattlesnakes."

I thought about the two we'd brought with us from Ehrenberg, the way Trepan had taken off after the Rhodes boy on top of the Dome Rocks and brought him back to safety, and the kindness in their voices outside of Tyson's Well when they'd tried to assure Missus Rhodes that everything was going to be all right. But then I recalled the way they'd acted at Tyson's Well, the cool and calculated manner in which they'd observed Pete and me as we tried to make sense of what had occurred at the station earlier that morning. Remembering their eyes, and the way they'd watched everyone so closely, made me think Noah was probably right.

"There were four of them at first," Noah said. "Leading two extra saddle horses. I figured they were here to pick up a couple of passengers, which I guess they were, in their own way." His lips thinned in frustration, and he went back to fastening the saddlebags in place, making sure they sat square above the rear skirt.

"You said four at first? Pete mentioned he only saw four of them ride out, including Trepan and Brown."

"There were four who came in yesterday, then three took off last night. Only one came back this afternoon. I couldn't say what happened to the other two."

"How were they dressed?"

"Decent. A little dust and dirt, like you'd expect from men on the trail, but good clothes overall. Mostly clean-shaven, too."

The same description would have fit Brown and Trepan, I mused. Although it seemed like a clue, I didn't know what to do with it.

"How were they armed?"

"Like most men. A rifle and revolver showing. I couldn't say about hideout guns."

We finished up and I loosened the jenny's lead rope and led her outside. Noah came with me, glancing to the west as we exited the stables. The sun was setting, the clouds above the horizon painted in shades of gold and crimson, and the sky was a soft turquoise. It was still hot, though, and probably would be until midnight or later.

"Lizzie is fixing something for your supper," Noah said. "You can eat it in the saddle if you're in a hurry."

"She's a good woman."

"Elizabeth? She's the best." He nodded toward the saddlebags. "She's got ham and biscuits and a jar of sweet cactus jelly in there, along with some simple cooking utensils. The rifle's a forty caliber and full loaded, although I didn't put a round in the chamber. There's more ammunition in the bags." He glanced at my revolvers, the shorter Smith and Wesson in the shoulder rig, visible beneath my vest after I removed my jacket, and the longer version on my hip. "I didn't have any of those stubby forty-fives you shoot in your Schofields."

"I've got extra in my warbag."

"What about your shotgun?"

"That goes with me."

Noah's saddle had one of those horn loops the old-timers used to use to tote their long guns with, back in the days before scabbards became so popular. I'd carry my shotgun that way, balanced crosswise in front of me and resting on my thighs. I'd been riding messenger for so many years by then that I just felt more comfortable with a scattergun than I did a rifle, despite the Parker's limited range.

I stopped the jenny at the water trough to give her a last drink. "Tell Pete I'll take good care of his girl," I said, retrieving my warbag from where I'd dropped it beside the trough earlier, after making up my mind to go after the bandits.

Noah chuckled. "That old fart's about to throw a fit in there, but he knows the stock is under my authority as long as it's at Desert Wells. She's the point mule, and did less pulling then the wheelers and swing team. She'll be all right as long as you don't push her too hard."

I fastened the warbag behind the bedroll, and when the mule was finished drinking, I coiled her lead rope and tied it close to the horn. Then, gathering the reins, I stepped into the saddle. The jenny flicked her ears a few times at the unaccustomed weight, but she'd been ridden before and didn't try to buck me off. Elizabeth came out of the house carrying my hat and a bundle wrapped in a square of cheesecloth. She handed both to me, then patted my knee. "Come back safe, Thomas."

I told her that I would, and thanked her for the food. Then she went back inside and I gingerly settled the hat over the lump on my head.

"Keep your eyes on the skyline, Slade," Noah said, backing off a few paces.

"Watch your own hide," I replied. "And take care of that crusty old man in there. He kind of grows on you after a while."

Noah smiled and I tapped the jenny's ribs with my heels, and we rode out of Desert Wells at a walking trot, heading west into the setting sunset.

SESSION FOUR

The outlaws' trail continued straight for several miles, then turned abruptly north. They weren't making any effort to hide the prints of their horses as they crossed the harsh terrain, for which I was grateful. There are men out there even today who can track a fly across a dead badger, but I'm not one of them.

It was already gnawing on me to know the road agents were making better time than I was. Aboard a jaded mule, I knew my odds of catching up were slim, yet I still found the jenny's lagging gait aggravating. After a while the trail began to angle more to the northwest, toward the northern tip of the Plomosa Mountains, and for the first time since pulling out of Tyson's Well at noon, I began to feel a stirring of anticipation. I tried to caution myself not to get too excited. The bandits had already changed directions twice in a few hours, and might do so several more times before striking out for their final destination. Still, I was beginning to sense that we were actually going somewhere, and not just fleeing.

Twilight lingers for a good long time in that country, but ultimately, darkness wins out. I pulled up when I could no longer make out the bandits' trail, and dismounted with a small groan. I'd been a messenger for five years by then, riding coaches all over southern and western Arizona, but except for that one excursion after the Desert Wells holdup, I've probably never ridden more than thirty miles or so in the hard, leather cradle of a saddle. I'm not complaining, though. The way that little jenny heaved a drawn-out, hacking sigh as I stripped my rig from her sweating back told me I hadn't yet begun to suffer.

After dumping my tack out of the way and fastening the lead rope to her halter so I could remove the bridle, I poured half the contents from one of the canteens into my hat, then held the makeshift bucket under her nose. She drained her ration in three long swallows, then followed the beaver-felt hat with her muzzle when I pulled it away. I sympathized with her thirst, but I was only carrying two gallons of water with me and didn't have any idea of what might lie ahead. I couldn't risk giving her any more, and took only a couple of small swallows for myself. I will admit it felt pretty good when I put that water-soaked lid back on my head, though—mule slobber and all.

Since the jenny had been fed before we left Desert Wells, I saved the little bit of grain Noah had sent along and stretched out on my bedroll. I didn't kindle a fire. I didn't want to advertise my presence to the men I was following, in case they were watching, plus I'm not sure there would have been enough wood nearby even if I had wanted one. Besides, I was content to lay quietly while the darkness closed in and the air finally began to cool off.

I was using my warbag for a pillow, holding the jenny's lead rope in my hand. She'd showed no inclination to wander or seek out fresh graze after I pulled the saddle from her back, and it wasn't long before she laid down nearly at my side, tucking her nose into the protection of the slot between her lower belly and leg, like a dog will do on a winter's day. It would have been a perfect opportunity for me to drift off as well, but I couldn't seem to let go of my thoughts. I kept running the day's events over in my mind, all the disjointed deeds that shouldn't have been related, but which I felt certain were—the Mohave arrows at Tyson's Well, the rustled livestock, even the two strangers Pete had pointed out that morning as we rolled out of Ehrenberg. Like pieces of a puzzle scattered across a kitchen table, yet the picture remained unclear.

The moon came up while I lay there thinking. Bright and three-quarters full, it bathed the land with a soft radiance. The jenny didn't take any notice of the increased light, or even wake up when I pushed stiffly to my feet. Dropping the lead rope on the ground, I rummaged around inside my saddlebags until I found the sandwich Elizabeth had made for my supper. It was ham with jelly and some kind of hard cheese, and it tasted pretty good, although I knew I'd regret the meat before the night was through. Salt-cured like it was, it was going play hell with my thirst. After allowing myself a single swallow of water, I roused the sleeping mule and cinched the saddle in place.

My original plan when I'd stopped was to push on after a few hours' rest and hope I was somewhere near the outlaws' trail when dawn broke, but I soon discovered there was enough light for me to make out the tracks of the bandits' horses just fine, like dark scabs stippled across the waxen plain. Knowing I wouldn't be able to push for speed, I decided to walk and give the jenny a break.

The trail continued northwest, paralleling a dry, shallow wash. If you've ever been through that part of the country, you know it's just as barren as that stretch of road east of Tyson's Well. No water and not enough graze to keep a rabbit hopping, although I could hear coyotes off in the hills, so I guess there was something out there big enough for them to feed on. Probably lizards, I reflected glumly.

I stopped at dawn to water my mule, draining my first canteen into my hat and holding it under her muzzle. When she finished, I slung the empty canteen back over the saddle horn, clamped the cool, water-soaked lid over my head, and brought down the second canteen for a couple of short swallows for myself. After walking all night, my feet were throbbing, and I'd been correct as far as the effects Elizabeth's ham would have on my thirst. I was already miserable, and the day hardly begun.

I tightened the cinch, then eased into the saddle. The jenny moved out of her own accord, quickly settling into that familiar walking jog that was so easy on the tailbone . . . mine, not hers. I was feeling pretty confident by then that I knew where we were going. If we continued on like we were, we'd eventually reach the Colorado River. From there the bandits could take off in any number of directions, but the two most likely ones would be either upstream or down. I was caught a little off guard when the trail abandoned its northwesterly course shortly before noon to veer almost due west across the rugged plain, but since we were still heading for the Colorado, I didn't let it bother me.

The jenny's gait began to slow as the hours slid past. I didn't push her. Around midafternoon, with the temperature moving well into the nineties, I finally dismounted and loosened the cinch. She was breathing pretty heavily by then, and I was feeling kind of light-headed myself with thirst and fatigue. I gave the mule half of the remaining canteen of water, but decided to forgo a drink myself. If things got tight, it was going to be me who would have to depend on the jenny's fortitude to get us out of there, not the other way around.

I walked for a couple of hours, until we had the Plomosas off our left shoulders, then gave up and crawled back into the saddle. The outlaws' trail continued across the broad plain, but I noticed they weren't hurrying anymore. It was a brutal, blistering country, griddle-flat save for the far-flung mountain ranges to the east and south, and the sun seemed to hammer everything in sight with equal indifference. It was in there somewhere that I began to notice that the prints of the outlaws' horses appeared to be making less of an indention in the flint-like soil, as if the farther west we traveled, the less the earth was willing to give of itself.

I stopped again late in the afternoon and took two long swallows for myself, then poured the rest of the water into my hat for the jenny. My head was really swimming by then, and my lips felt like twisted ropes of jerky. A man can go for a good long way in that kind of country without food, but he needed to drink regularly. Without water and shade, and with temperatures nudging the century mark, he wasn't likely to last more than a day or so. I remember glancing toward the sun as I recorked the empty canteen and wondering what it would be like to die out there, withered away to a dry husk, as crisp as a discarded snake's skin.

A person's mind can follow some mighty strange paths in those kinds of conditions, and mine was wandering freely. I eventually became aware of a blinding light shining under the brim of my hat, and without having any real sense of time passing, realized it was the sun, squatting on the horizon like a ragged yellow hole punched through the sky. That was . . . what . . . fifty-odd years ago? Yet even today when I hear people talk about near death and the bright light that seems to beckon them forward, it always takes me back to that afternoon crossing La Posa Plain, moving unsteadily forward in a chimerical daze, my tongue grown thick and unresponsive, my eyes scraping in their sockets like kiln-fired clay marbles.

I was feeling so loose-reined when the sun finally slipped below the horizon that I didn't even notice the line of greenery that came up in its stead. My mule did, though, and quickened her pace. The unexpected increase in speed—just a trot, yet faster than the shuffling walk she'd fallen into through most of the afternoon—rocked me in my saddle. Grabbing the horn in surprise, I forced my thoughts back to roost, my head swiveling rapidly to see what had startled my mount. It was only then that I noticed the line of trees in the distance. Firming my grip on the reins, I urged the mule into a choppy gallop. Although I realize now that I was pushing her too hard, I was feeling pretty goosey at the time, and not thinking clearly. I remember how nothing seemed quite real except for those trees, and my desire to reach them. In her thirst, the jenny didn't protest the pace.

The mesquite in that part of the country is fairly scrubby compared with other locations, yet it's often a sure sign of water. As we drew closer, I could feel a definite moistness against my face, a softening of the desert's aridity. I brought the jenny to a walk as we entered the fringe of trees, my thirst—and hers—struggling against my need for caution. When I spotted the stolen C&P stock grazing within the chaparral, I slid the Parker from its saddle-horn loop and moved it to the crook of my left arm. I tried to rein the jenny to a stop, but she wasn't having it. She kept fighting the bit in her desperate need for water, until I finally swung to the ground and let her go.

Keeping my thumb curled over the shotgun's right-hand hammer, I made my way through the feathery, low-hanging mesquite. The stage stock watched my progress warily, their soft brown eyes shifting from me to the jenny, already knee deep in the shallows of the Colorado, sucking greedily at the muddy water to douse the burning in her throat. I could appreciate the urge, but couldn't allow myself the same luxury. I also knew I'd have to get her out of there soon, before she drank too much and colicked herself.

I didn't see any hint that the bandits were still around, nor did I expect to. They'd left Desert Wells with a several-hour head start, and weren't likely to slow down anytime soon, even if they weren't expecting pursuit. Coming to a grassy spot close to the bank, I glanced briefly at the ashes of a dead fire and the trampled vegetation surrounding it. They must have either stopped there briefly, or left someone at the site to look after the stolen stock while the rest of the gang robbed the coach. Either way, it was clear that they'd pushed on well before I got there, which suited me, as fuzzy-headed as I was feeling.

I set the shotgun aside, then waded into the river to retrieve the jenny. She balked when I tried to pull her out, but I kept a steady pressure on the lead rope and she finally gave in and followed me back to dry land. After hitching her to the stout trunk of a mesquite, I walked back to the river and bellied down to bury my windburned face deep in the Colorado's soothing currents. I felt a moment's empathy for my mule when I finally forced myself away from the river. My stomach was full, but my thirst was far from quenched.

The Colorado was probably seventy-five yards wide there, deep and powerful, although there was a shallow sandbar, furred over with slim willow saplings, not too far upstream that slowed the current directly in front of me. California lay flat and featureless across the river. Thick brush lined its banks, but there were no trees, and not much cactus. The land was largely unimpressive on this side of the river, too, just scattered chaparral and some decent graze for the stock. There was a low buff about a hundred yards to the north, crowned with clumps of sage and small boulders, but no real timber.

The C&P stock was still watching me suspiciously. Recalling how they'd shied away as I came through the trees, I figured they were going to be hard to catch. I was going to have to get my hands on at least one of them, though. The jenny was played out.

Dragging a sleeve across the dripping stubble of my chin, I walked over to the abandoned fire. Although the ashes looked cold, I could detect a lingering warmth when I held my palm close. They'd been there, all right, and not as long before as I'd at first thought. They'd built a fire and maybe had a meal and some coffee before pushing on. My stomach rumbled at the thought of hot coffee and a warm supper, although I've got to admit that at least with a full belly of water, I didn't feel nearly as addled as I had earlier.

Shoving to my feet, I began a slow, outward spiral away from the ashes, searching for some clue that might give me a better idea of the men I was dealing with, and what direction they'd taken after leaving their riverside camp. I soon wished I was better at reading sign. There was sure plenty of it around. Boot prints and crushed cigar and cigarette butts, spent matches and the circular indentation of cups or bottles, not to mention all manner of scuffs and gouges. Unfortunately, the whole site was as meaningless to me as a Shanghai newspaper. It wasn't until I approached the river's edge about forty feet downstream from the fire that I got my first solid lead.

For a moment I couldn't figure out what I was looking at, other than a smooth, shallow channel notched into the mud. It was six feet wide, deeper toward the middle, and sliced cleanly through the brush. Like something heavy had been pulled ashore there, then shoved back into the water. When it dawned on me what it was, my head reared back in surprise.

Do you remember me telling you about Ed Granger, the Ehrenberg fisherman who was convinced someone had stolen his skiff? This was it. It had to be, and it made sense, too. All the planning and hard work that Trepan and his crew had gone through to pull this holdup off so smoothly, it all came together right there on the Colorado's left bank. I felt a growing excitement as the story unfolded in my mind.

They—whoever the others were—had taken the boat first, sailing it upriver and hiding it there amid the willows, while Trepan and Brown came inland with the gold, disguised as mine officials. Meanwhile the men who had stolen the boat had gotten their hands on some bows and Mohave arrows, and staged a fake Indian attack on the Tyson's Well station, knowing that the threat of fresh hostilities, after so many decades of Apache warfare, would keep the station keeper and his tenders cowering inside until help arrived.

Pete's team of six would be tired when they rolled into the Tyson station shortly after noon, but they'd be wrung down to weary spirit and trembling muscle by the time they reached Desert Wells. Only the jenny, being one of the leaders and not expected to pull as hard as the swing team and wheelers, had retained enough pluck to continue the chase, and that only because I'd forced pursuit onto her. If I hadn't been so stubborn, if I'd done what so many others would have done and waited for the next stage to come through from Prescott, then ridden that back to Ehrenberg to report the robbery to the sheriff's office, the outlaws' trail would have become so cold and tangled, it probably never would have been unraveled.

The only thing the road agents hadn't counted on was my determination to recover what I considered mine, at least until it could be turned over to the district manager in Prescott. Now they were on their way downriver, and if their timing was right, they'd sail into Ehrenberg sometime late Sunday night, in time to catch the *Cocopah* before she pulled out for Yuma on Monday morning.

My shoulders began to slump with the realization that they'd won, that the chase was finished almost before it had begun. Even with a fresh mount, I'd never be able to beat the outlaws to Ehrenberg. Yet after a moment or so of melancholic reflection, doubt began to stir within me. Their plan appeared flawless. It was just so . . . damned . . . *perfect.*

Too perfect, I thought suddenly, eyeing the skiff's deep gouge in the mud. Yeah, they'd beat me back to Ehrenberg, but not by much, and a telegraph could easily reach Yuma before the *Cocopah* did. Even if they cut the line, Ira could send a message overland, pony express–style. The Coltrane manager in Yuma could have the sheriff and a posse waiting dockside for the whole gang, not even a stone's throw from the city's infamous territorial penitentiary.

It might have been a good plan. I'm not saying it wasn't. It just wasn't as perfect, as open and shut, as someone obviously wanted me to believe.

With my grip tightening on the Parker's stock, I eased toward the river's muddy bank for a closer look. The gentle lapping of waves kept the sandbar willows moving rhythmically, and clouds of tiny insects swarmed above the foliage. I stopped when my boots slapped water, but still couldn't see much. The brush was too thick, the Colorado's current too intimidating to a desert-bred boy who'd never learned how to swim. Recalling the sandbar upstream, I backed out of the scrub and headed in that direction.

The sun had been down for quite a while by then, and dusk was thickening into a sooty paste. Sensing that time was running out, I lengthened my stride, ignoring the jenny's plaintive whimper as I passed the sturdy mesquite where she was tied. [*Editor's Note:* Although a mule doesn't make exactly the same sounds as either a horse or donkey, it does have a diverse vocabulary of intonations, including the "plaintive whimper" described here by Slade.]

The sandbar was probably a hundred feet long, but no more than twenty across at its widest. Like both of the river's banks, it was covered with those slim, red-barked willows that are so common along Western streams, most of them anywhere from waist- to chest-high, pullulating with clouds of mosquitoes and other biting or annoying insects. After locating a shallow spot to wade out to the sandy island, I bulled through the thick growth to the lower end, where an open beach offered a better view of the main channel.

At first I didn't see anything out of the norm, and my disappointment started to build. I'd been so damned sure, although of what, I couldn't have said. I was turning away when a shadow in the water caught my peripheral vision. Pivoting back around, I squinted into the gloom. Even then, it took a moment to locate what I'd spotted only seconds before from the corner of my eye—a turtle shell–shaped image lying just beneath the water's surface, maybe thirty yards downstream, but only a few rods from the left bank.

I remember thinking: *What the hell,* then edged closer to the sandbar's tip, as if another half dozen more inches might actually make a difference. A slow smile began to worm across my face. I felt like whooping, but didn't. I was turning away a second time when I heard a distant boom, followed by a club-like blow to my ribs. I grunted loudly as I was sent spinning into the river. The current grabbed me, twirling me toward deeper water. I tried to cry out, but the sound became garbled as I slipped beneath the surface, the Colorado's powerful undertow dragging me toward the bottom.

Excerpt from:
Minutes of Military Inquest
Reedcatcher Insurrection
28 May 1882–8 June 1882
Major Leandro Marcus, Presiding
13 July 1882, Fort Yuma, A.T.

"**Captain [James] Reynolds, you were in command of the troop sent into the field to pursue and capture the Reedcatcher war party, were you not?**"

"Yes, sir, I was."

"**What was the result of that mission?**"

"We captured fourteen Mohave warriors, and killed five more. Our own casualties was one man wounded, none killed."

"**If I may take a moment, I'd like to note the success of Captain Reynolds's patrol, and its outstanding completion. I trust the wounded trooper has fully recovered?**"

"Yes, sir. Trooper Ames was restored to full duty within the week."

"**Well done, Captain. Now, to return to the subject of this inquiry, what, in your opinion, was the nature of the Reedcatcher raid? Were they after scalps and plunder, or were they only interested in killing?**"

"As far as I could tell, Major, none of those. In questioning the prisoners afterward, I was informed that their raid was in retaliation for the death of a Mohave youth who was tortured and killed by white men."

"**Were you able to uncover any proof of these claims?**"

"No, sir, just the conversations I had with the captives on our way to Fort Yuma, although I reported their accusations to the commander at Fort Mohave at my earliest opportunity, via a telegraph from Fort Yuma."

"**Fort Yuma, not Fort Mohave?**"

"Yes, sir. It was suggested by the agent at Fort Mohave that if prisoners were taken, it might be prudent to escort them to Yuma, rather than back to Mohave. In my opinion, that was sound advice, and we boarded the steamer *Alice* at Hardyville on June ninth. We disembarked at Fort Yuma five days later."

"At any point during your interrogations, Captain, did the captives allude to any fear of a planned act of military retaliation against the Bosque Wash Mohaves for the theft of horses near Eldorado Canyon?"

"It was mentioned a few times, but never very seriously. For the most part, I'd have to say they were more angry about a youth being tortured and killed."

"The one you mentioned a moment ago?"

"Yes, sir."

"What was the name of that youth, Captain?"

"Whip. That's the English translation. It actually refers to the scorpion, and the curve of its tail. As I understand it, the boy's full name was Fast Stinger, or something along those lines. My interpreters were unable to provide a literal translation."

"But he was called Whip?"

"Yes, sir, after Arizona Whiptails."

"Scorpions?"

"Yes, sir."

"You claim the war party's route was contorted. Explain that."

"Reedcatcher appeared to be leading his men in a zigzag pattern, primarily north to south, but with a southeasterly bent. It was my opinion at the time, and that of my scouts as well, that the war party was in search of someone they expected to find in that vicinity."

"What area, specifically, Captain?"

"The Black Mountains, Sacramento Valley, and Dutch Flats region, all in northwestern Arizona. The Mohaves were moving fast, but continued to double back on themselves."

"Did your captives state a reason for this seemingly random course?"

"Yes, sir. They confirmed what I and my scouts suspected, which was that the Reedcatcher party was looking for the men responsible for the torture and murder of the boy called Whip."

"At any point in your pursuit of the Reedcatcher party, did you venture south of the Bill Williams River?"

"No, sir."

"At the point where your scouts picked up the Reedcatcher trail, was there any indication that the renegade Mohaves had crossed to the south of the Bill Williams River, or had in any way been below that river?"

"No, sir. My scouts picked up the Mohaves' trail less than ten miles off the reservation, and stayed on it the entire chase."

"Captain Reynolds, in your opinion, did the Mohaves under Reedcatcher's command, or any faction of it, attack the Colorado and Prescott Stage station at Tyson's Well, east of Ehrenberg, on the morning of two June of this year?"

"No, sir. It's my opinion that the Tyson's Well station was too far south for Reedcatcher or any of his men to strike there, then return north of the Bill Williams River in the time available to them."

"Thank you, Captain. You are dismissed."

SESSION FIVE

As I was saying before we were interrupted, I'd just gotten slammed into the Colorado River by what I at first assumed must have been either a mule's kick or a battering ram. I hit that river nose-first, and for the next several minutes was caught up in a nightmare of flailing limbs, murky water, and pure terror.

Although I've already mentioned I couldn't swim, fear can do wonders when it comes to survival, and I soon corked back to the surface, pounding at the Colorado's powerful grip like I used to pound at my ma's legs when she was dragging me toward a haircut or a dose of tonic. Fortunately, the current below the sandbar curled inward, which helped keep me away from the deeper water at mid-channel, although, even relatively close to the bank, I was in way over my head—no pun intended. I knew because at one point I tried to stand up, just to get my feet on something solid, and immediately sank below the surface, catching a snout full of muddy water for my troubles and escalating my already rapidly inflating fear. Yet even as I continued to slam my fists against the river's relentless tow, I realized I was gradually edging closer to shore.

Those sandbar willows I told you about earlier almost always lean noticeably toward the water, kind of like brass rings on a carousel. I'd reach for them every time I got near a bunch, but my fingers kept slipping off. About the fourth or fifth time that happened, my panic started kicking in. My boots were full of water, my saturated clothing seemed to weigh a ton, and the twin revolvers strapped around my waist and chest felt like grasping arms trying to pull me under. My strength was fading rapidly, and it occurred to me that I could very well drown out there, waterlogged and alone and half froze from the Colorado's chilly currents, straight out of the snowcapped Rocky Mountains—a humiliating end considering the thirst and blazing heat I'd endured all day.

With a final burst of determination, I grabbed a lungful of air, then deliberately allowed myself to sink below the surface. I'd wager my head was at least three feet under before my boots finally touched bottom. I went even lower when I tried to push off, my toes sinking into the tacky mud. Caught off guard by the riverbed's clinging muck, I was disheartened when I broke the surface and found myself no nearer the bank than I had been when I went under.

Gasping and half blinded, my limbs growing heavier with every feckless stroke, I wanted to cry out in rage and despair. When I sank the next time, I'm not a hundred percent certain it was a deliberate act on my part, although I did manage to grab a lungful of air before sliding from sight. Had I not done that, I kind of doubt I would have come back up. But I did, and that time, remembering the gooeyness of the river's bed, I adjusted my upward lunge accordingly.

Breaking the surface brought a hoarse but barely audible roar of delight from my throat. Although the water was still over my head, the bank was only a few feet away. Still, my escape wasn't guaranteed. I was growing weaker; my muscles ached, and my limbs seemed to respond only haphazardly to the commands my brain kept sending them. Spying a clump of willows thrust deeper into the channel than any of the others I'd passed so far, I knew I was going to have to make it work this time. If I lost my grip again, I wouldn't have enough strength for another try.

In that liquid-hazed world, it almost seemed like the willows were speeding toward me, rather than the other way around. Despite my efforts against it, I could feel myself starting to slide under. It took just about everything I had to raise my left hand out of the water that last time, to close my fingers on a pair of jouncing red stems and allow the current to twirl me toward shore in a neat little allemande.

Hacking water and snot in what seemed like equal portions, I reached for another handhold to pull myself deeper into the willows. Tentatively lowering one foot, I quickly found bottom, while my head and most of my torso remained above the surface. Drawing air in over my tortured throat, I floundered toward dry ground, forcing a passage through the thick, resisting growth. Soggy mud and brown water streamed from my clothes as I lurched into the shallows close to the bank. My sinuses felt raw and my lungs burned, and every time I coughed, little spurts of water would shoot up the back of my throat or out my nostrils. Blackness hovered above my head like the wings of a thousand crows. I fought it back until I felt solid ground under my feet, then fell limply forward.

I don't remember passing out, but I guess I did. When I opened my eyes, it was to stare into a tiny green face no more than six inches from the tip of my nose. At first I thought it was a frog. Then a splinter-thin tongue, split at the tip, flicked out to test the air between us. Apparently deciding I was still alive and large enough to be a threat, the snake turned and slithered off through the reeds. I watched it leave with one side of my face pressed into the mud, admiring the smooth, undulating movement of the reptile's slim form as it vanished from sight. It was a small one, some kind of grass snake, I suppose, and probably more afraid of me than I was of it—ironic, since I was pretty sure from the way I felt that it could have taken me without much effort.

The sky was gray with early morning light, the air damp and cool. Although I was chilled all the way through, I mostly ached. Brother, did I ache. My muscles felt as stiff as rusted iron and my joints hollered at every little twitch. It was as if I'd been beaten from head to toes with clubs, then stomped on for good measure. You wouldn't think plain water could pummel a body so viciously, but there's power in a river that can shame even a sideshow muscleman.

I pushed awkwardly to my feet, grunting like my grandpappy used to do whenever he got out of his chair on cold winter mornings. Grandpappy had gnarled hands and a hunched spine, and could just about spit venom when the weather turned cool in the fall. That night on the Colorado, I finally understood why he acted that way. My hat was gone, my boots squished with every step, my still-sodden clothes clung to my body like dead flesh, and my head throbbed as it did after a night drinking cheap booze down at Molly Herriman's Saloon, back in Ehrenberg. After fighting my way clear of the willows, I turned north toward where I'd left the jenny.

It was a lot farther going back than I anticipated. Dawn was already etching the jagged skyline above the Plomosas by the time I stumbled into the small riverside clearing. I paused at the edge of the chaparral to stare at the sandbar where I'd gone into the water. Although I tried to remember what had knocked me off my feet, I couldn't quite wrap my thoughts around the actual event. It was like a spotty fog had drifted across my brain, obscuring bits and pieces, while others shone clear.

The jenny stood where I'd left her, hitched to a mesquite. She watched with sad eyes as I stumbled into the clearing, and although she seemed to perk up when I approached, I had to once again ignore her silent plea to be turned loose. I was trembling so violently by then that I could hardly loosen the straps holding my warbag to the saddle. With the day's heat still several hours away, I knew I had to get a fire going soon; otherwise, I was going to be in trouble.

Mumbling reassurances to the mule that I hadn't forgotten her, I walked over to the gray ashes of the outlaws' fire and eased down on creaking knees. The little pasteboard box of matches I carried in my pocket was soaked and useless, mashed into a glob of pasteboard and red phosphorus, but I had a spare box in my warbag, and dug it out. There was a tiny stack of mesquite limbs piled on the ground next to the ashes, and with those, a fresh match, and a wad of last winter's dried grass for tinder, it didn't take long to get a fire burning. Wiggling so close I was practically hunched over the top of the small, wooden pyramid, I waited eagerly for the warmth I knew was coming. Although the heat was sparse at first, it gradually strengthened, and after a while my tremors slowed, then stopped.

Hunger was gnawing at my stomach, but I was determined to take care of the jenny first. After tightening the cinch, I crawled into the saddle, then rode out to circle the stolen C&P cavvy. The stock was scattered and wary, and would trot off with high heads every time I got close. I finally had to fashion a lariat out of my picket rope, which I was able to drop over the neck of a tall sorrel wheeler. After hitching the mare to the same sturdy mesquite where the jenny had spent the night, I went back for a second mount. Ignoring the mules, I finally snagged a short-coupled bay gelding and led him back to camp. With both horses tied off, I pulled my rig from the jenny's back and slipped the bit from between her teeth.

"You did real good, girl," I told the mule, giving her hip an affectionate slap as she dodged clear.

I guess she didn't appreciate the sentiment, because she took a swipe at me with a rear hoof as she went past, a kick I just barely dodged. With a condemning bray, she trotted to the river, and soon had her muzzle dipped into the purling waters. I smiled without resentment, although I'm sure I would have felt differently had her iron-shod hoof connected with my body. I was stiff enough as it was, without the added insult of a mule's shoe imprinted on my hide.

It was only while walking back to the fire, my near miss with the jenny's hoof fresh in my mind, that I began to recall the events of the previous evening, especially that mule kick–like thump that had sent me ass-over-teakettle into the Colorado's surging currents. I halted uncertainly, my thoughts ranging backward. Although my body throbbed from the beating it had taken from the river, my hand rose almost instinctively to press on the short-barreled Smith and Wesson, still in its shoulder rig under my left arm. The pressure, light as it was, ignited a spasm of pain across my side.

I flinched and swore, then unbuttoned my shirt down to mid-chest, which is only as far as shirts went in those days, being mostly slip-overs. Pulling the damp material away from my body, I stared in bewilderment at a grapefruit-sized bruise under my arm. Frowning, I closed the shirt and pulled my vest back, revealing the torn leather of my shoulder holster.

In looking back, it seems like it took me forever to realize what had happened. I remember trying to pull the Smith and Wesson from its holster, and how it wouldn't come until I grabbed the toe with my other hand and gave the gun a yank. My confusion deepened as I stared at the crippled revolver. The cylinder had been knocked askew in its frame and refused to rotate, and a piece of wood had been chewed from the grip, leaving a pale, splintered scar in the checkering.

As if in a daze, I turned toward that low bluff to the north that I'd dismissed with barely a glance the night before. A pair of cactus wrens were flitting above a sprawling patch of prickly pear below the summit, and a C&P mule grazed near its base, but nothing else stirred in the calm gray light. Shifting my gaze toward the river, I recalled the shadowy image of Ed Granger's skiff beneath the Colorado's rippled surface, and mumbled a gentle curse, almost in awe, of the things I'd neatly forgotten until a mule's misplaced kick brought it all crashing back.

I glanced again at the bluff but felt certain whoever had taken a shot at me there the night before had long since moved on. After a moment's pondering, I returned to the fire. There was plenty of wood left, and it didn't take long to rekindle a fresh blaze. Sitting close for warmth, I dug my gun kit and a box of .45 Schofields from my warbag and set about repairing the damage. I cleaned the big revolver I carried at my waist first, oiling it thoroughly afterward, then reloading with dry rounds. Next I plucked the dozen cartridges I carried in the loops on my belt—already faintly green with verdigris—and replaced those. Although still damp, the gun's leather had been well greased before my dunking, and would be dry again by sundown.

I peeled out of the shoulder rig and tossed it aside. I hated to leave the shorter revolver behind, but figured the odds were better that I'd need to travel light and fast than it was that I'd cross paths with a competent gunsmith who could make any needed repairs in the field. It was so out of whack I couldn't even get the latch released to empty the cylinder. Finally I stood up and heaved it into the river, and like as not it's still there, way down deep in the mud.

Leaving the shoulder holster on the ground, I threw my saddle over the sorrel's back and cinched it down. The fire had burned to ashes by the time I was ready, but I kicked dirt over it anyway. Then I swung a leg stiffly over the cantle and, with the bay horse in tow, reined toward the bluff.

I rode around to come up the back way, keeping my shotgun handy. There were no trees, but lots of greasewood and cactus. I kept my eyes on the ground all the way to the top, looking for sign and finding plenty of it. Dismounting below the crest, I went the rest of the way on foot. It didn't take but a few seconds to find where the ambusher had laid in wait. Whoever had taken that shot must have been there for a while. Cupped inside a cluster of greasewood were more than a dozen ground-out cigarette butts, gouges where he'd apparently plunged a knife repeatedly into the hard soil—maybe out of boredom—and finally, the marks of elbows and knees and square-toed boots, all in a line with the riverside clearing. Hunkering down where the man had waited, I had a clear view of the campfire, as well as the tip of the sandbar. From below, I'd estimated the distance at around a hundred yards. From up here, I guessed it closer to one hundred twenty, still well within range for a competent marksman, even one armed with a small-caliber rifle.

Noah's words echoed faintly in my mind. *They're an ugly bunch . . . corner them and they'll turn as mean as a sack full of rattlers.* I'd believed him at Desert Wells. I believed him even more, there on the Colorado.

The sun was all the way up by the time I left the bluff, its heat already spreading across the valley. For the first time that morning, I began to feel whole again. A fire can be real nice when you're chilled to the bone, but it can't take the place of a summer sun.

Leaning back in my saddle, I dug the sack of food Elizabeth had sent along from my bags then fumbled around inside that for some ham and what was left of her biscuits, mostly crumbs at that point. I ate as I rode, following the river north through scattered patches of mesquite and an occasional small grove of cottonwood or river elm. I hadn't gone quite half a mile when I came to where my ambusher had left his horse, staked in a verdant clearing under some tall cottonwoods. The grass all around where the picket pin had been driven into the sod was cropped close to the ground, telling me the animal had been there a while.

I stopped but didn't dismount, my gaze roaming the tiny vale. I would have expected the others to have waited for the ambusher, but from the looks of things, they'd gone on without him. I found that puzzling. Why leave a man behind when they didn't know how many might be following? And why would anyone consent to be left behind under those circumstances? It crossed my mind that maybe they'd done something as simple as draw straws to see who would stay back and watch for pursuit, but I've got to admit, they didn't seem like the straw-drawing kind.

It was probably another mile upstream when I ran into my second mystery of the morning. I stopped again, scowling at the trail where it peeled away from the river to angle back to the northeast. I could feel the muscles drawing tight across the back of my skull as I studied the bandits' tracks.

Leaving the Colorado didn't make sense, unless it was another ruse to throw off pursuit, like what they'd tried with Ed Granger's skiff. But if that was their plan, I couldn't find the reasoning behind it. Deciding that I didn't have a choice, I reined away from the shady riverbank, back into the full blast of the sun.

Even with fresh mounts and the ability to switch horses when needed, I didn't hurry. At that point I was content to hound their trail from a distance. Sooner or later, they'd have to go to roost. I could decide then what my next move should be. I did notice that they also weren't pushing very hard, which made me wonder if they were settling in for a long haul. I tried to picture what might lie ahead. It was all empty country as far as I knew, desolate and inhospitable. Way off in the distance I could see the Buckskin Mountains, humped up on the horizon like an arthritic spine. There was a fair-sized river on the other side of those, but no towns that I'd heard of.

It didn't take long before I began feeling the effects of the sun. The memory of my near hypothermia that morning seemed like a bad joke as I dug the gray silk ascot from my warbag and fashioned it into a bandanna to cover my head. I wondered what would become of my hat, likely still floating downstream from my dunking the night before. I hoped someone found it and put it to good use; it was a damned fine hat, made of good quality beaver felt, and less than a year old.

There's really not much to tell about the rest of that day. It was just trudging forward under increasingly brutal conditions. It took a lot longer to reach the Buckskins than I thought it would. The sun was already setting by the time I rode into the foothills. Darkness caught me well below the summit, forcing a halt in the middle of a deep, sandy wash. There wasn't any graze for the horses, and I had to do the best I could watering them from the canteen by trickling it carefully into the cupped palms of my hands, then letting them to suck it up as best they could. I spilled more over my boots than I got into the horses, and had yet another reason to regret losing my hat to the Colorado.

The next morning, after a skimpy breakfast of what remained of the food Elizabeth had sent along, I saddled the bay and moved out. Although I'd briefly considered plowing on through the night before, I was soon glad that I hadn't. Less than two hundred yards from where I'd camped, the bandits abruptly left the wash. I scrambled my horse out of the deep arroyo after them, but had to toss the sorrel's lead rope halfway to the top to keep from being pulled from the saddle. I cursed as the taller horse spooked back down the wash, holding its head off to one side to avoid stepping on the lead. Although I briefly considered going after it, I quickly decided against it. A frightened horse can be a bear to catch, and could have led me a merry chase all the way back to the Colorado. Prodding the bay's ribs with my heels, we continued on our way.

The sun wasn't even up yet, but I was already sweating. It was warm down there among the rocks, and my nerves were drawn taut. I don't think there was a spot anywhere on that mountainside that didn't harbor at least one handy place for an ambush. I was an easy target, and knew it. Still, I kept on, and after a while the trail dropped into a narrow slot-like canyon, the tracks winding steadily deeper into the mountains. The bandits were riding single-file now, squeezing through places where I could have kicked both sides of the canyon at the same time if I'd wanted to.

I kept my shotgun free and handy, my eyes constantly scanning the canyon's rims. It's kind of interesting how a bullet in your side, even if it doesn't kill you, can knock the chocks out from under your confidence. Being ready to kick loose of my saddle at the first hint of trouble is probably why I reacted the way I did when I heard a commotion coming up fast behind me.

I swore and yanked hard on the bay's reins, but it was so narrow in that slot canyon the horse had to partially rear up on its hind legs to get turned around. In doing so, it slammed my back against the wall, sending a spasm of pain shooting across my tender ribs and loosening a small avalanche of stones and dirt and clouds of dust that only added to the confusion. Snapping the Parker to my shoulder, I was about to holler for whoever was back there to stop immediately and throw down their guns, when the sorrel suddenly appeared around the corner. I swore again, then heaved a long sigh and lowered the shotgun.

"You damned fool," I told the sorrel. "It's a wonder I didn't blow your head off."

The horse snorted deer-like, then came timidly forward. Although aggravated with the mare's unexpected return, I was relieved, too. Next to water, a knife, and a gun, a good horse is about the most important thing you can have in that kind of country.

The sorrel came close and I grabbed the lead rope, but I didn't keep it. Looping it into a tight butterfly coil, I fastened it under the mare's halter, where it would be out of the way. A horse is a herd animal, and while the sorrel probably wouldn't have followed me away from the rest of the C&P stock on the Colorado without the lead, she apparently had no intention of abandoning me—or more likely, the bay—way out there in the middle of nowhere.

I dismounted to get the bay turned back around, then crawled into the saddle and continued on. The sorrel fell in naturally behind, and I no longer had any concerns about her staying close. Thirty minutes later, we came to a flat spot near the crest, and I hauled up to let the horses catch their wind. After loosening the bay's cinch, I walked to the edge of the flat where I'd have a clear view of our route in from the Colorado River. My gaze hardened at the cluster of boot prints in the dirt around me. Somebody had been watching, and had likely spotted me crossing the cactus-studded plain far below. They knew I was coming, and they'd also know by then that I didn't intend to give up. The next time they tried to stop me, they'd likely make damned sure they got the job done . . . permanently.

I've been on posses before, either as a representative for Coltrane or one of the express companies I've worked for over the years, and more often than not, after a group road-agented a stagecoach, they'd cut a bug out of there in a straight line for wherever it was they planned to go. If they were more organized than most, they might have a relay of horses waiting somewhere down the trail. Or if they envisioned themselves the wily sort, they might try to hide their tracks for a few miles, until panic took over and they made a beeline for their destination. No one

I'd chased had ever left such a convoluted trail as this bunch, and I'll admit it was starting to bother me. I couldn't decide if they were smarter than the average highwaymen, or just thought they were and had gotten lucky so far.

By now, word would have reached both Ehrenberg and Prescott that Pete Driscoll's eastbound coach had been hit by bandits. There would be posses out from both locations, and, with a little luck, the division agent at Prescott might have talked the commander at Fort Whipple into sending out a patrol, or at least loaning them a couple of good trackers. But based on my experience with earlier posses, I doubted they'd find anything. Not even with a couple of native scouts cutting for sign.

Noah Hoffman would have sent word in both directions that the bandits had been heading west when they left Desert Wells, and that was the direction the posses would take when they finally hit the trail. A more or less natural route was eventually going to lead them to the clearing where I'd taken my dunk in the Colorado, and once they reached the river, the sign was going to be fairly easy to read. My fear was that they'd come to the same conclusion I initially had—that the bandits had abandoned their mounts at the river to sail downstream in Ed Granger's stolen skiff. It had been only pure luck that I hadn't fallen for their ruse, and poor thinking on my part not to have left some kind of message behind for them to find.

It wasn't much farther to the top. The trail led over a low saddle between a pair of stunted peaks. I halted again, this time to study the country before me. I could see the Bill Williams River way off in the distance, a line of dark green threaded across a rolling tan landscape, but nothing else. Noting the broken terrain below the saddle caused the muscles in my jaws to tighten. It looked like good ambush country. Even better than what I'd come through that morning.

It was midafternoon when I finally emerged from the

Buckskins, my hide all in one piece save for a few scratches from a manzanita bush the bay had stumbled into. Hauling up at the edge of the foothills, I eyed the distant line of foliage warily. Nothing there seemed out of the ordinary, no smudge of smoke nor hint of movement, yet I felt strongly that was the direction the bandits had taken, and that they might still be there. The Bill was the only source of water for miles around, and they'd need to stop, no matter how briefly, to refill their canteens. The trouble was, so would I, and my blood cooled at the thought of crossing that long, empty expanse of cactus-studded plain, exposed to the bandits' rifles.

From what I could see from the chaparral, the trail seemed to head straight across the valley to the river. The sorrel, growing impatient with thirst, started toward open ground. I kicked the bay after it, grabbing the lead rope and hauling the mare back to cover.

"We'll wait a bit," I said, as if an explanation might curb the horses' restlessness.

I don't know if you've noticed, but I'd begun talking to my horses more and more as the miles reeled off behind us. Although I'd only been on the trail three days by then, the emptiness of the land was starting to work on me. I've never been the pioneering type, for all that I grew up in that country. I always liked a town, that sense of safety and community that comes with the company of others. I'm not saying I was intimidated by the wilderness, because I wasn't. It's just that, given a choice between the hunter's trail and a warm meal and a cold beer with family and friends, I'd take the latter every time.

Reining back into the scrub, I hitched both horses to sturdy limbs, then crawled through the thickest part of the chaparral to where I'd have a clear view of the trees along the Bill, probably three quarters of a mile away. I left the Parker on my saddle, but had the Marlin with me, figuring the rifle might prove wiser in such open country.

Settling down with my back against a boulder and the Marlin slanted across my lap, I waited and watched. It was miserably hot inside the chaparral. Sweat saturated my bandanna, turning my shirt dark and leaving gray whorls of salt under both arms. Eventually the sun set and the light drained out of the sky. The shadows grew thick and a breeze began to stir, rattling the limbs around me and making my scalp crawl with images of skulking bandits and wily Apaches. I waited until the moon came up, then pushed stiffly to my feet and returned to where I'd left the horses. Shoving the Marlin inside its scabbard, I loosened my coat from behind the cantle and slipped it on. A crazy country, Arizona, but I loved it then and still do today.

"Well, I guess I've put this off long enough," I told the bay. Leading the weary animals out of the chaparral, I stepped into the saddle and reined toward the distant river, keeping the sorrel on a short lead at my side.

My nerves were tingling as we crossed that lumpy plain. In my mind I kept hearing the hollow boom of the gunshot that had sent me tumbling into the Colorado, remembering how far away it had seemed at the time, yet how I'd been almost instantly knocked off my feet. As if it had been the sound of the report, rather than the bullet thumping into the Smith and Wesson in its shoulder holster, that sent me into the water.

No shot rang out that night, and I began to breathe easier as we entered the deeper darkness under the trees. I could feel the moisture off the river almost instantly, and the scent of the tall grass that brushed the bottoms of my stirrups was soothing after the harsh aridity of the desert. Even though the horses were suffering terribly for water, they kept reaching for that long-stemmed June grass all the way to the river's edge. Strands of it jutted from around the bay's bit like scraggly whiskers by the time I dismounted on a sandy shoal and pulled the headstall so that the gelding could more easily drink. The sorrel was already standing knee deep in the river, the sound of her slurping loud but gratifying above the purling of the Bill's waters.

I stood vigilantly as the horses drank, my eyes and ears attuned to the surrounding darkness, but everything seemed quiet. Finally deciding it was safe, I began scooping up palms full of water for myself, likely making as much racket as my horses but too parched to care. It was only after slaking the worst of my thirst that I tied off both animals and made a quick scout through the trees, even though I was fairly certain the outlaws were nowhere nearby. Had they been close, the horses would have let all of us know with their questioning whickers.

I made another cold camp that night, pulling my blankets over my shoulders and using the slanting trunk of a cottonwood as a backrest. I kept the Parker across my lap, the Marlin at my side. Although I didn't anticipating falling asleep as quickly as I did, I guess the near hundred-degree temperatures of the past few days were beginning to take their toll.

My stomach was rumbling the next morning as I saddled the mare, but there wasn't anything I could do about it. I'd cleaned up the last of Elizabeth's food the day before, even picking the crumbs out of the bottom of the saddlebags with the wetted tip of my finger. Although there were fish in the river and probably deer along the bottoms, I wasn't going to take time to hunt.

I'd lost the bandits' trail the night before, but picked it up again less than a half mile from where I'd spent the night. They'd crossed the Bill the previous evening, but hadn't stopped. That baffled me. Even with my limited skills as a tracker, I could tell that their horses were beginning to fade. If they hadn't held over here at least long enough to allow their mounts time to graze and recoup some of their strength, it meant their destination had to be close.

Tight-jawed and stubbornly determined, I reined after them. Their trail wound up into the foothills of a mountain range I didn't know the name of, following a rocky trail toward a V-shaped pass several miles to the north. I made pretty good time considering the roughness of the terrain, and pulled up on top around noon to have a look around and give my mounts a chance to catch their wind.

While the horses grazed, I walked forward on foot, the rifle hanging loose in my right hand. A column of smoke was curling into the sky in the distance, wind-tattered and twisted. Although curious, I didn't necessarily believe it had anything to do with the men I was chasing. I've already mentioned how there were mining camps all through that country, ranging in size from a couple of hundred hard rock miners, to just a handful of men joining together for safety against Indian attacks and bandit raids. Some of the larger camps might have a store or a saloon, as often as not set up in tents in case the mines played out and they had to move on in a hurry, but very few of them had any dwellings more permanent than a stone hut or mud *jacale*.

Other than their tracks in the flinty soil, I didn't see anything of Trepan or his men, but after eyeing those scuffed prints a moment longer, my gaze involuntarily shuttled back to that far-off column of smoke—too big to be a campfire, too singular for a mining camp—and a niggling sense of foreboding settled heavily in my gut. I stared a while longer, then walked back to fetch my horses and resume the journey.

We were several hours coming down out of those hills north of the Bill. Although the outlaws' trail continued forward without pause, I could tell their horses were about played out. They'd gained quite a bit of time on me by not stopping at the river the night before, but their haste was costing them dearly now, the heat—especially among those winding canyons and rock-strewn ridges—growing nearly unbearable as the afternoon advanced. Even the lizards looked thirsty, their paper-thin flanks pumping rapidly as they contemplated my passage with reptilian indifference.

The land finally leveled out late that afternoon, dun-colored and bleak, but without the upthrust of earth on every side that caged the heat and held it close. A long, broad valley opened to the northwest, while the country to the east and north remained crinkled with small, boulder-strewn hills and shallow canyons. Although the smoke I'd spotted from above had vanished, I can't say I was surprised when the outlaws' trail led me to its source. I hauled up about a hundred yards away, eyeing the burned-out wreckage of an adobe house; a couple of smaller outbuildings were untorched, but damaged.

For a moment, the old fear of Apaches razored through me, even though I knew in my heart that the destruction here had been caused by white men. Although I didn't see anyone moving about, the outlaws' horses were scattered across the plain in front of the house, lathered and wrung-out, their muzzles nearly dragging the ground. Easing the Parker from its loop, I nudged the sorrel forward. The smell of the fire sharpened as I drew close, and my nerves were just about thrumming. I was trying to prepare myself for whatever macabre discovery awaited me, but not doing a very good job of it.

The house was larger than I would have expected for such an isolated location. It had a flat roof, a verandah across the front, and a pair of windows with real glass on either side of the open door. A squatty barn was set off to one side, with a corral nearby and a lean-to shed between that and the house, covering a couple of ricks of split firewood. A wooden chicken coop lay on its side next to the lean-to as if blown over, although the carcasses of dead, bullet-torn poultry dotting the flat ground around it seemed to challenge the idea of a twister.

Before the fire, it would have been a nice-looking spread

under any circumstances, but what really set the place apart in that sun-blistered country was the patch of greenery to the rear. Maybe two acres of tall grass, young fruit trees, and berries climbing short fences made of saguaro ribs, sagging beneath the weight of its just-beginning-to-ripen crop. I wondered briefly if the source of water was another hand-dug well or a natural spring. Then my gaze returned to the dead chickens and the worn-out horses, and I rocked the Parker's hammers to full cock.

The closer I got, the more certain I became that the place was deserted. The extent of the damage was a large part of my conviction. The front door hung open on broken hinges, the entire frame twisted, as if about to tear loose from its adobe mooring. The glass in the windows had been shattered by bullets, and tongues of pale gray smoke curled from the various ports and openings like dancing wraiths. Other than the low hum of the wind, there wasn't a sound. Not even a curious whicker from one of the horses.

I stopped again when I noticed a pair of graves to the north of the house. The nearest one had a simple rock for a headstone, and looked like it had been there for a while. The farthest nearly closed my throat. The soil was dark and freshly turned, and the crumbling dirt atop its crude headstone seemed to suggest that it had only recently been pried out of the earth and moved there. Although nearly twice the size of the first marker, it sat atop a grave barely a third as large as the older mound.

My gaze returned to the barn's dark entrance, then moved on to the little orchard out back. If anyone was left, that would likely be where they were holed up. I don't know why I glanced over my shoulder, toward the long, flat valley that stretched away to the northwest, but I did, and the muscles across my shoulders immediately tightened when I spotted movement far out on the plain—a solitary individual, afoot.

Although too far away to make out any details, I felt certain it was a woman. Even though I was eager to know who she was and what she was doing out there alone, I couldn't turn away. Dismounting, I tied my reins to a post jutting from the wreckage of the chicken coop, then made my way toward the house. The stench of the fire, of burned leather and scorched wool and ruined meat, intensified at the door. It was an odor unique to house fires. As if all within had been tainted with a miasma of charred dreams and singed memories. I was still confident that the house was empty, but let the Parker's twin muzzles enter the building first. Both hammers were drawn all the way back, and my finger rested firmly on the right-hand trigger.

If you've been thinking that adobe doesn't burn, you'd be right, but a well-set fire inside any structure can cause a tremendous amount of damage, no matter what its outer hull. From the underlying odor at the door, I was guessing kerosene had been used to bolster the fire's destruction. Most of the furnishings had been piled in the middle of the front room before being set ablaze. Among the fire-blackened debris, I recognized a table and chairs, a hutch, cabinets, bed and bedding, various crates and boxes. Very little had burned all the way down to ash, but it was all equally ruined. What hadn't been consumed by flame now stunk of oily smoke, an essence worse than that of a cornered skunk.

The one thing I didn't smell, and for which I was grateful, was charred flesh. I'd seen the burned remains of an emigrant family outside of Prescott some years earlier, and had no urge to ever witness anything like that again. [*Editor's Note:* Slade is probably referring to the Oskar Gedman family, of Trosa, Sweden; the Gedmans were found murdered south of Prescott in 1877, and although blame at the time had been attributed to both the Mohave and Apache (Tonto) Indians, the perpetrators were never positively identified, and no one was ever brought to justice for the crime; in addition to Oskar and his wife Stina, three of the Gedman's children—William, Viktor, and Emma—were found near the incinerated prairie schooner; a fourth child, twelve-year-old Hans, was never located.]

Breathing as shallowly as possible, I made a quick pass through a pair of back rooms, then hurried outside, the stink of the blaze already adhering to my clothing. I checked the barn next, but it was empty, and looked like it had been for a long time. There were fresh tracks in the corral, though, and eyeing the gang's saddle-worn mounts scattered across the plain to the northwest, I decided Trepan and his men must have come here to pick up fresh horses. That was why they hadn't lingered at the Bill the night before. Meanwhile, my own horses were showing the strain of the long desert trek. I was glad I'd brought along a second mount, though. As tired as they were, I hadn't completely exhausted either animal yet.

Lowering the Parker's hammers to half cock, I went back to where I'd left the sorrel. I had to thread my way through at least a dozen dead birds to reach the mare's side. The chickens—all hens—looked like they'd been cut down with shotguns as they fled the toppled coop. Staring somberly at the murdered fowl, it occurred to me that Trepan's crew seemed to be getting steadily meaner as the days wore on. First, the ambush at the Colorado, then the callous way they'd pushed their horses through the night. And now this.

Even though the chickens had obviously been dead for a while, I was hungry enough to overlook the potential hazards of eating spoiled meat. But first I wanted to learn the identity of the woman I'd seen walking away from the burned-out homestead, and find out how she was tied in with Trepan and his crew.

Stepping into my saddle, I reined toward the flats, only to pull up a few minutes later when I realized the woman was no longer in sight. I sat there for a moment, my gaze roaming the distant reaches. Finally deciding that if she'd spotted me poking around the wreckage of the house and barn, she might have simply gone into hiding, I lifted the sorrel into a short lope. I rode with my feet light in the stirrups, in case I had to leave my saddle in a hurry, the Parker balanced across the bows in front of me.

The sun was pretty low on the horizon by then, making it difficult to see what lay directly in front of me. Boulders, some of them as big as stagecoaches, dotted the plain along the foothills on my left, and shallow canyons cut back into the mountains like old scars. When I got to where I'd last seen the woman, I slowed the mare to a walk and began cutting back and forth for sign. The first tracks I found were made by horses, and I couldn't help a grim smile when I realized I'd probably saved myself a lot of trouble by not having to sort out which direction the gang had gone in when they left the house.

Swinging onto the bandits' trail, I followed it for another hundred yards, until I came to a new set of prints overlapping the sharper edges of the outlaws' iron-shod mounts. I pulled up, my brows furrowing in concentration. When I first spotted the woman, I'd assumed she was heading for civilization. Maybe a trading post along the Colorado, or some miners' camp back in the hills. Now it appeared as if she was also following the outlaws' trail.

When I thought about it, I could see where she'd have cause to, assuming the burned-out house belonged to her, and that it had been Trepan's men who destroyed it. But surely she didn't intend to hunt them down alone. What could a woman do against such a crew like this? Then I recalled something my grandpappy had told me when I was still a boy.

"*Tom,*" he'd said, watching his daughter—my mother—stomp back into the house after chewing the two of us out for some kind of foolishness I've long since forgotten, *"never underestimate the power of a good mad."*

He meant anger, of course, and I knew from my own experience that it could be a powerful force. Hell, it was a big reason why I was out there in the first place. So why shouldn't she be allowed to feel the same way toward the men who had fire-gutted her home?

With my curiosity piqued, I rode on at a quicker pace, hoping to catch up before darkness fell. It was barely half a mile farther on, with the sun's belly just touching the western rim of the horizon, when a high-pitched shriek on my left nearly curdled the blood in my veins. A ragged cry was torn from my throat, and the sorrel nearly came unglued as the woman burst out of the rocks not more than forty feet away. Her eyes were wide and wild, her hair disheveled. She continued her flesh-shriveling wails as she attempted to close the gap between us before I could get my horse under control, my shotgun swung around to face her.

She was carrying a pickax—one of those wooden-handled digging and trenching tools with one end pointed and the other flat and perpendicular for scooping or chopping through roots—cocked over her shoulder like she knew how to use it. Even with that fool mare of mine trying her damndest to unload me, I noticed how the piked tip was stained with dirt and what looked like dried blood. I kept trying to get the Parker up to cover her, but the sorrel wasn't cooperating; it snorted and crow-hopped and kicked up a fine cloud of grit as it clumsily retreated from the screeching woman, while I struggled to hang onto my reins and shotgun and, especially, my seat.

I think I might have actually yelped when the pick streaked past my knee, caught briefly in the coiled lead rope tied to the saddle's pommel, then jerked free as the sorrel lunged sideways. The mare's legs tangled in a clump of greasewood, and she went down hard on her side. I kicked free and rolled clear, but lost my shotgun in the process. The woman kept coming, howling madly as she dodged around the flailing sorrel. I was on my back, my hands raised futilely—

SESSION SIX

I'm not even going to begin to tell you how aggravating it is when I have to stop every time that damned machine of yours fills another disk. Just give me some warning next time, will you?

What I was saying was how that woman seemed to come out of nowhere with a blood-encrusted pick cocked over her right shoulder, acting like a hatter. [*Editor's Note:* Slade is probably referring to an abbreviation of the term "mad as a hatter" here, a colloquial phrase implying insanity; during the eighteenth and nineteenth centuries, mercury was a commonly used ingredient in the construction of hats made from the felt of fur-bearing animals such as the beaver and nutria; this led to a slow mercury poisoning in the men and women employed in the hat-making business, often resulting in severe dementia.]

I was still on my back when she finally got a clear swing, and only managed to jerk my head out of the way at the last second. The pick's steel tip buried itself in the hard ground next to my ear, spraying dirt against the side of my face and into one eye. She was already yanking the heavy tool free when I swung my legs in a roundhouse sweep that took her feet neatly out from under her. She dropped on top of me with a startled squawk, and I brought my elbow around with everything I had, connecting solidly with that space between the tip of her chin and her lower lip. She grunted and her head slammed back, and I tumbled her off to the side and tried to scramble clear. She kept fighting, cursing and spitting like a wildcat, kicking at my knees and lower legs with her heels, although thankfully never getting the proper leverage to do any serious damage.

She was determined, though, and didn't give up until I finally staggered out of range. When I did, it was as if all her vigor suddenly abandoned her. She fell back with a gasp, her chest heaving violently. I moved off a few more feet, but kept my hand on the Smith and Wesson, and I don't want to hear a word from you or anyone else who ever listens to these disks about what a horrible person I was to strike a woman, or be ready to shoot her if I deemed it necessary. That damned pick had come too close to my jaw for me to feel any remorse for my reaction.

She wasn't unconscious, but she looked dazed, and wasn't moving. I stood above her for nearly a minute, my heart pounding, sweat streaking my face. I used the back of my hand to wipe the dirt from my lips, then eased off a few more paces and took a look around. She seemed to be alone, and was apparently unarmed save for that pickax. I went over and snatched it off the ground, discovering upon closer examination that what I'd at first taken for blood was actually dried earth with a reddish tinge, like you find in that part of the country. It was a relief, and it toned down my concern for her sanity, although I continued to keep my distance.

As if finally gathering her senses, the woman sat up, glaring daggers my way but keeping her mouth shut. I told her to stay where she was and went to fetch my horse, keeping the pick with me. The bay had hung back at the homestead at first, as if wanting to stay with the outlaws' horses, but I guess its familiarity with the sorrel finally won out. It was standing a few yards away, watching our antics with a child-like curiously. I was reaching for the coiled lead rope tied to its halter when I heard a noise behind me, and whirled lightning quick to find the woman coming after me with a curved butcher knife raised over her shoulder. Instinctively palming the Smith and Wesson, I thumbed the hammer all the way back, and she came to an abrupt halt.

"If you come near me, I'll kill you," she promised huskily, the first coherent words I heard her utter.

"I'd say a revolver trumps a knife."

"I don't care. You'll have to kill me from where you stand, because if you come any closer, I'll drive this blade straight through your heart."

"Lady, I don't mean you any harm, but I'm not keen on getting a knife jabbed between my ribs, either. You need to make a move and let me shoot you, or quit trying to kill me. I favor the latter, but I'll leave the decision up to you."

She hefted the knife a few times, as if judging its weight—or more likely, her odds against my determination to follow through on what I said I'd do—then slid back a step and lowered her weapon. "All right, just so you know I mean what I said."

I nodded and cautiously moved the Smith's hammer to half cock. "My name's Slade. I'm a messenger on the Colorado and Prescott stage, which this bunch robbed three days ago. I've been following them ever since."

"How do I know you're not one of them?"

"I had similar thoughts about you."

"You saw what they did to my home." An odd hitch came into her voice with the word *home,* and whatever doubts I'd had immediately vanished. "They took away everything, stealing it or burning it or . . ." She looked away, blinking rapidly.

"They're a low bunch, I'll grant you, but I'm not one of them," I said gently.

"You're just following them? All by yourself?"

I had to laugh at the undisguised skepticism in her question. "You mean like you were doing?"

That gave her pause, and I sensed that her distrust might have softened a little—not that I was ready to turn my back on her just yet.

"What did you say your name was?"

"Thomas Slade, out of Ehrenberg."

I'll bet you think I told her my friends called me Tom, and that that's what she should call me, but I didn't. The fact is, very few people used my Christian name in those years. Most just called me Slade, and that never bothered me.

A frown had creased the woman's slim brows. "They mentioned you," she said after a pause. "Or Trepan did, and Jim Bowers tried to kill you."

"Someone took a shot at me back on the Colorado." I brought my left hand up to press lightly against my bruised ribs. They still hurt, although not as bad as that first morning.

"It was Bowers," she replied matter-of-factly. "They didn't think anyone would follow them so soon, but Trepan had Bowers stay behind to watch, just to be certain."

"Trepan's their leader?"

She hesitated, then shook her head. "I don't think so, but he was the one who gave the orders here."

That didn't add up at the time, but it would eventually.

"They thought you were dead," she went on. "Bowers told everyone that you were, and that he'd thrown your body into the river. Trepan was especially angry when he realized you were still alive, still following. Bowers said that if he ever had another opportunity, you wouldn't survive."

"I can't say that surprises me, although I don't intend to give them the chance." I hesitated. "If I holster this gun, do I have your word you won't try to poke a hole in me with that knife, or the pickax?"

She seemed to give my proposal some serious consideration, then nodded. "If you keep your distance. I've put up with

111

enough lunacy the last few days. I won't suffer it any further."

"Fair enough," I allowed, returning the Smith to its holster. "I've still got to go after Trepan and his men, but I'll do what I can to help you before I leave."

"I don't need your help, Mister Slade. I intend to go after the Trepan gang myself. I owe them, and Miller, especially."

"Miller?"

"Sam Miller. He was the one they sent here with the extra horses."

"Is he the one who set fire to your house?"

"He set the fire, but no one made any effort to stop him. He's also the one who . . . who killed . . ." She looked away, and her lips trembled; after a moment, she lamely added: "My chickens."

I felt a heaviness in my heart at her words, and recalling the smaller, more recently dug grave north of the house, I wondered who Miller had really murdered. I didn't pry, though. She seemed too raw at that moment, too close to a brink I couldn't know the bottom of. Keeping my voice even and calm, I said: "It's getting late, and my horses are worn out. If you aren't opposed to it, I think we ought to go back to your place. There's water there, and hopefully something for us to eat . . . maybe some chicken, if those hens haven't been laying out too long."

"This afternoon," she replied absently. "After they burned the house."

"Is there anything else?"

"Foodwise? I'm afraid they didn't leave much. There are some green apples coming along in the orchard, and the blackberries are starting to turn. The berries are extremely bitter yet, but the apples should be edible, if you don't mind them small and hard as rocks." She brought her eyes back to mine— gray ones, I noticed, narrowed in vigilance and conviction. "I haven't changed my mind, Mister Slade. If you attempt to come close, I'll kill you, just as certainly as Miller did my hens."

I nodded gravely. "I believe you, ma'am, I surely do." I caught the sorrel's reins and led her over to where I'd dropped the Parker and slid that back through its loop on my saddle. I was still carrying the pick, but after a moment's hesitation, I set it on the ground, leaning it against the same trampled stalk of greasewood that had tripped my horse earlier. Then I stepped into the saddle and rode over to grab the bay's lead rope. "You can ride back with me, if you'd like."

"I'll walk," she replied, and when I hesitated, she bluntly added: "I'd rather be alone."

Nodding acceptance, I reined away, wondering all the while if she'd really intended to return, or if she'd make a run for it as soon as I was far enough away. Since there was only one way of knowing for sure, I headed for the house, and didn't look back.

After picketing my horses on the tall grass of the orchard, I lugged my saddle back around front and dumped it under the lean-to with the firewood. Then I cut a couple of green mesquite limbs for spits and got a fire started. The woman was still some distance away, but trudging steadily toward the house, the pickax riding easily atop her shoulder. I'll admit I was kind of surprised she hadn't taken off, but pleased, too. After three days on my own, some company was going to be welcomed—assuming she didn't try to disembowel me in my sleep.

With the fire going strong, I gathered up all the dead chickens and hauled them behind the barn where the woman wouldn't have to look at them, keeping only what looked like the two freshest for our supper. I plucked them with some trepidation. Although they hadn't yet started to smell, they'd obviously been out in the sun longer than they should have been, and I was afraid eating them was going to be dicey. Had I even a few dried biscuits left in my saddlebags, I probably wouldn't have risked it.

When the woman finally arrived, I asked again if there was any more food, but she assured me there wasn't.

"Spoiled chicken and green apples completes our fare," she said, propping her pick against the side of the lean-to. "Neither are likely to kill you, although you may wish for death before it's over." She gave me a challenging look and a small, taut smile. "How hungry are you, Mister Slade?"

"Hungry enough, I guess." Squatting beside the fire, I began skewering the hens. I'd already checked the apples and blackberries in the orchard, and dismissed them as too green for digestion.

As I held the first hen close to the flames to burn off the smaller feathers and fuzz, it became obvious that she didn't want to watch me prepare the birds for grilling. Her gaze kept sliding off to one side or the other as if she couldn't decide where to look, although she was clearly making an effort to avoid the pair of graves north of the house. After a while, as if having nowhere else to turn, she looked at me.

"I'm sorry I don't have anything better to offer. Trepan's men took most of the best of what I had, and Miller burned the rest."

"Sounds like Miller was harboring some pretty deep resentment over something."

"I believe his stay here was more of a disappointment than he'd anticipated. His bad luck seemed to amuse the others, although not enough to entice intervention on my behalf."

I considered her words—not so much what she said, but how she said them. There was a hint of an accent in her voice—British, perhaps—and traces of a higher education in her choice of words. Yet there was nothing in her appearance to suggest anything other than a work-roughened frontier woman. She was tall and slim, and moved with what I suppose you might call a willowy grace, now that her initial anger had subsided. Her skin was deeply tanned, already showing signs of aging around her eyes and at the corners of her mouth. Her hands were brown and callused, the nails blunted from labor. She wore her curly blonde hair pulled back in a loose ponytail under a wide-brimmed straw hat, and a plain blue cotton dress with pink and yellow vertical stripes. I've already mentioned that her eyes were gray. Her voice was faintly husky, although that could have been from swallowing too much smoke from her burning house.

I wanted to know her name, but wasn't sure how she'd take my asking. She seemed touchy to questions, and was probably still leery of my intentions, for which I couldn't blame her. I inquired about her chin, instead, where I'd struck her with my elbow. She gave me a sharp look, as if maybe wondering if I was mocking her, but then admitted that it was sore, although probably deserved.

"I abhor violence," she added quietly, "so my behavior these past few days has been a little disheartening. And, I suppose, a little eye-opening."

"I've been curious," I admitted, jutting my chin toward the gray lump of her burned-out home, barely visible in the gathering darkness outside the lean-to.

She was silent for so long I began to wonder if she was going to reply, but eventually she did.

"Trepan and another man came through here a month ago," she began. "They wanted to board some horses with me, but I told them no. I said they were welcome to water their horses at the seep, and to spend the night in the orchard if they wished, but that I didn't want to be responsible for their stock."

"Did they offer to pay?"

"Money wasn't the issue. I was uncomfortable in their presence. Neither of them had introduced themselves, and that also made me uneasy. There was something almost sinister in their presence, and I was relieved when they declined to spend the night."

"Was that other man with them today?"

"No. There were six of them here, but not the other one . . . the tall one."

"Who was here today?"

"Trepan. He was traveling with Henry Brown, George Anders, Merle Stratton, and Jim Bowers. Miller appeared several days earlier with the extra horses."

"What's Trepan's first name, did he say?"

"John. His name is John."

[*Editor's Note:* Research into known outlaws of that time and approximate location failed to turn up references to any of the above names, although a Melvin D. Stratton, no address, was convicted of stealing a "tall dun gelding, mark'd with Rocking T brand, one used saddle & bridle" in Pima County, Arizona, in October of 1879; Melvin Stratton served eighteen months in the territorial penitentiary at Yuma, and was released in 1881; no evidence linking this man to the Merle Stratton mentioned in the Thomas Slade transcripts could be found.]

"Did they mention that other man?" I asked. "The one who came here with Trepan last month?"

"There was some allusion to another man, but no mention of a name. From the way Trepan spoke, I assumed he was the mastermind behind whatever mischief they were up to." She gave me a thoughtful glance. "Robbing a stagecoach, you said?"

"Yes, ma'am, the Colorado and Prescott line. They made their move at Desert Wells."

"Was anyone hurt?"

"Some busted heads, but nothing serious," I replied.

It's kind of ironic that at about the same time I was making that statement, Jethro Hanks was slipping into his coma, back at Desert Wells. Of course, I didn't have any way of knowing that at the time.

Studying the oblong knot still prominent above my ear, the woman said: "You're lucky no one was murdered. They . . ." She stopped and looked away—to the south, I noticed, rather than toward the two graves north of the house.

"Trepan and Brown acted like gentlemen on the coach," I said vaguely, when it became clear she wasn't going to continue.

"But they weren't, were they?"

"No, ma'am, they weren't."

"They weren't here, either. They weren't as bad as Miller or Anders, but they made no effort to control the situation, either. I think that as far as Trepan and Brown were concerned, I didn't exist as a person. What the others did, what they said or how they acted, was of no more significance to those two than the howling of coyotes in the hills." She stopped and wiped her eyes as if to dry them. "If you're wondering, and I suspect you are, they didn't assault me. At least not in the way you . . . but what they did." She motioned toward the house, then the chicken coop. "This matters to me, Mister Slade. You probably can't fathom such feelings over inanimate objects, a home or domestic stock, but . . . it matters to me."

"Yes, ma'am, I expect it does. For what it's worth, it would matter to me, too."

A smile played briefly over her lips. "I wish you'd stop calling me *ma'am*. My name is Claire Adams, and I have been curious about something as well, Mister Slade. What happened to your hat, and why are you wearing that ridiculous pirate's bandanna?"

I laughed and told her how I'd lost it, explaining Bowers's shot and my dunking in the Colorado; I even described my nose-to-nose encounter with the snake the following morning. I didn't mention how close I'd come to drowning, though. That was a little too recent yet to make light of.

"I didn't know this was how a pirate dressed," I added. "I'd have pictured a tricorn hat and a fancy coat with lots of braid."

"There is a story being published in a magazine that I've read the first installment of . . ." [*Editor's Note:* Adams may be referring to either Robert Louis Stevenson's "Treasure Island," serialized in *Young Folks Magazine* in 1881 and 1882, or "The Black Scourge of Hispaniola," by Haywood Coyler, published in two parts in *Adventures Magazine* in 1880; both contain images of pirates wearing bandannas.]

Claire's voice trailed off as if in thought, then she abruptly stood and headed for the house. Although it must have been as dark as pitch inside, she entered without hesitation, and returned a few minutes later with a broad-brimmed, high-crowned, genuine Boss of the Plains.

"Try this," she said, handing me the hat. "It smells of smoke, but it'll cover your neck and face better than a bandanna, and might keep your nose from searing any worse than it already has."

Well, she didn't have to tell me my nose was sunburned. I could feel the heat coming off of it like a tiny blaze, and my lips were starting to crack as well.

"Thanks," I said, accepting the battered Stetson. The hat had seen some hard use even before the fire. It was stained and dented and pocked throughout with burn holes, some of them tiny, others large enough to poke my thumb through, but it was still going to be a hell of a lot better than a bandanna. I tried it on and found the fit tight but not uncomfortable. I gave it a good soaking in the water trough before we pulled out the next morning. That helped stretch the fibers a little, but it never did lose that house-fire stink.

It was full dark by the time the chickens were ready. The smell wasn't the best and the taste was worse, since I'd grilled it past well done for safety's sake, but it was filling, and neither of us suffered any ill effects that I'm aware of. Afterward I added more wood to the fire, and we sat back without speaking, watching the flames and listening to the pop and sizzle of the burning wood. I wanted to ask Claire about a bedroll, but was hesitant to do so, not wanting her to get the wrong idea. Finally, deciding I couldn't put it off any longer, I said: "I've got two blankets on my saddle. You're welcome to one of them, if you'd like. It'd be a fair trade for the hat."

"Thank you, Mister Slade, but there's a saddle blanket in the barn that I can use."

"I noticed an old saddle in there, too."

"Yes, a McClellan."

"If you don't mind my asking, why didn't you use it?"

"On one of the horses Trepan's men left behind?"

I nodded, and she sighed.

"I suppose I should have, even as exhausted as they so obviously are. To be honest, I suppose I wasn't thinking very clearly this afternoon. I . . . had some matters to attend to after Trepan and his men left, and I'm afraid that afterward, my thoughts were rather consumed with the idea of revenge. I had given little consideration to the necessities of life when I set out this afternoon, either to food or water, let alone a method of transportation swifter than my own plodding gait. I actually owe you a debt of gratitude for coming after me, Mister Slade. It's forced me to consider the larger picture, outside of emotion."

"Does that larger picture include you going somewhere to get help?"

"No," she replied with a flat bitterness that caught me off guard. "I intend to seek my goal under my own terms, and to be certain that the punishment fits the crime. I can appreciate your desire to have your money returned, and to see these men jailed for their crimes against the Colorado and Prescott company, but it is my intention that justice is served for the crimes they committed here, not elsewhere."

"What crimes are those?" I asked gently. She was silent a long time, staring into the lowering flames. Finally, taking a chance, I said: "The grave?"

Her reply was barely audible. "Yes."

"The newer one?"

She nodded.

"I'm sorry for your loss."

"Thank you."

"What about the older grave?"

"An Indian. Last year."

"An Apache?"

"I'm afraid I'm not very knowledgeable on tribal differences. He was dressed partially in white man's clothing, the rest in native attire. He showed up unexpectedly one morning, acting very bold. I gave him some bread and meat, but he wanted to go inside. I told him no, but he was determined and wouldn't quit."

"Did you kill him?"

"Yes. I'd managed to lock myself in the house, but he kept trying to break inside. I finally pulled the latch on the door and allowed him to enter. When he did, I shot him."

"You did right," I told her, although I'm not sure she needed the assurance. She seemed like a hardy woman, capable of taking care of herself. Or at least she had been until Trepan and his bunch showed up.

"I've no regrets, Mister Slade," Claire continued. "I may detest violence, but I won't willingly suffer it upon my person. The man's intentions were quite clear, as were mine when I ordered him to leave."

"So you had a gun?"

"I did. Miller took it, along with an ax and a shovel. I've no insight into his intentions for them."

"Is that why you're carrying the pick?"

"It should prove adequate," she replied, somewhat defensively, I thought.

"I don't doubt that it'd get the job done," I agreed, then tipped my head toward the graves, lost in the darkness. "What about the other one?"

Her head came around sharp as a pistol shot, and I immediately wished I'd kept my mouth shut.

"That one is none of your business, Mister Slade."

I nodded quickly. "I expect you're right, Missus Adams, and I apologize for the intrusion." Hoping for amends, I added: "If you'd like, I'll go fetch that saddle blanket now."

"No, I can find it." She rose and took up her pick, and the muscles across my shoulders drew taut. She stood across the fire from me for nearly a minute before she spoke again. "I'll sleep elsewhere tonight. Please don't look for me. If you do, I'll kill you."

Her words held a chilling conviction, and I didn't doubt for a minute that she meant them.

"I'll be right here if you need me," I replied, keeping my voice low, the tone mild.

"I shan't need you, Mister Slade. Good night."

"Good night, Missus Adams."

I suppose the gentlemanly thing to do would have been to rise and see her off, but I didn't feel any particular need to poke the tiger that night, and kept my seat instead.

You might think after my conversation with Claire that I'd have been too daunted to close my eyes, but I slept sound the night through and awoke more refreshed than I'd felt since leaving Ehrenberg. For some reason, I already trusted her. It was she who lacked faith in me, and judging by her appearance the next morning, I suspect her slumber had been quite a bit less satisfying than mine.

Ordinarily, I wouldn't have kindled a morning fire, but I

wanted to try again to talk Claire into giving up her intentions. I wanted her to go somewhere safe, someplace where she could keep her head down and out of the line of fire, and let others take care of John Trepan and his thugs. But as soon as I saw her that morning, I knew the odds of my changing her mind were slim.

"There's some chicken left," I said, rolling the remains of last night's supper closer to the flames.

"You can have it."

"There's plenty," I insisted, earning myself a withering glance for the overture.

"They're my chickens, Mister Slade. I don't need you to offer what I already have."

Leaning back with a sigh of resignation, I decided to give up on subtlety and get to the point. "You're just going to hold me up if you insist on coming along. The best help you can be is to stay here until I send someone out to bring you in."

"You misunderstand again. I'm not going with you. I'm going on alone. I'll allow you to travel with me if our paths should take us in the same direction, but I won't allow you to interfere in my objective."

"Missus Adams, I'm not your enemy. I'm after the payroll that was taken off that C and P coach, and that's all I want. Trepan and his men aren't my concern, although I'll bring them in if I can. But your safety is a concern, whether you want it to be or not."

The concrete stiffness of Claire's face softened in response to my explanation. She sat down opposite me and placed the pick at her side. "I need to apologize, Mister Slade. My rudeness is unwarranted. But you need to accept that my mind is made up in this matter. It won't be reversed."

I stared into the flames for a long minute, then reluctantly nodded. If I ever got her close to a town or a military post, I might have some options, but for the time being, I was going to have to accept the situation as it stood.

"All right," I conceded. "But if we're riding the same trail, going after the same men, we ought to try to work together."

Claire's eyes brightened. "That sounds splendid. What do you suggest?"

Tapping a chicken breast with the end of the stick I'd been using to keep the coals stirred, I said: "I'd suggest we eat a hearty breakfast, Missus Adams. It's going to be a long day."

"Agreed," she replied enthusiastically, then leaned forward to study the faintly smoking piece of meat. "Do you suppose it's warmed all the way through by now?"

"Probably not, although I doubt heat is going to improve the taste any."

I picked up the breast and handed it to her, juggling it in my fingers. I don't know if it was warm in the middle, but it was sure hot on the outside. I took a leg and a thigh for myself, all that remained of the two birds I'd grilled the night before, and brought them to my lips to blow gently against the fire-darkened skin. As I did, I noticed Claire setting her breakfast aside, then lowering her head and folding her arms under her breasts, and another piece of the puzzle fell into place. When she looked up from her prayers, I said: "You're Mormon." Then a second revelation occurred to me, and I added: "You're a second wife."

Her face reddened, but she refused to look away. "A third, actually."

I thought about that for a minute, then chuckled quietly. "What did you do to make the other wives so mad?"

"My relationship with either church or family is irrelevant to our current situation, Mister Slade," she replied tartly, and I knew that I'd angered her once more. She was right, though. It wasn't any of my business. I was just curious, and more about why she was out there, so far from civilization, than any of the sordid speculations that accompanied most conversations about Mormon men and their plural wives.

We ate in silence, and when we were done, I rose to bring in the horses. "Go get your saddle," I told her. "You can ride my bay."

She hesitated only a moment, then pushed to her feet and headed for the barn. By the time I returned, she had the McClellan, a saddle blanket, and a bridle waiting.

"Do you know how to ride clothespin style?" I asked, handing her the bay's lead rope.

"I am familiar with the method, and suspect it shall be considerably easier than riding sidesaddle, even in a dress." A smile played briefly across her lips, blunting the severity in her eyes. "I've often wondered, in fact, why it is that women are expected to ride in such an uncomfortable and unconventional fashion, while it is deemed perfectly acceptable for men to ride . . . what did you call it? Clothespin style?"

I didn't know what she meant at first. Then it dawned on me, and I did a double take. But when I turned to look at her, she was already reaching under the bay's barrel for the cinch. A grin spread slowly across my face, but I didn't pursue it. I was really starting to like her, though.

The morning was cool, but you could tell the day was going to be brutal. We pulled out just as the dawn's light began to spill down over the Hualapais to flood the valley. [*Editor's Note:* Although Slade never mentions this valley by name, its proximity to the Hualapai Mountains and Bill Williams River is a strong indication that he is referring to Dutch Flat, east of Lake Havasu City; later statements, made by both Slade and Adams, also support this location.]

Claire handled the bay like she'd been riding all her life, and even managed to keep most of her ankles hidden beneath the hem of her dress, although don't ask me how. She had the extra canteen hung off one side of her saddle and the pick on the other, its head tied off near the pommel, the handle hanging down in front of her knee. She carried no other baggage, no saddlebags or bedroll, not even a jacket against the predawn chill. Only her pick and knife, and that wide-brimmed straw hat, with a ribbon that tied under the chin to keep it on in the wind.

For a while after we pulled out, the outlaws' trail led us northwest. This was more or less toward the Colorado, and my hope began to grow that they were heading for the big river, but we hadn't gone more than a few miles when their tracks veered abruptly to the northeast, cutting diagonally across the long flats. Keeping my growing irritation with the bandits' seemingly aimless wanderings to myself, I reined doggedly after them. Claire noticed the tracks when I did, but didn't question the altered course, even though I could tell she was curious. We pushed on through the growing heat, stopping in the middle of the plain around noon to water the horses out of my leaking hat. Nodding toward the distant mountains before us, I asked Claire what was out there, but she could only shake her head.

"There is a place called Beale's Springs near the northern tip of the valley, but that's so far away. I'm sure there are springs much closer than that, but I'm not familiar with them." [*Editor's Note:* Beale's Springs, near present Kingman, Arizona, was named after Lieutenant Edward Beale, a naval officer in service to the US Army Corps of Engineers; ordered by President James Buchanan in the late 1850s to survey and build a federal wagon road across the thirty-fifth parallel in Arizona and California, Beale is probably best known for commanding the US Camel Corps in his 1857 survey of that route.]

Toward midafternoon, the trail swung back to the northwest, paralleling the foothills of the Hualapais, and not far beyond that we found where the gang had spent the night in a shallow arroyo. Claire and I stopped for only a few minutes, more to give our mounts a breather than to explore the camp, although I did take time to count the places in the sand where the outlaws had unfurled their bedrolls. It looked like all six of them were riding together now, which was a relief, since I didn't want a repeat of what had happened back on the Colorado.

We kept on until right before sunset, when the trail switched directions once more. This time, Claire brought her mount to a stop with a little sound of exasperation. "Now they're going west again!"

"A little south of west," I agreed.

"To what purpose?"

"I don't know, but if it's to confuse their pursuers, they're doing a hell of a fine job." I shut up and gave her a sheepish glance. "Sorry about the language. I hope I didn't offend . . ."

"I am hardly so delicate that words will scratch me, Mister Slade," she said as if amused. "And to be perfectly truthful, I'm not at all certain expressions such as hell and damn aren't appropriate in such an environment as this."

I couldn't help smiling. "You know, Missus Adams, I'm liking you more and more all the time."

And damned if that wasn't the wrong thing to say, too. The twinkle vanished from her eyes, and her expression turned cold as a desert night.

"We had best continue if we ever hope to catch up," she said sternly, then tapped the bay's ribs with her heels. She guided her smaller horse around me to take the lead, her spine as stiff as a fireplace poker. She was a hard woman to read, but I suspected even then that her darting moods were caused more by what she'd endured from Trepan's bunch than from any trespass on my part.

I'd been right that morning when I predicted the day would be unusually hot. Although I didn't have any way of measuring it at the time, Ira would tell me later that the thermometer he kept at the C&P offices in Ehrenberg had topped out at 107 degrees that day. I don't doubt it was just as broiling where Claire and I were. The sky shone above us like a shimmering white ceiling, and dust stirred on the eddies of wind that skirted the flats, sometimes lifting into dust devils that rose to towering heights, only to collapse upon themselves as if succumbing to exhaustion. My lips continued to crack like old leather, and even in the shade of the smoke-stained hat Claire had loaned me, my nose and cheeks burned like little pieces of coals pressed against my flesh.

Sundown brought only minimal relief. I called a halt in the shelter of a bluff below a range of mountains I didn't know the name of. Claire dismounted first, staggering like a drunk when her feet hit the ground. Having gone through this before, I hung onto the saddle horn until my legs didn't seem quite so wobbly.

"Good grief," Claire breathed, her face glowing red in the softening twilight. "How do miners and cattle drovers endure this heat all day?"

"I suppose they get used to it after a while. Give it another week, and you'll be feeling pert as a parrot yourself."

"I cannot speak for parrots, but I shall pray for the completion of our quest long before that much time has elapsed. Either that or the discovery of a lotion for . . . certain parts of the anatomy."

There it was again, that little spark of the true character she mostly kept hidden, but that I really wanted to see and know better. I'd learned my lesson, though, and kept my mouth shut.

We pulled our saddles and watered the horses as best we could, saving the last little bit for ourselves and draining the first canteen by the time we were through. I felt better afterward, but knew we were both still badly dehydrated. Claire's expression was somber as she eyed the empty receptacle.

"Is that all the water we have?" she asked, nodding toward the as-yet untouched canteen tied to her saddle.

"I'm afraid so."

"Then . . . we shall be without water by tomorrow evening?"

"More than likely."

"Are you worried?"

I gave her a level look and a truthful reply. "Yes, ma'am, I am. Let's hope we find some water soon. Otherwise, we're going to be in some real bad trouble."

She didn't have a response for that. I wouldn't have, either. The future hung over us like a dark cloud, and we both felt its measure.

We didn't bother lighting a fire that night. We didn't have any food to cook, and I would have been afraid Trepan's men might spot its glow even if we did, no matter how hard we tried to hide the flame. Although I'd debated bringing along a couple of those hens Miller had killed after pulling down Claire's chicken coop, I figured we'd already pushed our luck the night before.

I picketed the horses on what little grass the country afforded, while Claire rolled our blankets out about six feet apart, the saddles stacked between us like an old-time bundling board. [*Editor's Note:* Bundling was an archaic winter practice of eighteenth century New England, where courting couples would lie in the same bed while fully clothed, often with what was known as a bundling board placed between them for propriety's sake; although popular with descendants of the Dutch Netherlands and the British Isles, the custom was frowned upon by the more Puritan sects of the region.]

Stretching out on top of my blankets, I laced my fingers behind my head and stared quietly at the sky. What had appeared almost chalky that afternoon looked as black as polished jet with the sun's setting, heavily frosted with starlight. The moon's glow from behind the Hualapais wasn't enough yet to disrupt the beauty of the stars, although it would be up soon.

"A penny for your thoughts, Mister Slade," Claire said after a bit.

"I'm afraid you wouldn't get much for your money, Missus Adams. I was just stargazing."

"Hmmm, as was I. One could almost forgive the earth its daily brutality for the wonders nature sometimes offers her children."

"Missus Adams, I hope you don't take this wrong, but I surely do admire the way you talk. I thought I was fairly well-educated, having gone through all six grades, but I suspect you've got me beat."

Claire laughed softly. "I believe it's safe to say my pattern of speech is the result of a finishing school in New York City. I had only two years at Vassar, and concentrated mostly on the arts."

"Vassar? Where is that?"

"Vassar is in the Hudson Valley of the state of New York. I was born in Glens Falls, which is also in the Hudson Valley."

That surprised me. "You're not from England?"

"Heavens, no. How did you arrive at that conclusion?"

Now it was my turn to laugh. "I guess from the way you talk."

"I'm afraid I'm a New York girl, through and through."

We drifted into several minutes of silence after that, the natural direction of our conversation stopped by a locked gate only she had the key to. Maybe she realized that. Or maybe she was only starved for company, because when she began speaking again, it was without any prodding from me.

"Father always claimed my independence . . . my muleheadedness, was how he put it . . . was obtained from education. Perhaps it was. I know I was a different person when I returned to Glens Falls. I felt like a stranger among my old friends, and although I had several suitors, none appealed to me. Too bumpkinish, was my argument, which vexed Father no end. Then Richard Adams came to Glens Falls to seek converts to his religion, and I'm afraid I was swept away by his charm and education. I knew he already had two wives in Utah, but considered our relationship daringly risqué. We were married against my parents' wishes and traveled to Utah Territory within the year.

"As you might expect, my reception from Richard's first two wives, sisters, I might add, was chilly, at best. When Richard was called by Brigham Young to serve the Church in Callville soon after his return, he took all three of us, plus seven of his eleven children, with him.

"Callville was such a disappointment to all of us. It was supposed to be the head of navigation on the Colorado River, and a Mormon port for converts on their way to Salt Lake City, but the cost and difficulty of inland travel from there proved too overwhelming, and the town never flourished. In fact, it hardly existed by the time we arrived. Less than a dozen inhabitants, most of them thoroughly demoralized by the isolation of the place. Richard immediately wrote the Prophet asking for reassignment, and was granted a return to his home north of Salt Lake City."

"How did you end up here?"

"It would seem, Mister Slade, that before my banishment to this harsh land, I was considered somewhat attractive, and, as you've suggested, not totally uneducated. My sister wives had some mild problems with that, but it was the wives of my husband's friends who proved most difficult. Eventually, in order to keep the peace within his households and the community at large, Richard decided that he and I would return to Arizona. His plan was to raise sheep, as the Navajos do on such poor country to the east. His first order of structure was to begin the orchard. After that was established, he built the house and outbuildings that Trepan's men took such delight in destroying, using labor hired from the mining communities in the Bradshaw Mountains. Then left me there alone, while he returned to Utah for a flock.

"Unhappily, Richard was taken into the Heavenly Father's arms before he could return. It was suggested by our bishop, revealed to him in a revelation, no less, that I should remain here and prepare for the arrival of others of our ward who might wish to join me, but no one ever came." [*Editor's Note:* A ward, in Mormon nomenclature, is the physical boundary of a congregation, similar to political wards in other parts of the country.]

"How long ago was that?" I asked.

"Three years."

That got my attention. "Three years," I echoed, pushing up on one elbow. "By yourself?"

Her look was defiant. "And where would you have had me go, Mister Slade?"

"Ma'am, I wouldn't care where it was, as long as there were other people around."

She sighed and looked away. "I sometimes wonder if that isn't what Bishop Jensen had in mind, that I just . . . go away. Although he still has supplies sent down every six months, the men who deliver them and pick up my tithing of produce never stay, and are always vague in their replies regarding my future. I can only assume they are under orders to treat me as a discarded investment, otherwise I surely would have been sent for before now."

"Maybe it's Jensen's wives who gave him his revelation," I suggested.

"Yes," she admitted, her voice heavy with resignation. "I have suspected as much for quite some time."

"But you're still here?"

After a long pause, she said: "Yes, I'm still here."

"Is it . . . that newer grave. I noticed it looked like it was dug fairly recently."

Her silence seemed to stretch on for minutes before she finally replied. "It is freshly dug. A very dear friend is interred there. A friend whose . . . love, I suppose . . . allowed me to survive out here, both mentally and emotionally."

I wanted to ask, but couldn't. Sensing my reluctance, Claire responded.

"His name is Charlie Red, Mister Slade, and he was murdered by the Trepan gang."

SESSION SEVEN

We were slow putting out the next morning. I think we were both feeling the effects of the previous day's journey—the intense heat and the limited amount of water that we'd allowed ourselves. The horses were showing the strain, too, since I was no longer able to switch off from time to time. I'd expected our journey to become more difficult as time went on, but I hadn't counted on it happening so quickly.

The outlaws' trail continued westward, and my hopes began to rise once more that they might be making a run for the Colorado River, where Claire and I could refill our canteens. That didn't happen. The sun was hardly past its apex when the trail once more bent abruptly northward.

Hauling in on the sorrel's reins, I had to grit my teeth to keep from cursing. This back-and-forth business was really starting to grate on me. I could tell it was bothering Claire, too. Pulling up at my side, she blurted: "What in the world are they trying to prove?"

"They've been doing this ever since they left Desert Wells."

"Why?"

I told her briefly about my theory that they wanted to confuse pursuit, but I don't think she agreed. I'm not sure I did anymore, either. Trepan had something else in mind. I just didn't know what it was yet.

"Are they looking for something?"

"Maybe."

"What?"

I shook my head.

"If they went to so much trouble planning their robbery and escape, even to the point of having fresh horses waiting at the orchard, wouldn't they know where they were going?"

"Maybe it's not a specific location they're looking for. Maybe it's a person. Tell me about the man who came to your place with Trepan that first time."

"It was dusk, and they didn't dismount. He was tall and well-dressed, but I couldn't really make out his features. Even though I sensed he was in command, it was Trepan who did most of the talking." After a moment's pause, she added: "If that's who they are looking for, wouldn't they have designated a rendezvous point before the robbery?"

Leaning back in my saddle, I exhaled loudly. "You'd think so, wouldn't you?"

Claire waited for me to go on, but I didn't have anything else to add. Still, I've got to admit that, with the idea out there, it was beginning to sound more logical than believing the bandits were lost. As crazy as it seemed, Trepan's crew was now in pursuit itself, for its leader. The question, of course, was who that man was. And why was he so hard to locate?

"What now, Mister Slade?"

I knew what she was asking. We were out of food and low on water, and graze for the horses had become almost nonexistent. Meanwhile, the Colorado River couldn't have been more than a long day's ride to the west—water and grass and food along its banks for us, if we took time to hunt for it. But if we abandoned the trail then, I doubted that we'd ever pick it up again. Trepan and his gang would disappear into Arizona's vastness, never brought to justice, the mine payrolls never recovered.

"We keep on," I replied grimly, heeling the sorrel onto the outlaws' trail.

There was no protest from Claire, nor did I expect any.

She'd kind of surprised me with her confession about Charlie Red the night before. Not that she'd offered any further information on him, but she'd been so protective of his grave ever since I first mentioned it, so quick to close down into a stony silence whenever I approached anything even remotely personal, that I'd half expected her to do so again, after revealing Charlie's name and the fact that he'd been murdered by the Trepan gang. I guess that's why I didn't push her to tell me more. I was happy enough to have that much, without her turning mulish.

We rode on through the rest of the day, the sun baking the land with near-malicious intensity, leaching the juices from our bodies and turning our horses clumsy with fatigue and desiccation. Toward evening I spotted a mesa off to our left, and even though Trepan's men had passed on by to the north, I noticed something too tempting to ignore.

"What is it, Mister Slade?" Claire asked when I halted.

I jutted my chin toward a faint green smudge near the mesa's base. "What's that look like to you?"

She studied it a moment in the fading light, then said: "Trees. It looks like trees."

"It does to me, too," I replied, thinking that, where there are trees, there has to be water. Of course that water could have been fifty feet underground, like it was at Desert Wells, but I didn't mention that to Claire. "Let's go take a look," I said.

Well, they were trees, all right. A spindly grove of paloverdes, more scrub than forest, but with good grass for the horses and water, too, although it took us a while to find it. It was Claire who finally stumbled upon a small seep trickling out of the rocks. She gave a shout and I hurried over. The source was way back among some large boulders that had tumbled off the mesa's face who knew how many eons before. It was a tight squeeze to reach even for Claire, but the water, what there was of it, tasted about as sweet as anything I'd had since leaving Ehrenberg.

"There's not going to be enough for the horses," Claire said after we'd both slaked our thirst. She looked worried, but I wasn't concerned.

"We can dig a hole out a ways, then channel into it from the seep. After it's filled, we can bring the horses in one at a time to drink. It won't be as handy as a water trough, but we've got all night." I wiggled free of the narrow cleft and scratched an X in the dirt with the side of my heel. "We'll dig here. I'll give the horses what water we have left in the canteen, then we'll let them graze until I've got a hole dug. I'll need to use your pick to . . ."

"No!" She backed up a step, clenching her fists as if preparing to take a swing.

"Missus Adams, the ground here is pretty soft compared to what we've seen so far, but it's not soft enough for me to scoop out with my bare hands."

"Then I'll do the digging and trenching, Mister Slade, but the pick is mine, and you'll not touch it."

I hesitated, not sure how to respond to the quick flare of her temper, the rock-like finality of her words. Her fists were still clenched, the knuckles pale through the weathered tan of her flesh, and her eyes were sparking like lit fuses.

"All right," I said finally, carefully. "You can do the digging, and I'll watch the horses."

She nodded stiffly, then made a quick, shooing motion with one hand. "All right then. Go on and let me get started."

I walked back through the rocks to where we'd left our mounts. Claire followed as far as the bay, where she loosened her pick from the saddle, then disappeared back among the head-high boulders. I dumped our tack nearby, then picketed the horses toward the center of the small grove. As I was heading back, I spotted something small and dark stirring the grass, and jerked to a stop like a smart man does in that bristly land of rattlesnakes and Gila monsters. But it was only a desert tortoise, its hard, scalloped shell looking like a rock in the gathering shadows. If it hadn't taken a forward slide just as I came close, I doubt if I'd have noticed it.

I'd never eaten tortoise, but I knew that a lot of the desert tribes did, and I was too damned hungry to turn my back on a solid meal. My first in several days, if you don't count the sun-tainted chicken I'd choked down at Claire's.

I won't bore you with the details of the evening. I've seen bigger tortoises, but this one was large enough. I'm guessing maybe four pounds of meat, once the shell and entrails were removed. I grilled it over a small, drywood fire, my stomach raising all kinds of racket as the fat began to drip and sizzle. Claire came in before it was finished, her hands and the hem of her dress damp with mud, stray blonde curls falling limply over her forehead. She stared dully at the pale meat, just starting to brown around the middle, and said: "You found food."

"Tortoise," I replied needlessly, since the shell was sitting upside down in plain view next to the fire. "I thought I'd scrape out the inside for a water bucket for the horses."

"Primitive ingenuity comes to the rescue once more."

"It'll do until something better comes along," I agreed, but her slack expression and lackluster response had snagged my attention. "Are you feeling all right, Missus Adams?"

"Yes, I'm just . . . weary." She offered a wan smile. "Perhaps it's time we dispensed with some of the formalities, Mister Slade. For instance, if I called you Thomas, would you return the favor and call me Claire?"

"I'd like that."

"And do you favor Thomas, or is it Tom?"

"Actually, most people call me Slade."

"Then you prefer Slade?"

I thought about that for a minute. If anyone else had asked, I'd have told them to stick with Slade, since I was so used to it. But it was different with Claire. Or maybe I wanted it to be different. "Let's use Tom."

"Very well . . . Tom." She leaned forward to stare at the meat, rotating slowly on its spit of paloverde. "I wonder . . ."

"The grease?"

She looked up in surprise. "Don't tell me you're clairvoyant, as well?"

"No, but my nose still feels like it's on fire. I thought maybe a little grease might ease the heat." I glanced at Claire's face. Her cheeks were wind-buffed but hardly burned, although her lips looked about as chapped as mine.

"I wear a hat regularly, which has protected me thus far. I suspect had you not lost yours in the Colorado River, you would have fared much better yourself."

"Probably, but I'm going to try some of this turtle grease on my nose and lips. I'd suggest you add some to your lips. They look dry."

Her tongue flicked out snake-like to explore the arch of her upper lip, and for the first time since I'd met her, I wondered what it would be like to kiss her, or to run my fingers gently through that honey-blonde hair. I don't know, maybe I was staring too hard, but it was as if she read my thoughts, and there was that now-familiar hardening of her gaze, her spine and shoulders going defensively rigid. I silently cursed my forwardness and returned my attention to our evening's meal.

That tortoise didn't taste half bad. It wasn't great, and probably would have benefited from some salt and pepper, but hunger has a way of complementing most kinds of food, and the longer you go without, the better it flavors. Watching us from a distance, a stranger might have imagined us sitting down to a Fourth of July picnic of golden fried chicken, rather than bland reptile, barely cooked all the way through.

I was right about the water hole Claire had dug, even though it took most of the night before we had both canteens filled and the horses satisfied. We were saddling up early the next morning when, out of the blue, Claire said: "I know where they're going."

Looking up with my latigo just single-looped through the cinch ring, I waited for her to continue.

"There's a little railroad siding north of here called Kingman. Trepan's men will catch a train there, and be two hundred miles away before nightfall." She was standing beside the bay, her eyes shining but distant, as if she were there now, watching them board. "That's why they've led us on such a merry chase. The A and P didn't have a compatible schedule, so they've had to regulate their escape to a known eastbound departure. If they arrived too soon, they'd have risked a posse catching them at the siding." [*Editor's Note:* The Atlantic and Pacific Railroad, coming east out of Flagstaff, wouldn't reach the siding at Kingman, Arizona, until later that summer, a fact neither Slade nor Adams seemed aware of at the time; there is also some controversy regarding the date the siding received its designation as Kingman, although one would assume Adams, through Slade's recording, wouldn't have called it Kingman if the name hadn't been in use at the time.]

I ran my hand absently up the oiled latigo, turning Claire's theory over in my mind. Although it seemed like a solid argument, something about it troubled me. Finally, tentatively, I said: "If the track's already been laid that far, there's a good chance they've also got a telegraph. The two usually go hand in hand."

"Would it matter?"

"It might, if they thought we were close. We could wire Flagstaff and have a posse waiting for them. Or if not Flagstaff, then some other town down the line. If Kingman is their destination, they'd need to make sure we didn't get there until well after they left."

Or make sure we didn't get there at all, I mused gloomily.

"What if they destroyed the telegraph line east of Kingman, before boarding the train?"

Claire was making a convincing argument, no doubt about that, but something continued to nag at the back of my mind. When I didn't immediately reply, she went on.

"There's a place called Yucca, not far from here. There were surveyors there last month, mapping out the route for the railroad. They say the line will be completed to Needles by the end of the year."

"Who told you this? Charlie Red?"

Claire's head jerked back as if slapped, and her eyes misted over. "I . . . no, it was Trepan." She hesitated. "He didn't exactly tell me, either. I overheard him and Brown talking about it." Then her lips thinned with accusation. "You don't believe me, do you?"

"I believe you overheard them, but why would they allow you to eavesdrop on something as important as their escape?"

"Maybe they didn't know I was there."

"That's possible, but they've been real careful about that kind of stuff so far. Besides, the Atlantic and Pacific doesn't have a reliable schedule yet. No matter what the railroad says it'll do, Trepan couldn't know with any certainty when the next train would arrive, or when it might pull out again."

"Then your argument is that they continue to roam the wilderness like masked Moses?" [*Editor's Note:* One assumes Adams is referring to the biblical Moses here, who allegedly roamed the desert for forty years as leader of the Israelites.]

"I didn't say that. In fact, you could well be right. It doesn't seem likely, is all."

"Then offer an alternative that does seem more likely, Mister Slade."

"Missus Adams, the fact that I don't have a more likely alternative doesn't mean there isn't one." I scratched reflectively at my jaw, my whiskers sounding like sandpaper under my fingernails. As I did, a new thought occurred to me. The A&P might not have a reliable schedule yet, but the Colorado River Steamship Company did, including one for its flagship, the *Barbara Kay*, which, if it kept to its normal timetable, would soon be leaving Hardyville for the military garrison at Fort Mohave, before continuing its southbound voyage to Fort Yuma.

"What day is this?"

Claire frowned in thought. "I believe it's Wednesday, although I may be mistaken. I'm afraid I lost track of time after Miller's arrival with Trepan's remounts."

"Wednesday's about what I'm thinking, too." Then I told her about the *Barbara Kay*, and how she was due to leave Fort Mohave on Friday.

"Two days from now?"

I nodded. "If you're right about Trepan's men trying to keep us off guard until they can escape using some means other than horseback, then the *Barbara Kay* might be a more likely option. It's got a legitimate schedule they can depend on, and I doubt if Fort Mohave is any farther away than Kingman's Siding."

I could see Claire's excitement returning. "I like that scenario," she said softly. "Tell me . . . Tom . . . what is our next course of action?"

Her words brought a smile to my face. I don't know if you picked up on it, but we'd kind of reverted back to our old way of addressing one another as Mister and Missus for a few minutes there, so it was nice that she was willing to let it go so easily.

"We'll keep going north and hug these mountains until we cross their trail," I told her. "If we don't find their tracks by the time we reach the head of the valley, we'll know I was wrong, and that Trepan and his boys probably took their chances with the railroad. But if we're right, and find their trail heading for Fort Mohave, then we'll have shaved several hours off our end of the chase, and be all that much closer when we reach the fort."

"That sounds like a splendid plan. Let's hurry, before the heat worsens."

Brother, let me tell you, we were both feeling better when we rode out of those scrubby paloverdes that morning. Full bellies and full canteens, and that tortoise grease helped more than I figured it would on my blistered nose and chapped lips. Claire's lips were looking a lot better, too, and I thought again about how nice it would be to kiss them, real slow and gentle, and see how she'd react, although I was careful not to look her way with such thoughts rattling around inside my skull. I still didn't have a clear idea of who Charlie Red was, or how close he and Claire might have been, but I was pretty certain this wasn't a good time for me to start feeling romantic.

I pushed a little harder than normal that morning, but when the temperature started to climb in earnest, I eased the sorrel out of her easygoing jog and brought her back to a walk. You don't drive an animal too hard in that kind of climate, not unless you've got a reliable source of water and plenty of feed just down the trail.

We followed the base of the mountains like I'd planned, although every once in a while we'd angle up into the foothills for a better view of the broad valley that flowed away on our right. At one point we spotted a group of men way out on the flats, along with several wagons and some churned-up earth. Claire asked who they were and I told her it looked like a surveying crew, probably for the railroad. We discussed riding out to ask if they'd seen anything of Trepan's bunch, but decided against it. The distance seemed too great, and would have cost us too much time, considering the likelihood that the bandits had probably given the surveyors a wide berth, anyway.

It was later that morning when I called our first stop of the day. I dismounted and loosened the sorrel's cinch. Claire did the same with her bay, but instead of keeping her distance, like she normally did during our occasional breaks, she led the gelding over to where I was standing in the skimpy shade of a saguaro, watching a red-cheeked flicker inside its nesting cavity near the top of one of the cactus's thorny arms.

"I have decided I need to apologize for my behavior recently," she said, as if plunging into the conversation was the quickest way to get it over with. I suppose I could have been polite and acted surprised by her admission, then told her I hadn't noticed anything amiss, but I wasn't that kind of a guy. I didn't think Claire was that kind of a woman, either.

"Is it because . . . the grave?"

"Charlie's grave, yes." She averted her eyes, as if even speaking his name was painful.

"He must have been a good friend."

"Yes, he was a very good friend."

"You said it was one of Trepan's men who killed him?"

"Trepan himself, actually. Sam Miller mentioned how we were close, and Trepan wanted to hurt me."

"Any special reason?"

"Who knows what motivates such men as John Trepan," she replied bitterly, but then after a moment, added: "I suppose, in all honesty, I was less than cooperative during their stay. Trepan insisted I cook a large meal the night of his arrival. He wanted a chicken and dumpling stew, and, out of malice, I decided to spice the meal with a liberal dose of McIlhenny's Tabasco." [*Editor's Note:* Edmund McIlhenny (1815–1890) began commercial production of his famous brand of hot sauce in 1868, from his home at Avery Island, Louisiana.]

A faint smile twitched at the corners of Claire's mouth. "I thought the results were rather splendid, all things considered. The men were greedy, and the sauce produced such a slow burn that it allowed them several spoonfuls apiece before they began to experience the full effect of the Tabasco."

"You were taking a pretty big risk," I said.

"I've lived alone within a hostile environment for years, Tom. Risks are a daily factor of life in the desert." Her expression sobered. "Then Charlie arrived, and Trepan shot him in cold blood."

"Jesus," I breathed. Then: "It isn't any of my business, Claire."

"About Charlie?" She was quiet for a long time, as if considering how much she wanted to reveal. Finally, she said: "He was a friend, Tom, that's all. A very dear and trusted friend, but, it is . . . *was* . . . a complicated relationship. I doubt that . . . well . . . that anyone would really understand." She kept her gaze on the horizon, and although her cheeks were dry, I didn't think it would take much to bring on a fresh stream of tears. "He was so gallant," she went on in a faraway voice, and I knew she was talking about Charlie Red, about a time before John Trepan and his killers had bulled into her life. Then she looked at me and laughed softly, as if in embarrassment. "Listen to me, speaking like a schoolgirl, fantasizing of magnificent knights on magnificent steeds."

"Nothing wrong with having a good friend."

"He was that," she replied wistfully. "Perhaps in his own way, he was the best friend I've ever had." Then her eyes turned moist and her voice choked. "That's why I'm going to kill them, you see?"

"Them? All of them?"

"If possible."

"With just a pickax?"

"It's all I have."

"You've got my help now," I reminded her. "There's the law, too, if we ever get someplace with a badge."

"The law wouldn't care, wouldn't get involved with a . . ." She stopped suddenly, then turned away, gathering her reins above the bay's neck. "At any rate, I did want to apologize for my somewhat erratic disposition since we've met. I feel it only fair that you have at least a partial understanding of the cause."

I nodded but didn't reply, didn't have a clue what I could have said that might have made her feel better. Moving alongside the sorrel, I tightened the cinch, then swung my leg over the cantle. We rode on in silence after that, not speaking again until we came to a sharply defined trail shortly after noon, marring the bottom of a sandy wash that wound down out of the mountains on our left. I reined up atop the low bank of the arroyo and took a moment to savor the relief I felt at having guessed correctly about the direction Trepan and his men would take. It had seemed their most logical choice that morning, when I explained my reasoning to Claire, but logic doesn't always take you where you expect it to. I was glad it panned out this time.

"Is it them?" Claire asked, pulling up beside me and eyeing the hoofprints.

"I wouldn't know who else would be out here."

"Is it possible for you to gauge how long ago they may have passed this way?"

"I'm guessing not more than a few hours, as clean as those tracks look."

In Arizona, we used to call those broad, sand-packed washes "desert highways," since they were often the easiest route through a lot of that chaparral- and cactus-choked country. If the banks were high enough, it was also a good way to move about without being easily seen.

Claire and I turned west into the arroyo, the mountains rising above us like jagged teeth. The sun was just tipping toward night side, blazing down with a fierce intensity as we began to climb. Sweat trickled from beneath my hat, darkening my shirt in all the usual places. Claire suffered equally but silently, her features set in grim determination as we hounded the outlaws' trail. Figuring Trepan's men would follow the wash as far as it would take them toward the summit, I was more than a little surprised when they abandoned the wash barely an hour into the mountains, turning north toward the very heart of the knobby range.

"Now what?" Claire demanded, without bothering to hide her aggravation.

"Up to their old tricks again," I replied, although I noticed they'd left the wash along a rocky stretch of ground where tracking would be more difficult. Letting my gaze roam ahead, I spotted what looked like a trail winding through the rocks and cactus. We pushed on stubbornly through the increasingly broken landscape. Despite the graze and water of the night before, our horses were once more beginning to show the strain of the journey, forcing us to stop often to allow them some rest. It was during one of these brief breaks that I began to get an uneasy feeling, like we were being watched. Climbing back into my saddle, I motioned Claire forward.

"What is it?" she asked. "Did you see something?"

"No, but I feel it."

She didn't question my vague reply, but continued to study the serpentine path leading away from us, the prints of the outlaws' horses chiseled plainly in the hard soil. Although I couldn't see anything worrisome, the feeling that we were no longer alone continued to build. After a couple of minutes, I slid the Parker from its loop on my saddle horn and handed it to Claire.

"I know you've got your heart set on using that pick, but I think you might fare better with a scattergun."

She eyed the shotgun thoughtfully for a moment, then shook her head. "No, there's another reason I intend to use the pick. A promise I made."

"To Charlie Red?"

"No, to John Trepan."

For the first time I began to sense a kind of desperation in her demeanor, and wondered if she was afraid she'd made a promise she wouldn't be able to keep.

"It was the only weapon they'd left me, but when I approached Trepan with it, just before they rode away, he laughed." Claire's cheeks reddened at the memory. "They all laughed. Then Trepan drew his revolver and told me I'd never touch him with a miner's tool, that I should buy a gun if I wanted to do him any real harm." Her expression turned bitter. "Sam Miller rode over then, and held up my rifle. He offered to sell it to me for a price that, well, it wasn't cash."

Having developed an idea of the kind of man Sam Miller might be, I had a fair idea of the kind of offer he'd make.

"I told Miller, and Trepan, too, that I had no use for their offers, and that a pick would be all the weapon I'd need when the time came. That probably sounds as hollow to you as it obviously did to them, but their jeers only solidified my resolve."

I didn't answer right away, and the silence between us grew strangely uncomfortable. I understood what she was saying, and why she felt so strongly about it, but no matter how determined she believed she was, a pick wasn't going to be any kind of weapon against a gun. Then a flat, distant thump—like a book being dropped on its side in another part of the house—rolled over the hills toward us. I looked at Claire and she looked at me, and the sorrel perked its ears toward a craggy peak a couple of miles away.

"Was that . . . ?" Claire turned her head partially to the side to hear better, her brows furrowing in concentration.

"A gunshot? Yeah, I think it was." I strained to listen as well, to filter out the unrelenting chatter of birds and the faint rustle of the wind in the scrub, and damned if I didn't hear it again, a quick, rippling reverberation, barely audible, yet unmistakable. Then the wind picked up and Claire's bay shifted its weight from one side to the other, causing the old McClellan's leather to creak loudly. But we'd both heard it, and I think we both felt certain that Trepan and his men were somehow involved.

"What poor souls have those animals fallen upon this time?" Claire whispered, more to herself than to me.

"Take the shotgun, Missus Adams," I said tersely.

Claire hesitated only a moment, then accepted the shortened firearm and laid it across her saddlebows. I reached behind me to dig a box of 12-gauge shells from my saddlebags and handed it to her.

"Do you know how to handle that?" I asked, nodding to the scattergun.

Her reply was a curt: "Yes." Then, wedging the box of double-ought buckshot in the open channel behind the McClellan's pommel, she broke the Parker at the breech to make sure it was loaded. Watching the practiced ease in which she handled the shotgun, I decided not to worry about her ability to shoot it.

Drawing the Marlin from its scabbard, I said: "Whatever's happening up there is likely going to be finished long before we get there, so let's not go busting in until we know what we're facing. I don't want to ride into a trap."

Claire nodded resolutely. "I trust your judgment, Tom. Lead on, and I shall follow like the dutiful soldier."

I grinned big; damn, I liked the way she talked sometimes. Then I slapped the sorrel's ribs with my heels and we moved out at a good clip. Claire kept the bay's nose close behind the sorrel's copper-shaded tail as we wound past sprawling beds of prickly pear and stubby barrel cactus; saguaro dotted the hillsides around us like startled sentries, and beneath the tracks of Trepan's horses, our path was stippled with the shoeless prints of wild mustangs and desert bighorns.

Despite the roughness of the terrain, we made pretty good time. Gunfire continued to roll down from the higher peaks, and I found myself hoping that whomever Trepan and his men had jumped up there would continue to make a good showing for themselves until we arrived—foolish thinking, perhaps, since I didn't have a clue what kind of help we'd be, possessing only a rifle, a revolver, and a short-range scattergun. And Claire's pickax, of course.

The sound of shooting grew louder as we approached the broad mouth of a rocky canyon, its floor curved as if scooped out with a giant's round-bitted shovel. I levered a round into the Marlin's breech and waited for Claire to come alongside.

"They appear to be making quite a fight of it, aren't they?" she observed.

"It sounds like Trepan's boys might have bitten off more than they can swallow," I agreed, although I was already beginning to doubt my earlier assumption that the outlaws had ambushed a mining camp or a party of prospectors. The fighting seemed too intense for a bunch of rock busters.

"What if it's the other way around?" Claire asked quietly. "What if it's Trepan and his men who were ambushed?"

"By who?"

"A posse? Didn't you say Fort Mohave was nearby?"

"Fairly close, although I'm not real sure where we are right now, or how far away Mohave might actually be."

A ragged staccato of gunfire tumbled down out of the canyon, and the sorrel shifted nervously under me and tried to turn away.

"I believe she senses the danger ahead as clearly as we do," Claire said.

I glanced at her, but she was already shaking her head no.

"I'll not turn back at this point, Tom. Lead the way, and I'll be close behind."

"Watch yourself, that's the main thing. If it gets too chancy, we'll back off and try again later."

She nodded grim accord, and we eased cautiously into the canyon. The walls rose quickly on either side of us, steep slopes with a sheer, vertical cliff at the top. Shallow, arched-roofed caverns, kind of like grottos, or what you sometimes see in photographs of ancient cliff dwellings, pocked the upper rim.

The trail wound through the center of the canyon toward a sharp bend probably a quarter of a mile in. The gunfire came from beyond that, more sporadic now than it had been earlier, as if both parties were digging in. I'll admit I was pretty nervous about the whole thing. My palms were sweating around the Marlin's wrist and the sorrel's reins, and the muscles across my shoulders and the back of my neck were drawn as tight as a miser's wallet. The closer we got to the canyon's rocky elbow, the more I licked nervously at my lips, the faint taste of tortoise grease still lingering from that morning. We weren't quite a hundred yards away when a shot rang out that sounded closer than the others, followed by a gentle tug on my shirt sleeve and the sharp smack of lead on rock at my side. Throwing a startled glance to our rear, I saw a trio of Indians racing their ponies across a shoulder of the canyon toward us.

"Tom!" Claire cried in warning, but I was already pulling my horse around, yelling for her to make a run for it.

Shouldering the Marlin, I snapped off a round, but with the sorrel dancing so frantically under me, my shot went high and wide. Then a barrel cactus exploded into a spongy mass next to my left foot, and I dug my heels into the mare's ribs, racing after Claire on her bay while the Indians closed in behind us.

Excerpt from:
Minutes of Military Inquest
Reedcatcher Insurrection
28 May 1882–8 June 1882
Major Leandro Marcus, Presiding
14 July 1882, Fort Yuma, A.T.

"Please state your name and occupation."

"I am José Gómez. I translate for the army."

"Translate? You mean you are an interpreter?"

"I am translate. I speak Mohave, Cocopah, Pima, Yavapai, Mexican, English, a little bit Latin. I translate these words for the army."

"As an interpreter?"

"Explain to me what is interpreter."

"An interpreter . . . translates."

"Words, for the army?"

"Yes, sometimes. He might also translate for territorial delegates, officials from the Bureau of Indian Affairs, or any number of business or political leaders wishing to converse with our local tribes."

"Like the army?"

"Yes, the military depends heavily on good interpreters."

"That is who I translate for, the army. Not those others you say."

"Gentlemen, and I am addressing the court at large, if I hear one more snicker from the civilian section, I will have this room cleared immediately. And if I hear even a hint of mirth from any military personnel, I will have that man severely reprimanded. Do I make myself clear? Very well. Now, Mister Gómez, you stated for the record that you were an interpreter for the military during the

Reedcatcher insurrection, is that correct?"

"Sí, I translate for the army."

All right, let's move on. You were employed by sub agent Alvins at Bosque Wash village at the time of the Reedcatcher uprising, were you not?"

"Sí, yes, I worked for Mister Alvins, for the army."

"Yes, the military is in charge of the Fort Mohave Reservation."

"Sí, that is who pays me, the army, but I translate for Mister Alvins."

"Good, now we're getting somewhere. Mister Alvins has stated that there were rumors of unrest among the Bosque Wash Mohaves, including a fear that they might be blamed for the theft of horses from the Eldorado Canyon region of Nevada. Were you aware of any such rumors?"

"Yes, many rumors before Reedcatcher jumped the reservation."

"Including the Eldorado Canyon rumors?"

"Sí, yes."

"Mister Gómez, were you aware of white men in the vicinity of Bosque Wash, trading in either whiskey or guns to the Mohaves?"

"I believe there were white men, yes, but not traders."

"Not traders? Then what were they doing there?"

"They bring whiskey and guns to the young men, make big talk about the army coming to arrest them."

"For the theft of the Eldorado horses?"

"Sí."

"To what end, Mister Gómez?"

"Explain to me what you ask?"

"I mean, to what purpose were these white men spreading rumors and handing out guns and whiskey. What did

they get out of it?"

"Ah, yes, sí. The unrest you talk of, I think that is what they get out of it."

"They wanted the Mohaves to leave the reservation?"

"Sí, yes."

"To what . . . why did they want the Mohaves to leave the reservation?"

"To what Captain Reynolds said earlier, I think. To confuse the white men in Arizona, scare them."

"Again, sir, why?"

"I don't know."

"All right. What do you know of the youth called Whip?"

"Fast Stinger?"

"Yes. He was called Whip, was he not?"

"By the white men, sí."

"Was he tortured, Mister Gómez?"

"Yes, tortured, then killed."

"By the white men who brought guns and whiskey to the Mohaves at Bosque Wash?"

"Sí."

"Do you know their identities . . . their names?"

"No."

"Could you describe them, based on information obtained from the Bosque Wash Mohaves?"

"No. One was tall, they said, very tall. The other I do not know. Just a man, I think. The tall one, he was the chief, but that is all I know of them."

"Why did they kill Fast Stinger, Mister Gómez?"

"Because Big Reedcatcher would not go to war. The white men wanted this, but Big Reedcatcher did not want to anger the army. He did not want to bring trouble to his family at Bosque Wash."

"So these men kidnapped Whip, then killed him, in

order to force Reedcatcher into an act of aggression?"

"Sí."

"What was Whip's relationship with Reedcatcher?"

"Explain to me relationship."

"Was he a friend? Did Reedcatcher know his parents?"

"Ah, yes, I see. Fast Stinger, who you call Whip, was Big Reedcatcher's son. That is why they killed him, and that is why Big Reedcatcher left the reservation, to kill these white men who wanted him to go to war for them."

SESSION EIGHT

Even as hammered down as our mounts were after their long journey from the Colorado River, they seemed to sense the danger coming after us from the rear, and scrambled over that rocky trail like fleeing pronghorns.

Rounding the canyon's bend, we immediately spotted the source of the gunfire that had been reeling us in for the last couple of miles—a handful of abandoned buildings, clumped together near the center of a little flat on the south side of the canyon, like a small village or an old *rancho* from Spanish Colonial days. Later on, I'd count a dozen structures altogether, some of them constructed with flat stones, likely gathered from below the canyon's rims, and others made of adobe. All were roofless or in some form of disrepair, and the haze of powder smoke that hung over the tiny plain only added to the sense of desolation. [*Editor's Note:* In his report to the commanding officer at Fort Mohave, and later during the Reedcatcher Inquiry conducted at Fort Yuma, Arizona Territory, Captain James Reynolds identifies this location as "the old Santiago Ranch"; no other references to this site have been located.]

Indians had the buildings surrounded, yet even from a couple of hundred yards away, I could see white men scattered among the sturdiest structures—broad-brimmed hats and sun-burnished faces, though pale in comparison to the dark-skinned warriors who had them trapped.

Realizing that the trail we were following was going to lead us straight into the fray, I shouted for Claire to make a break for the canyon's wall. She glanced wildly over her shoulder, and I used the Marlin to point out a shallow, grotto-shaped cavern about halfway up the north wall. I don't know if she heard what I was saying, but she understood what I meant, and quickly reined her mount into the scrub. I was right behind her when we hit the rock-strewn slope below the arched mantle high above us, ramming my heels into the sorrel's ribs.

Our progress slowed as the grade steepened, and I finally jumped from the saddle and tossed my reins over the mare's neck. The horse snorted and jumped sideways, stumbling over a twisted branch of sage and falling to her knees. Then she lunged to her feet and clambered after the bay, her hooves kicking loose a small avalanche of dirt and stones.

Dropping to one knee, I threw the rifle to my shoulder and tried to find a target, but the trio of Indians who had herded us into this trap had already given up the chase and were scattering for cover. I managed to get off only a single round before they vanished into the rocks at the base of the canyon's wall, and had the satisfaction of a sharp yelp as my bullet sang off the upper corner of a stagecoach-sized boulder, just as the last warrior urged his mount into its shelter. I was pretty sure I hadn't seriously injured him, but I hoped I'd gotten my message across. We might have been outnumbered, but we weren't going to go down without a fight.

With those three warriors temporarily out of sight and the others—the rest of the Indian war party and what had to be Trepan's men holed up in those deserted buildings—occupied a couple of hundred yards away, I broke from cover and sprinted up the side of the canyon to where Claire was hitching her horse to a flimsy manzanita branch at the side of the cavern's broad mouth. She grabbed the sorrel and had her secured next to the bay by the time I stumbled into the cave, my breath wheezing in the dried-bone air, my legs trembling from the climb. Claire tried to pull me deeper into the cavern, but I shook her hand away and told her to get back.

"There's hardly any space to get back in to," she replied pragmatically, although she did get down on her hands and knees where she wouldn't make quite so much of a target.

I've probably been misleading in referring to our shelter as a cave. It was more like a hollowed out pocket in the side of the cliff, maybe twenty feet tall at its apex and fifty wide across the mouth, but no more than a dozen paces from front to rear, and that on a ledge gently inclined toward the canyon's floor. The slope below us was dotted with chunks of pale sandstone that had broken out of the cliff's face over the ages. Some of those chunks were pretty big, but most were about the size of a pickle barrel on down. Cactus and woolly brush covered the slanted earth like a ragged, prickly carpet, none of it tall enough to hide a man on horseback, but plenty thick enough to crawl through, were those three hiding in the rocks below so inclined.

I'd already caught brief glimpses of them, making their slow way through the scrub. Probably no more than eighty yards away at that point, but still difficult to spot through the thorny cover. Although I figured it would be a wasted shot as shaky as my limbs were after my frantic, lung-busting climb to the cavern, I decided to take one anyway, just to let them know we were aware of what they were up to, and I was pleased as punch when my bullet came close enough to the nearest Indian to send him diving for cover. The others faded from sight before the Marlin's echo could bounce back off the far wall, giving me time to catch my breath and take stock of our situation.

I don't guess you'd need a sixth-grade education to know we were in a real bind. With that sheer rim above us, we were cornered like rats in a box, and no way to chew ourselves out that I could see.

Claire crawled up beside me to peer over the edge. "Where are they?" she asked, meaning the trio who had chased us into this hole.

"Yonder," I said, pointing out where the warriors had gone to cover—although I doubted they were still there. If it had been me, I'd have started belly wiggling to other locales as soon as I hit the dirt, to avoid a bullet fired blindly into the scrub where I'd dropped.

Staring across the canyon toward the little rancho, Claire said: "I couldn't tell from below. Is that Trepan and his men over there?"

"I think so."

Her lips thinned in a grimace. "I hope the Indians don't get them before we have our chance."

"Right now, I'd settle for the Indians not getting us."

"Are they Apaches?"

"I don't believe so. I think they might be Mohaves, maybe the same bunch that hit Tyson's Well last week."

"You told me the other night that you didn't think it was Indians that attacked the station, because they used bows and arrows instead of rifles."

"That's what I said."

"I didn't notice any of these men using bows. The ones I've seen have all been armed with rifles."

"I noticed that, too," I agreed, then raised my voice to shout across the canyon: "Trepan. John Trepan, is that you?"

We waited as the echoes of my question faded. Then a voice came back, made small by the size of the gorge. "Slade?"

"Well, I guess that answers that," I said to Claire.

She was staring across the canyon, her jaw clenched in barely contained fury.

Laughter floated out of the dilapidated rancho. "You

should've stayed back at the woman's place, Slade, and kept her with you."

I wasn't expecting Claire to reply, and flinched when she shouted: "I said I'd come after you, Trepan. All of you."

More laughter echoed across the canyon; one or two of the gang made a few lewd comments. Then the Mohaves opened fire against the rancho, and talking ceased. When the shooting tapered off several minutes later, I glanced at Claire.

"I know how you feel about Trepan and those boys, but we'd be a lot better off if we could get down there with them."

"Join with our enemies?"

I nodded toward the lower slope, where the three Mohaves were still hidden. "Better to fight alongside Trepan than be overrun by Indians."

"I'd rather be dead."

"I'm not sure we'll have a choice. Trepan's men are better armed than we are, and they've probably got a lot more experience in this kind of fighting than you or I do."

"I am well aware of what John Trepan's butchers are capable of," Claire replied. "At least up here, we won't have to worry about turning our backs on our allies. Trust me, Tom, if we joined Trepan and came out victorious, we'd soon find ourselves at the mercy of the very men you believe will save us. And you can believe me when I say that mercy is a concept none of those men are familiar with. Especially not after all the trouble we've been to them."

Well, she had a point, but I still held that we'd suffer less at Trepan's hands than if we were captured by the Mohaves, and stand a better chance of getting away afterward, too. I tried to gauge the distance between our little grotto and the outlaws' enclave, and figured it at two hundred yards, give or take a few rods.

"It's too far," Claire said, as if reading my mind.

"Maybe," I replied, but I'd already spotted a possible avenue of flight, a shallow, twisting arroyo off to the side that, while it wouldn't afford much in the way of protection, would at least provide an uncluttered route to the lower end of the rancho.

Claire and I were stretched out shoulder to shoulder on the cavern's floor as we peered down toward where the Mohaves were still keeping out of sight. The fighting across the canyon had tapered off considerably by then—scattered shots and little flurries of gunfire that would rock back and forth down the canyon's walls, only to fade out slowly in the distance. I'd guess there were at least a dozen Indians surrounding Trepan's men, although I may have missed a few in the dense scrub. [*Editor's Note:* According to the Fort Yuma military inquiry on the 1882 insurrection led by Big Reedcatcher, nineteen Mohaves participated in the fight at Santiago Ranch.]

It was hotter than a raw chili pepper pegged out there on the canyon's wall. The sun was shining directly down on us, and the air was dry and still. I was keeping a close watch on the brush near the canyon's floor where I figured those three Mohaves were hunkered down in hiding, but couldn't spot them. There wasn't a speck of color nor a trembling bush to give away their position. It was only when they opened up on us once more that I realized they were half again as close as they had been, spread out in a shallow arc that had us pinned down from every direction.

They only fired half a dozen or so rounds, the bullets digging into the soft stone at our backs and showering us with rock fragments. Claire shrieked when a ricochet struck the floor at her side, kicking up a powdery geyser of pale dust. I thought at first she'd been hit, but she insisted she wasn't. Then she showed me her sleeve, where the fabric had been torn below the elbow.

"Almost," she said.

I glanced over my shoulder to study the stone panel behind

us, the curved ceiling and high, smooth walls. There was no point in urging her to crawl back or find cover. She'd already pointed out there wasn't any place to get back to, and no cover, either. There wasn't even a decent-sized rock to curl up behind. I swore under my breath when I realized how desperate our position had become. When I'd spotted this shallow den from below, the possibility of ricochets hadn't even entered my mind. Now the likelihood that this little grotto could very well become our tomb—especially if those Mohaves figured out how vulnerable we were to bounced bullets—filled my ears with a tempest-like roar.

"Tom," Claire said softly, breaking the moment. I looked at her, waited for her to go on. "I . . . for some reason, I feel a need to apologize."

"For what?"

"For the stubbornness, my stubbornness, that led us here."

"I was chasing Trepan long before I stumbled across you and that pickax," I reminded her.

"If . . . if there was some way . . ."

"It ain't over yet, Claire," I said gently.

She nodded and forced a smile. "Of course not. Worse odds than these have been overcome by desperate men. Surely the gods would grant the same privilege to a man and woman."

I didn't reply, partly because she was talking strange again—like I imaged women who attended colleges with names like Vassar might do on a regular basis—but also because of her use of the word gods, rather than God. It seemed an unusual choice for a good Mormon woman, although it was more than I wanted to explore at the moment.

Turning my attention back to the slope below us, I was startled by a hint of dull red, where I was pretty sure only tan had been moments before. Recalling that one of the Mohaves who'd run us up here had been wearing a rust-colored cloth shirt, I eased the Marlin to my shoulder and drew a bead on the patch of color. I estimated the range at sixty yards, although downhill, which made it somewhat more difficult to judge. Thumbing the hammer to full cock, I took a deep breath and held it. My finger tightened on the trigger, but before I could fire, a shot rang out from my left. The bullet whined shrilly as it passed overhead, smacking solidly into the grotto's wall, then flying back into space. I cursed and fired, but my aim was off, and I knew even before the smoke cleared that I'd missed.

Two more shots whipped past us before I could lever a second round into the rifle's chamber. For a couple of minutes then, we kept up a steady fusillade. Although the Mohaves were getting off three and four shots to every one of mine, I feel like I made a good showing of it, and kept them from advancing, even if I didn't do any serious damage. Then the shooting stopped and a deep silence drifted over the slope. I was breathing hard, as if I'd made a dash to the canyon's floor and back in those few hectic moments, although I hadn't moved at all except to lever and fire as fast as I could work the Marlin's action.

"Tom," Claire said, nodding toward the rancho.

Listening, I could hear one of the outlaws shouting, but with the ringing in my ears from all the shooting, I couldn't make out who it was or what he was saying. I glanced at Claire, but she shook her head.

"I think he's asking if we're running out of cartridges," she said.

It seemed an odd question, and Claire would tell me afterward that the query had seemed more sarcastic than curious, as if they were making fun of our predicament.

"It would be like him," she said bitterly, adding that it had sounded like Miller's voice to her, although her hearing had been affected, too, and she couldn't be sure.

Not really caring what Trepan or his men had to say, I turned my attention back to the Mohaves. That patch of red was gone, which brought a satisfied grin to my face. Then a fresh burst of gunfire raked the cavern's wall, and Claire and I ducked. A shot ricocheted into the dirt close to the bay's hooves, and the gelding snorted and yanked hard on his lead rope. The limb Claire had tied him to arched back until I thought it might break, before the horse finally stepped forward again, releasing the tension.

"We've got to get out of here," I told Claire.

And there was that look again, our closeness of only moments before trampled beneath an acrimonious hatred for the men across the canyon. "To die from one of Trepan's guns, rather than an Indian's?"

"Our odds are shady enough as it is. If we lose our horses, we ain't likely to leave here unless it's our bones being carried off by coyotes."

"Then you go, but I won't."

I'm not proud of how I responded to that, and I won't repeat it now, other than to admit it included more than a few obscenities, spoken loudly and vividly, and fueled, no doubt, by my own sense of helplessness. Claire waited until I was finished, her expression as hard as stone.

"Go on," she insisted, once I'd run out of steam. "I'll be perfectly safe here."

"That's the stupidest goddamned thing I've heard you say yet, and you're not a stupid woman." I paused then, scowling as a new thought began to worm its way through my brain. "What aren't you telling me?" I finally asked.

Her lips moved, but no words came, and I knew I'd struck a nerve. Then another shot rang out, the sorrel's scream all but drowning out the sound of the ricochet. The horse reared, and I swore and started to push to my feet, but Claire pulled me back just before two more shots raked the air where I would have been standing if she hadn't grabbed me. I swore again and flopped back to my stomach. The sorrel fell heavily, then slid a dozen or so feet downslope without kicking, a small avalanche of broken limbs and small rocks preceding it. The dust was still floating above the torn scree when I pushed toward the lip of the cavern's floor.

"Tom," Claire cried, reaching for me.

I shoved her hand away. "Stay down," I snapped, wanting to hurry before the dust settled. Leaving my rifle behind, I wiggled swiftly down through the scrub to where the sorrel had come to rest against another manzanita, the bush bent nearly flat beneath the animal's weight. The mare was dead, no doubt about that. The bullet had struck her squarely in the chest, but there was only a faint smear of blood, and her eyes were already glazing over. Staying low, I fumbled at the saddlebags, digging out all the extra ammunition I could reach. Unfortunately, the cartridges for my Smith and Wesson were lodged under the sorrel's hip, and I couldn't get enough leverage to pull the bags free and still keep my head down. Settling for what I had, I grabbed the canteen off the saddle horn, then scurried back into the skimpy shelter of the overhang. The dust had cleared off enough by then that I kept expecting a shot in my hind side all the way up, but managed to slither inside the shallow cavern without attracting a bullet.

"What now?" Claire asked when I was safely back at her side.

"We're getting out of here," I replied curtly, and didn't make any effort to soften my words when I went on. "We're going to make a run for Trepan's position, even if I have to tie you to the back of the bay's saddle to do it. I don't know what'll happen if we all get out of this alive, but I damn sure know what's going to happen if we stay here. As soon as they figure out what happened to the sorrel, those Mohaves are going to start bouncing bullets off these walls, and it won't take long after that before we're both either dead or too tore up with slugs to care whether we live or die."

I gave her a moment to consider my words, hoping that she'd see for herself how we didn't have a choice anymore, but I was dead serious about my intentions. I was leaving that ledge come hell or high water, and I wasn't going alone.

Finally, almost meekly, Claire nodded. "All right."

"That's it?" I asked, not really sure I believed her.

"Yes. I owe you that much, whether I think we're doing the right thing or not."

I nodded awkwardly, caught strangely but pleasantly off guard by her quiet acceptance. Breaking open a new box of cartridges for the Marlin, I replaced the rounds I'd fired, then shoved the rest of them into the pockets of my trousers and vest. Claire scooted over with the Parker in one hand, the box of double-ought buckshot in the other.

"What do you want me to do?"

"As soon as we're ready, I'm going to open up with my rifle. I want you to wait until I've fired at least three rounds, then make a run for the bay. Don't spook him any worse than he already is, but get into that saddle as quick as you can."

"What about you?"

"I'll stay here and keep on firing until you're set, then I'm going to jump up behind you. You hammer that horse's ribs with everything you've got, Claire. Turn him straight downhill and don't hold him back. We won't have time to pick an easy route, just make sure he's going as fast as he can. I'm going to be shooting over your shoulder all the way to the bottom. I might not hit anything, but if I can get my bullets close enough to where those Mohaves are burrowed, we might make it off this damned wall." I hesitated, debating how much more I wanted to say, then decided that she was bullheaded enough that I'd better spell it out.

"Use that arroyo I pointed out earlier, and head straight for Trepan's position. I mean it, Claire. That's going to be our only chance. If you try to circle back the way we came, we'll never make it. Even if we did get past the Mohaves, they'd come after us, and we wouldn't be able to outrun them. Not two-up on a horse that's already been pushed to the point of exhaustion the last few days. They'd run us down before we reached the mouth of the canyon."

"I said I'd do what you wanted," she replied stiffly.

"Fair enough," I said, and it was. Claire Adams might have been maddeningly pigheaded and as touchy as a skinned toad when it came to John Trepan, Sam Miller, and Charlie Red, but I'd trust her with my life. Hell, that's exactly what I was getting ready to do.

I racked a shell into the Marlin's breech, added another to the magazine to replace it, then set the rifle aside. Drawing my Smith and Wesson, I double-checked to make sure all six cavities were filled, then returned it to my holster. Claire broke open the Parker, then gently closed it on full chambers. That was it—eighteen rounds to make an eighty-yard dash to the canyon floor, then another two hundred to the nearest building, where we could come under the protective cover of Trepan's guns—assuming the son of a bitch didn't decide to finish us off before we reached the little rancho's shelter.

"Do you believe in prayer, Mister Slade?" Claire asked quietly.

"My name is Tom," I reminded her.

"That doesn't answer my question."

"I reckon prayer might not hurt, although I intend to shoot until my guns are hot, and save any biblical recitals for later."

She smiled faintly. "I was a religious woman once. I'm afraid my faith has taken a series of blows in recent years." She tightened the belt around her waist, hiked the hem of her dress up above her ankles where they wouldn't be as apt to get in the way, then loosened the knife in its sheath. "I shall fight like a demon, though, and not easily give up my life, no matter our final destination in the afterlife."

"You about ready, Claire?" I asked gently.

"At your word."

I tipped my head toward the slope. "Remember to wait until I've fired three or four rounds before making a break for the bay."

She nodded resolutely and gathered her legs under her. The Marlin's hammer sounded loud in the stillness of our bullet-pocked grotto, the sun's light unusually brilliant. The land seemed sharply drawn all of a sudden, the air pure . . . and then that damned Mohave in the red shirt popped up from behind a clump of greasewood, and I shot him before he could pull the trigger.

I fired twice more at a sturdy, middle-aged man with shoulder-length gray hair and bowed legs as he lunged from cover, and drove him back into the dirt. Then I swung my rifle toward the third Indian, surging from the brush; vermillion streaked his right cheek, and his left was painted black, for death—mine, not his. He raised an old Springfield Long Tom as he ran, but when I put two bullets into a patch of cholla at his side, he dropped from sight without having fired a shot.

So you know, I wasn't deliberately missing. It's just kind of hard making a long shot like that when people are shooting back, and my aim was slightly less than true, even if my efforts weren't.

Shoving to my feet, I started down the slope just as Claire yanked the bay's reins free of the manzanita where she'd hitched him—Lord, how long ago had that been? How long had we laid up there, our hearts thumping with adrenaline, our words taut with fear? It seemed like hours, but when I think back on it, I doubt if it was more than twenty or thirty minutes.

I was moving slowly downhill, working the Marlin's action with cool deliberation, as if my limbs were being manipulated by factors outside my control. I was aware of Claire gaining the bay's seat, of her reining the terrified beast toward me, but I never took my eyes away from where I'd last seen the two remaining Indians dart into the scrub about a third of the way up the canyon's wall. I think I still had three or four rounds left when Claire finally got the bay over to where I was standing. I lifted the rifle's muzzle as she crossed in front of me, then slid smoothly across the gelding's hips. Claire shouted for me to hang on, then reined toward the canyon's floor and slammed her stirrups into the bay's ribs.

We raced downhill at an insanely breakneck pace, crashing through the thorny brush, leaping small boulders, dodging larger ones. It was crazy and wild, and I think I might have actually laughed out loud at one point, because I can remember Claire looking back at me in surprise, her mouth agape. Then the middle-aged Indian with the gray hair jumped from hiding and rushed to cut us off. He was shooting as he ran, and I felt the bay's stride falter, his whole body shuddering beneath us as if momentarily brought up against something hard and unforgiving. Then my bullet cut the Mohave down, and the bay regained its stride. It ran like a damned bird, swooping off the side of that canyon with its nose low and flat, its tail flying.

The Marlin was empty by then. I wedged the smoking rifle across my thighs, between me and the McClellan's cantle, and palmed the Smith and Wesson. I'd lost sight of the third warrior, the one with the painted face, but fired near where I'd last seen him, wanting to keep his face in the dirt, the image of his two fallen comrades fresh in his mind.

The bay hit the bottom of the slope and started up the other side without breaking stride, toward the small, flat plain and its scattered, abandoned buildings. I was twisted around and firing behind me by then, but that third Indian wasn't showing himself. I didn't think I'd hit him, not unless it was with an incredibly lucky shot, but I must have put the fear of hot lead into him, and that was good enough for the short haul.

Then the Parker roared and I whirled to the front, spotting an Indian coming fast through the scrub. He was short and stocky and wore a blue, military-styled jacket with the sleeves cut off—one of the warriors who had been engaged with Trepan's gang, I guess, but he'd spotted us coming through the sage and was racing to intercept us. Claire's shotgun put a swift end to that effort, and the Indian fell hard with the side of his left leg glistening red with blood and torn meat.

That arroyo wasn't as smooth as it had looked from above, but it was still our quickest route to the rancho. I'd quit shooting by then, down to just two live rounds in the Smith's cylinder and wanting to hang onto those in case of a last-minute emergency. I was kicking at the bay's flanks with my heels, but I could tell something was wrong. The horse's gait was slowing, growing choppier as the grade steepened.

"Tom," Claire shouted over her shoulder.

"Keep going!"

"He's bleeding!"

"Keep going!"

She cried out in frustration, but kept pounding at the gelding's ribs. Although the rancho was less than a hundred yards away by then, I began to sense that the little horse wasn't going to make it. Even more worrisome were the several Mohaves who were darting through the brush to cut us off. Reaching around Claire's waist, I slid the Parker from her fingers and told her to get down. She bent low over the McClellan's hornless cantle, allowing me a clear field of vision. I was gripping the shotgun with its single remaining charge in my right hand, the Smith and its two rounds in my left.

"Tom!"

I saw him, and squeezed the Parker's trigger. The Indian spun to the side and went down, his long hair flapping like an ebony sheet when his bandanna flew off. The shotgun recoil was too stout to hang onto it with one hand, and the gun bucked free of my suddenly numbed fingers. I shook my right hand once, then switched the Smith into its tingling palm. Even aching like it was, I knew I'd stand a better chance of hitting a target with my strong-side hand than firing from my left.

A young Mohave, not much more than a kid, appeared next, jumping out from behind a saguaro with an old cap-and-ball revolver already raised. I snapped off a shot that took him just above the knee, and he tumbled into a carpet of prickly pear with a strangled cry.

Shooting that boy in the leg wasn't an act of mercy. It was a lucky shot at a moving target from the back of a running horse. Despite the kid's tender years, I would have killed him if I could. He was sure as hell trying to kill me.

We were still a good forty yards away from the nearest building when the bay's stride began to falter badly. I grabbed the Marlin with my free hand, intending to take the rifle with me if the horse fell. At one point the gelding's front legs started to buckle, and Claire only barely managed to haul back on the reins enough to keep his head up. His breath was ragged and loud, and I imagined I could feel the rapid beating of his heart through my calves as he struggled to continue. I didn't hear the shot that finally killed the horse, but I felt the bullet's impact. The bay's entire body seemed to catch in midstride, and then its legs just stopped working.

I pushed free as the horse went all the way down, making sure to drag Claire out of the saddle with me. We rolled for several feet, then, keeping our heads low, crawled back to where the bay had fallen. Although the body was still warm, the horse's flanks were no longer moving, and I knew he was gone.

Shoving the Marlin into Claire's hands, I told her to reload. She reached unhesitantly into a side pocket of my vest to scoop out a handful of cartridges, but, in her haste, fumbled several of them at the rifle's unfamiliar loading gate until she finally got the hang of it. [*Editor's Note:* Because of patent conflicts—specifically Winchester's King's Improvement Patent of 1866—Marlin marketed its 1881 lever-action rifle with a spring-mounted, forward-sliding loading gate; with the expiration of the Winchester patent approximately twenty years later, Marlin was able to switch to the more familiar springboard pattern.]

Meanwhile, I tripped the Smith and Wesson's top latch and pulled down on the muzzle. The cylinder and barrel pivoted clear of the butt and hammer, and I turned the revolver upside down to let the empty brass rain down over my knees. It took only seconds to reload. As I snapped the Smith closed, I heard a quick, angry buzz dart past my ear, so close I swear I could feel the heat of the bullet's passage on my lobe. Shots were coming sporadically by then, most of them thumping into the bay's body, a few striking closer to Claire and me. The shooting tapered off after a few seconds, and I raised my head for a quick look around, but no one was advancing.

"What do we do now?" Claire asked after I ducked back down beside her.

"I'm not sure yet." I was studying the distance yet to be crossed if we wanted to reach the nearest of the standing buildings, a roofless adobe structure with crumbling walls and a single, low door. It was no more than twenty-five yards away, but the terrain between it and us seemed frightfully bare of vegetation. Just a few tiny clumps of sage and cactus, not enough cover to crawl, and too far away to make a run for it—at least without some covering fire from the other buildings.

"Trepan," I shouted.

"That you, Slade?"

"It's me."

"Damnit, son, you're a tough man to discourage. You're starting to irritate the hell out of me, too. You and the woman both."

"We can help."

Trepan laughed. So did several of his men.

"Tom," Claire said softly.

Following the direction of her gaze, I saw a fine skiff of dust floating above a cactus bed maybe thirty yards away. Rocking the Smith's hammer to full cock, I waited with the muzzle pointed toward the pale cloud, not daring to even blink.

"Watch sharp," I whispered to Claire. "They might be trying to slip in on us from several directions at once."

The Marlin's hammer snicked back smoothly. I didn't ask if she knew how to shoot a lever gun. After witnessing the authoritative way she'd handled the Parker, I felt confident she'd be just as handy with a rifle.

"You still there, Slade?" Trepan called, unaware that someone was creeping stealthily toward us through the scrub.

"I'm here," I confirmed, keeping my eyes on that little patch of cactus.

"Tell me, what's in it for us if we let you come in?"

"Two more guns."

"Hell, son, we've got plenty of guns. What else you got to offer?"

"He's toying with you," Claire said. "With both of us."

"I know, but as long as he's talking, he's not trying anything underhanded, and right now I've got something else on my mind." I shifted the Smith's muzzle about two feet to the right, where another quick puff of dust had spun briefly toward the sky, then drifted back to earth.

"I think we'll just keep you where you are," Trepan called. "You can help watch our flank, without getting too close to . . ."

I fired, the Smith's report shutting off whatever else John Trepan might have said. Over by the cactus, I saw the bare, brown shoulders of an Indian rise partway into the air, then flop back out of sight.

"You got him," Claire breathed.

I didn't reply. I was pretty sure my bullet had struck the skulking warrior, but I wasn't as confident that it had done enough damage to keep him out of the fight. Something about the Indian's quick reaction hinted at more mobility than a solid hit should have allowed.

Twisting partway around, I pushed up until my eyes were level with the bay's hip, scanning the ground between where Claire and I were lying and the nearest structure, but the distance hadn't changed, and our odds hadn't improved. The bay was offering some protection, but only from one side. Going the other way, there was only low-growth cactus and some scraggly shrubs. If the Mohaves made a rush, Claire and I were going to be in a tight fix.

"How about if I start shooting, while you try to make it as far as . . ."

"No."

"Hear me out, damnit."

"Tom, it's going to be both of us, or neither of us."

Leaning back against the bay's rapidly cooling body, I stretched my legs out straight to ease the threat of cramps in my calves. I've read since then that dehydration can cause a lot of the symptoms Claire and I were experiencing on that journey, which doesn't add anything to the story, I just didn't want you thinking I was getting ready to take a nap, or give up in any way. Claire, I noticed, kept squeezing her eyes shut for seconds at a time, and I finally reached across the saddle to loosen one of the canteens. Without a need to conserve water for our mounts, we both drank deeply, and I immediately began to feel better. My thoughts seemed clearer, too, and after a few minutes, I scooted around for another look.

I'd been pondering all along about how we could reach that nearest structure without getting shot, but now that some of the fog had lifted from my brain, I realized there was another option. A low, stone wall ran about fifteen or twenty feet past the smaller building. Although the wall was farther away than the building, the arroyo that we'd followed up from the canyon's floor curved to within a few yards of its near end, increasing our chances significantly.

Keeping my voice low and my eyes averted, I told Claire my plan.

"Can we do it?" she asked.

"I think so. It'll be risky, but better than staying here."

"All right, what do we do?"

The bay had gone down outside of the arroyo, but we were only a few feet from it. The banks were no more than a foot high up here near the top, the bottom more V-shaped than flat or curved, as it had been below. Although even shallower toward its head, I figured it would still be less dangerous than trying to make a run across such open land, even though, toward the end, the Mohaves would probably be able to see what we were up to, and know we'd have to expose ourselves to their guns if we wanted to make that final dash for the wall.

I was still trying to work out a better option, one that wasn't as apt to get either of us shot, when a warning cry echoed over the rancho from somewhere down canyon. I couldn't make out who was shouting or what he was saying, but I think we were all equally surprised when the Mohaves started pulling back. It was kind of a shock to see how close some of them had been able to crawl without being seen, not only toward our position, but toward Trepan and his men as well. Two of them were probably within a dozen yards of the small building where Claire and I had hoped to find shelter.

"What's happening, Tom?"

"They're leaving."

"Why?"

I could only shake my head. At first, I feared the Mohaves' increasingly hurried retreat might be some kind of trap, but within a few minutes, I knew they weren't trying to lure us anywhere. They were fleeing, just as fast as their moccasined feet could take them.

Staying low behind the bay, Claire and I watched eight or ten Mohaves stream out from behind some large boulders several hundred yards away, where they must have kept their horses during the battle. A few more came from somewhere up canyon, circling wide around the buildings, then quirting their mounts after the others. I spotted the warrior with the painted face, the last of the three who had trapped Claire and me in the shallow cavern, come out of hiding with his pony streaking across the ground. Several, I noticed, were swaying atop their wiry mounts, including the kid I'd shot in the leg and the warrior Claire had blistered with the scattergun.

"They're afraid of something," Claire said quietly, her gaze scanning the canyon's rims. Then she whirled toward me with a look of sudden anxiety. "We made it, Tom. We're alive."

"Looks like," I agreed uncertainly.

Downslope, the dust from the Mohaves' horses was already settling back over the canyon floor. I glanced toward the little rancho, scowling. I hadn't heard a peep out of Trepan or his men, and that seemed odd, too. Thinking back on it, I probably should have figured it out sooner—Trepan's bunch, and Claire's reaction as well—but at the time I just flat didn't see it.

"Trepan," I shouted.

After a long moment, his reply floated back, more subdued than it should have been, considering the Mohaves' retreat.

"We're pulling out, Slade. Stay where you are and we'll let you live."

Claire started to rise, but I pulled her back.

"They're going to get away," she cried.

"Let them. For now, just let them go."

"What . . . Tom, it's why we've followed them. It's why *I* followed them. I'm not going to let them ride off."

"We couldn't stop them even if we tried. We couldn't get close enough to stop them. The only thing keeping them from killing us here is that they know it would be too costly for them. It's a standoff right now, but we know where they're going. We can follow along behind, then pick our own time to move in."

Claire was practically in tears. "Are you a coward, after all, Mister Slade? Is that why you wish to cower here like a . . . like . . . *damn you*. If you're afraid, then stay, but don't try to prevent me from what I've come so far to accomplish."

She tried to jerk free of my grasp, but I held firm and pulled her back. "Revenge doesn't suit you, Missus Adams," I said, low but sharp.

"Quite the contrary, Mister Slade, I find it rather empowering." Her jaw was thrust stubbornly forward, her eyes blazing. "Let go of my arm."

"No."

"Slade, you still there?" Trepan shouted.

I didn't reply, but continued to stare into Claire's face until she finally relented, flopping back against the bay's stomach in defeat. I still didn't loosen my grip. I said earlier that I trusted her, and I did, just not when it came to John Trepan or his men.

"Slade?"

"I'm here," I bellowed. "Give it up, Trepan. Come on into Prescott and take your chances with a jury."

Trepan and several of his men laughed, and Sam Miller made a vulgar comment about Claire that I won't repeat. When he was finished, Trepan said: "That's brassy talk for a man pinned down under a dead horse."

"It's your only chance, Trepan. There are posses closing in from three different directions. You can't escape."

"I figure that's a lie, Slade, but I admire your pluck for trying. No, you stay where you are until we're gone. I'm running short on time now, and would rather not have to pry you two out of that hole if I don't have to. But you listen tight now, son. You give up following us, because I'm flat out of patience, and if you and that gal keep dogging us, I'm going to sic my crew on the both of you, and they won't stop until you're both feeding the buzzards."

"You tried that before," Claire shouted.

"I didn't try real hard, missy. If I had, you'd be dead by now. You, too, Slade. So far, I've been real lenient, hoping you'd come to your senses and go home. Now goddamn it, give it up before someone gets killed."

"It's a little late for that," I fired back.

"I don't know what you're talking about, Slade. We've been real careful not to hurt anyone, and I'd as soon keep it that way. Folks don't get as upset if it's just a mine payroll that's been taken, and not some innocent person's life."

"Tell that to Charlie Red," I countered.

Claire's head swiveled toward me, her gaze wide with terror. After a long moment of silence, laughter rolled out of the crumbling buildings and down the slope to where Claire and I were crouched behind the bay.

"Is that what she told you, Slade?"

"You killed him, didn't you?" I challenged.

"Slade!" Claire hissed. "Let it go!"

I looked at her in surprise. She'd mostly called me Tom, or Mister Slade when she was angry or put out about something, but she'd never referred to me by just my surname, no matter how upset she'd been.

"Let it go?" I echoed. "Why? It's what brought you here, isn't it? What's kept you going ever since we left your place."

"You don't . . . just let it go, Tom." Tears were streaming down her cheeks, and her face was twisted with anguish. "Please, just . . . let it be."

From the rancho, Trepan shouted: "We're pulling out, Slade. Take the woman home. Tell your boss that you tried, but that by the time you figured out where we were going, we were already out of the territory."

I didn't reply, but continued to watch Claire, baffled by the look of sick fear in her eyes.

"Claire," I said gently. "What is it?"

She shook her head and looked away. I could hear the gang moving around, the clatter of iron-shod hooves clipping stone as the men led their mounts out of whatever building they'd kept them in during the attack.

"You tell him yet, sweetheart?" Miller shouted. "You tell him about good ol' Charlie Red?"

I could hear the others hooting laughter, and Trepan telling them to shut up and get mounted. I moved around on my knees to peer over the top of the bay toward the rancho. The men were riding out single-file, weaving up the canyon through the scrub to pick up the trail again out of range of my rifle. I counted only four of them, instead of six, but two of the gang were leading extra mounts.

I turned slowly toward Claire, and she said: "Oh, Tom, I'm so sorry. So, so sorry."

Session Nine

I didn't trust Trepan, and Claire and I kept our heads down as the outlaw band rode out. We waited until they'd disappeared around a distant bend in the canyon before we cautiously rose and stepped away from the dead horse.

"Tom?" Claire said softly. When I didn't answer, she said my name again. I knew what she wanted, but I wasn't ready to discuss it yet.

"They didn't know about the Indian ponies," I said.

"What Indian ponies?"

"The two that were left behind from that bunch that had us pinned down in the cave."

She made a small sound of understanding, recalling, I suppose, the mounts that belonged to the two men we'd killed coming down off the canyon's wall. I'd noticed when the Mohaves fled that they hadn't taken time to retrieve those two horses, which meant they were likely still there, if they hadn't spooked during all the shooting or been killed by a stray bullet.

"Stay here," I told Claire. "I want to have a look around before I go after the horses."

"Tom . . ."

"Just do as I say," I interrupted curtly.

"I'll go get the horses."

"No, leave 'em. I'll bring them in after I'm through up above."

She stepped angrily in front of me. "I am neither an invalid nor a fool, Mister Slade. Either go exploring, or find the Indian ponies, but whichever you choose, I shall do the other." After a pause, she added: "I'm not asking your permission. If Trepan is indeed on his way to Fort Mohave, then I'll not contribute to wasting time on injured male pride."

She sure wasn't doing much to placate my mad, but then, she never had. Growling low in my throat, I told her to go find the ponies. "Take the shotgun with you," I added, nodding toward where the Parker lay in the middle of the arroyo some fifteen yards away. "Be sure it's loaded before you get into those rocks, and if you see anything that so much as twitches, you blow it in half with that scattergun. Use both barrels if you have to."

"I know what I'm doing," she snapped, then spun away.

I waited until she had the shotgun reloaded, then made my own slow way toward the upper end of the rancho, where Trepan's gang had done most of their fighting. I kept the Marlin with me, figuring that if Claire needed anything, the Parker would do her more good than the rifle.

You're wondering about Charlie Red, and I'm going to tell you, but not yet. You see, I hadn't forgotten those two empty saddles Trepan's men had left the rancho with, and, to be honest, they were bothering me a lot more than the truth about Charlie Red. I started up that slope real easy, my eyes darting every which way, although lingering most on the buildings where Trepan and his crew had holed up. I didn't walk straight toward them, either, but circled around to come at them from a different angle.

I flinched when I saw the body in the corner of the first building I looked into. He was dead, but the blood on his shirt had a tacky appearance that told me he hadn't been gone long. I eased inside for a closer look, but there wasn't much to see. What was missing seemed more significant. The man's pockets had been emptied, the insides cocked away from his trousers and vest like stubby ears, and his boots looked worn where spur straps had ridden across the vamp, although there were no spurs there now. I held the back of my fingers against his cheek to be sure, but he was already colder than anything in that country had a right to be, sending a shiver floating up my spine.

Moving to a nearby window, I peered through it toward a second building about twenty yards away. Spent brass glinted in the grass and weeds out front, and when I got over there, I found even more empty cartridges inside, suggesting this was where the others had taken refuge. As soon as I glanced out the windows, I could understand why. The building sat higher than any of the others, with a clear field of fire in every direction except for the smaller building where I'd found the first dead man.

I say first, because the second was just outside the larger building, lying on his face in the hot sun. There was a bullet hole in his lower back. Although not nearly as much blood stained this man's shirt as the first, the flies seemed thicker. I walked over with my rifle gripped tightly in both hands, and tipped the body over with a toe. Even half expecting it, I nearly jumped out of my boots when the man groaned. I rolled the Marlin's hammer all the way back and told him not to move, but I doubt that he even heard me. His guns had been taken and his pockets were turned inside out, revealing blue-stained cotton and wads of gray lint. Just to be certain, I did a quick check for a hideout gun, but he'd been stripped clean. Leaning the Marlin against the wall, I knelt at the outlaw's side and gently rolled his shoulder. Another small moan escaped his lips, but he didn't open his eyes. I said: "Can you hear me?"

There was no answer. Not even the flutter of an eyelid. Recalling the bullet hole in his back, I pulled a folding knife from my pocket and sliced the material away from his chest and stomach, but there was no exit wound. Not knowing what else to do, I probed the area under his ribs as gently as possible, feeling for a bullet beneath the surface, but couldn't find anything. The man's words caught me off guard.

"It ain't there."

I swayed back, instinctively moving my hand to the Smith and Wesson's grips but not pulling it.

"You're alive?"

"You askin', or tellin'?"

"I'm surprised, is all. Your partner's dead in that other building."

"I reckon I soon will be, too."

"Maybe not. You sound strong."

The guy tried to laugh, but it didn't come out very well. "You Slade?" he wheezed, after catching his breath.

"Yeah. Who're you?"

"Bowers."

"Jim Bowers?"

"The gal mention me, did she?"

"Not much, which I take as a good sign. She has harsh feelings for Miller and Trepan."

"Ain't their real names." Bowers voice was raspy, and seemed to be fading a little with every word he uttered. "Mine is," he added after a pause. "If you take a notion to bury me, you might scratch that on a rock for a headstone."

"I'm not sure we're going to have that much time, but I'll remember the name, and send someone out to fetch your body when I get to a town."

"It ain't no bother, either way. By the time anyone gets back here . . ."

His words trailed off, but he didn't have to spell it out. The only reason a man like Bowers would even care about being buried was to keep the carrion-eaters off of him. If I didn't do something for the body before we left, there wasn't likely to be much left by the time someone else got out here to bury him.

"You want me to pull you out of the sun?" I asked.

"Naw, I reckon it'd hurt too much to be moved. Just leave me be."

I edged over until my head and hat were shading his face, which he seemed to appreciate.

"Listen, Slade, I want you to catch that son of a bitch."

"Trepan?"

"Yeah, only his real name's Hulce, or House, or something like that. I didn't catch it real clear the first time, and he started going by Trepan almost as soon as I joined up."

"What about the others? What are their names?"

Bowers shook his head. "Couldn't say about the others. I know Miller and Brown took on aliases, but I don't know about the rest. I didn't. My name's Bowers, from San Antonio. You get a chance, send a telegram to my ma over there, tell her . . . tell her not to wait for me to come back." He frowned. "Jesus, Slade, it's getting cold. Do you feel that, or am I really dyin'?"

I laid my hand against his shoulder. "Hang on a while, Bowers. I need to ask some more questions."

The wounded man smiled up at me, his lips peeling back to reveal bloodstained gums, and I knew then that he was right. We both were. Jim Bowers wasn't going to live to see his ma or San Antonio ever again.

"Listen, you get that bastard Trepan, and when you do, you tell him I know . . . know it was him that shot me. You tell him that, Slade, so the damned skunk knows . . . knows that I know."

"Why'd he shoot you?"

"Because he got the chance in all the fighting, and because he's a greedy son of a bitch who wants all the money for himself."

"Is he the one who killed the man in the other building?"

"Naw, that's Merle Stratton. He got plugged comin' into the

canyon." Bowers chuckled, spitting up a few drops of blood that glistened in the sunlight. "They double-crossed us, too."

"Who?"

"Them Mohaves. Was supposed . . . to stop anyone followin'. Throw folks off our tail, but they called . . . called the ol' boy's bluff."

"What ol' boy? What are you talking about, Bowers?"

The outlaw shook his head, his gaze roving and kind of frightened, as if he sensed something approaching that I couldn't see.

"Christ, Slade, it's cold. You got a . . . got a blanket, or . . . or something?"

"I'll get you a blanket in a minute," I said, feeling a need to draw him out in the dwindling amount of time I figured he had left. Trepan's double cross had opened Bowers's mouth, but I was afraid his bullet was going to close it before I had the information I wanted.

"Chili," he said, out of the blue. "Chili'd be good. Ma . . . she used to make good chili . . . back in San Antone."

"Where's Trepan headed, Bowers?" I spoke sharply, trying to pull the dying man's wandering thoughts back to the abandoned rancho. "Who's his accomplice? Claire says there was another man, that he and Trepan set all this up more than a month ago."

Bowers nodded weakly. "Was another." He touched his cheek, smiling. "Scar, right here, damn that Charlie Red."

"Charlie Red marked him?"

"Deep, too."

"What's his name?"

"Don't know. Just . . . just saw him that one . . ."

"When, Bowers? When did you see him? And where?"

"Back . . ." He made a small, meaningless gesture with his hand. "There . . . I think it was. There . . ."

"Where?"

The outlaw closed his eyes, and after a minute I rocked back on my heels. Bowers was still breathing, but the sound was rattily now, as if his lungs were starting to fill.

"What did he tell you?"

I rose and turned. Claire stood a few yards away with the shotgun in her hands, a pair of mustangs on long lead ropes standing behind her. The ponies were smaller than the C&P stock we'd lost, but wiry and tough, and would probably fare better in that harsh desert climate than stable-fed mounts ever would. There was a tall gray and a shorter sorrel-and-white pinto, both of them kind of walleyed at the thick, cloying scent of blood.

Motioning toward the fallen outlaw, Claire repeated her question.

"Nothing."

"Did he tell you about Charlie Red, about what they did to him?"

"He said he marked the man who came to your place that first time."

She smiled coldly. "Charlie knew what kind of men they were. Even then, he knew."

I remembered the chill Bowers had mentioned, and felt it myself at Claire's words. Like the temperature had suddenly dropped about forty degrees.

"You think I'm crazy, don't you?" she asked.

"I think we'd better get started." I nodded toward the taller horse. "I'll take the steel-dust, you can have the pinto. We'll use our own saddles instead of those Mexican torture racks they're carrying now. Why don't you take a look around while I get my rig off the sorrel. See if you can find some water. There's probably a well nearby, if it hasn't caved in or gone dry."

She nodded and I walked past her, slipping the gray's lead

rope from her fingers as I did. She watched as I moved away, and I felt that chill again, then scolded myself for letting it get to me.

I led the gray as far as the base of the slope and tied him off in some manzanita, then moved on up through the scrub until I came to where the second Indian I'd shot lay sprawled on his back. He was middle-aged and craggy-faced, and, judging from his expression, he'd died hard and in a lot of pain. A Winchester carbine lay in the dirt at his side, and there was a half-filled bandolier across his chest. Farther up the slope I found the Indian in the rust-colored shirt, a younger man than his partner, but no kid, either. He'd died fast, and there wasn't much blood to stain the ground under him. A second Winchester lay nearby, although I didn't see any extra cartridges. I considered bringing both rifles along, as we could have used some additional firearms, but the thought of robbing the dead has always made me feel queasy, and I left the guns where they were.

I scrambled up the rest of the way to where the sorrel had come to rest, and without having to keep my head down for fear of having it shot off, it didn't take long to uncinch the saddle and pull it free. I worried some that the gray might throw a fit when I tried to switch rigs—a lot of those Indian ponies were barely green broke—but he accepted the saddle without flinching, and I was soon mounted and riding back to the rancho.

Claire was standing near the smaller building where Merle Stratton lay dead. She had a distant look on her face, making me wonder if she'd actually looked for a well at all, or if she'd just wandered aimlessly among the abandoned buildings, lost in a swirl of emotions. Tying the gray to a *viga* jutting from a collapsed roof, I walked over to where Jim Bowers lay in the dirt outside the largest building. He was still alive, still unconscious.

"What are you going to do with him?" Claire asked, coming over.

I shook my head, not sure what to do. "Any ideas?"

"Kill him."

I studied her quietly for a moment, wondering if she was serious, if Claire Adams was really as bloodthirsty as she was trying to sound. Finally I said: "No, I won't do that."

"Then we'll have to leave him."

"I won't do that, either."

"Then you've got a choice to make, Mister Slade, because I'm going after Trepan."

"Did you find any water?"

"What? No, I . . . no."

"Did you look?"

"You are avoiding the situation."

"It's a long way to the Colorado, Missus Adams. Let's look for some water to refill our canteens. Maybe we won't have to make a decision about Bowers."

"I won't wait." She walked over to where she'd left the pinto tied to a stubby bush and slid the pickax from its cradle across the McClellan saddle. As she stalked back toward Bowers, I moved deliberately into her path.

"Get out of my way, Slade."

"So you can kill a man who's already half dead?"

"So we can get out of here without you fretting over leaving a wounded man behind."

"I won't let you do it."

"You can't stop me," she grated through teeth clenched so tight it's a wonder she didn't bust off a couple of them. Her face could have been carved from ice, so lacking was it in any form of warmth or mercy—and suddenly, I'd had enough.

"All right," I said, stepping out of her way. "He's going to die anyway, so go ahead and finish him off. Let's see if that makes you feel better."

She shoved past me, so clumsy in her rage that she stumbled over the hem of her dress and nearly fell. I watched in rigid disbelief as she approached the outlaw, and clenched my fists when she raised the pick above her shoulder. The head passed its apex, then started forward, sweeping downward with a faint *whoosh,* and I remember thinking: *Aw, hell, she's going to do it.* But at the last minute she twisted at the waist, plunging the heavy spike into the hard earth with an explosion of dirt. My shoulders sagged and my breath escaped in a tightly drawn exhalation. I had to force my fingers open.

"Damn you," Claire said quietly, staring at the pick where it was buried several inches into the flinty soil next to the outlaw's shoulder, and to this day, I'm not sure who she was speaking to.

Turning away from the unmoving outlaw, she glared at me for several seconds, as if she hated me more than she did Trepan or Miller or any of the others. Then she walked over to a low rock wall and sat down heavily. The look on her face at that moment haunts me to this day—a combination of exhaustion and utter defeat.

"Claire," I said softly.

"Go away, Slade. Just . . . go away."

I walked over and sat down about a foot from her. I wanted to reach out and touch a shoulder or a knee, or lay my hand on top of the back of hers, but something told me that I'd approached as close as I dared for the moment, and that whatever support I hoped to offer would have to be conveyed from a distance.

"I seem to have failed once more," Claire said after a moment, her voice quivering.

"There wouldn't have been much success in driving the head of a pick through a dead man's chest."

"He's not dead yet."

I glanced at the body, the spastic rise and fall of Bowers's chest and the hoarse rattling deep inside. "About as good as," I said, then lifted my gaze to the lower canyon, what I could see of it from the small flat. "We need to find some water, Claire, if there's any to be found, then move on. We'd be in a hell of a fix if those Mohaves came back."

"They won't come back."

I looked at her. "What makes you so sure of that?"

"I just am." Then, after a pause, she added: "Ask yourself why they ran, when they had us so neatly cornered."

"I've been asking myself that question ever since they cut out of here like their britches were on fire. I haven't come up with an answer yet. Have you?"

"A probable one, yes. A war party that large is going to attract attention, which means the cavalry will be after them. I think there's a reason those three warriors spotted us when we came into the canyon. I think it was because they had been left behind to watch for pursuit. I think there were others back there, and that they saw something that made them feel they needed to evacuate the canyon."

"The army?"

"Perhaps, or some other large body of well-armed men."

"And you didn't say anything? Why, Claire? We could have brought this all to an end right here, instead of letting Trepan and his men ride out of here like they owned the world."

"Because I don't care about your payroll, Mister Slade. I have only one goal left in life, and that is to avenge Charlie's death. I shan't allow either you or the United States cavalry to deter me from that."

For a long moment, I could only stare. I'd thought I was getting to know Claire Adams, to understand her anguish, her need for revenge, but this seemed to go way beyond that, and it made me wonder how bad it had been out there, all alone except for her precious Charlie Red—a goddamned chicken.

So now you know, the truth laid out as bare as a frog's ass. Maybe you thought Charlie Red was going to be some kind of noble guardian, a benevolent champion of womanhood. Or maybe, like me, you suspected he might be a secret lover, maybe some land-loping miner or shepherd who'd come down out of the hills from time to time, as needful as he was giving. But in the end, he was just a rooster. So you can decide now, like I'd promised when I began this tale, whether I'm a liar, demented, or just a damned fool for believing in a woman who may or may not have been all the way there. If you feel like you've been made a fool of, expecting something more imperial, well, join the club, brother.

"I knew you wouldn't understand."

"I guess you're right. I don't. He was a chicken, Claire. A bird."

"He was a rooster, a red leghorn. And he was my friend."

"A bird?"

"Is that so hard to understand? Surely, when you were a boy, you had a dog or a horse or a cat for a companion. Someone who would listen to you when no one else would, someone you could tell your dreams and fears to, and not be afraid that they'd laugh or make fun of you."

"I had a dog," I admitted, which was kind of an omission on my part, since I'd actually had two of them at different times in my childhood—both of them damn good friends for a lonely kid like myself. But a chicken? I just couldn't get my brain wrapped around that image. "I guess . . . most of the chickens I've known in life were fried, sooner or later." I hesitated, afraid I might have overstepped again, but she didn't reply. After a while, I said: "Claire, we both ate chicken back at your place."

"I know. I've probably eaten a hundred of them in my life. But Charlie was different."

That didn't make a lick of sense to me, but I suddenly wanted to know. "How?" I asked.

"He was all I had left after Richard's death. Someone had stolen my horse, a rattlesnake killed my cow, and a wolf got the calf. My dog ran off with some stray bitch, and coyotes killed both of my cats. The chickens survived only because I had a solid coop to keep them in and the foxes out, but the hens never paid me any notice. They were too intent upon their laying, chattering amongst themselves like backyard gossips. Only Charlie seemed to know I existed.

"Oh, we had our difficulties at first. He was a male, and like all males, he thought he was the cock of the walk. He tried to put me in my place more than once, and came near doing it a time or two, until I took after him with a broom. I tried to kill him, and very nearly succeeded. Fortunately I failed, and we worked out a kind of truce after that. In time it became almost a partnership. I never dominated him . . . he was too proud for that . . . but he knew he couldn't dominate me, either. Eventually I gave him free access to the place. I was concerned that coyotes might kill him, of course, but I felt he deserved more than to be cooped up with a bunch of nattering hens all day. One evening, a coyote very nearly did get him. I was at the orchard when I saw it come streaking out of the rocks. I yelled for Charlie to look out, but he'd already spotted the dirty canine, and swung into battle."

Claire's face seemed to light up as she recalled the incident.

"He was magnificent, Mister Slade. Feathers flew, but so did fur, and the dust was so thick I could barely make out what was happening. I was running to help as fast as I could, but Charlie had the situation under control long before I arrived. The coyote took off even faster than it had advanced, with Charlie running after it in that long-legged stride of his, like: 'Who are you to invade my castle?'

"He was somewhat the worse for the skirmish, I'll admit, missing a few feathers and the rest ruffled or broken, yet rather gloriously intact, considering his adversary. And do you know what I found amid the feathers and fur, Mister Slade? Lying in the dirt like a discarded trophy. It was an eyeball, brown and bloodied, but unmistakable. Charles had taken it out with his spur, don't you see, and won the battle because of it." She laughed then, remembering something else, and said: "I didn't tell you how he attacked Trepan and that other man when they came to my place last month, because . . . well . . . because I didn't think you'd understand, but it was equally magnificent. They never dismounted, but that didn't matter to Charlie. He flew right up to meet them, spurs flashing like knives. Their horses were terrified and bucking, while the men flapped their hats and hollered like children. In the end, they were forced to retreat, leaving Charlie to strut back and forth in our yard like the true master of all that stood before him."

In spite of my frustration, I had to smile. I was remembering Bowers's remarks from earlier, about how Charlie Red had marked the other man, the one whose identity I still didn't know.

". . . *damn that Charlie Red*," Bowers had said, and as strange as it might sound, I found myself wishing I could have met him myself, at least to see what he looked like. [*Editor's Note:* Leghorns originated in the Livorno (*Leghorn,* in English) area of Italy, and were first shipped to United States in the mid 1800s; by the beginning of the 1900s they were the most popular egg-laying fowl in the states; colors range from white to black, with various solid and mottled shadings in between; male red leghorns are sturdy birds with broad chests, sturdy spurs, and short, stout beaks; cocks can weigh up to six pounds when fully grown; although not a fighting bird, they can be aggressive when threatened.]

"Are you angry with me, Tom?"

I thought about it for a moment. I had been earlier, but it hadn't lasted long. Especially not after her description of Charlie Red's scuffle with the outlaws. "No, I just hope your decision not to signal the cavalry doesn't get us killed."

"We don't know that it was the cavalry," she reminded me.

She was right. We didn't know what had made those Mohaves give up their attack, before seeing it through to what should have been its inevitable conclusion, but something had sure as hell spooked them off.

"Do we go after them?" Claire said.

"You asking, or telling?" I replied, echoing Jim Bowers response from earlier, when I'd questioned if he was still alive. I glanced toward the body, then shoved to my feet and walked over to where he was laid out. Claire joined me, staring down silently at the corpse.

"I'm glad I didn't kill him," she said softly, then turned her face toward mine. She was weeping gently. "But I'm going to kill the rest of them, Tom. I swear it."

"Then I guess we'd better get started," I said.

Excerpt from:
Minutes of Military Inquest
Reedcatcher Insurrection
28 May 1882–8 June 1882
Major Leandro Marcus, Presiding
14 July 1882, Fort Yuma, A.T.

"Thank you for your patience, Captain [James] Reynolds. I know you're anxious to return to your post."

"Not at all, Major."

"Very well. This won't take too long, but I'd like to add some clarification to the record in regard to your final encounter with the Reedcatcher party outside of Santiago Ranch Canyon, and especially as it pertains to the testimony given earlier today by Mister Slade."

"I'm afraid I may not be able to shed much light on that, as I was unaware of any white men in the vicinity of Santiago Ranch that day."

"But it was at Santiago Ranch that you engaged the Reedcatcher party, was it not?"

"Not exactly, sir. I'm told the actual ranch site is farther up the canyon from where we took up Reedcatcher's trail."

"Were you not on their trail the entire way, Captain?"

"Yes, sir, but always at some distance. It was only at the mouth of Santiago Ranch Canyon that we finally caught sight of our prey, and were able to conclude our pursuit."

"At the mouth of the canyon?"

"No, sir, several miles north of there. My scouts were spotted by the Reedcatcher party, and the Indians immediately fled. We maintained a vigorous pursuit along the eastern foothills of the Black Mountains to a location known as Wild Horse Seep, where we . . ."

"Seep, as in a watering hole?"

"Yes, sir, a small one."

"And you engaged the enemy there?"

"Yes, sir. Although Reedcatcher's men held the seep, we were able to surround them and prevent further flight."

"And the actual engagement, Captain?"

"We were stretched rather thin due to the poor cover available to us, and as nightfall approached, I began to fear we wouldn't be able to maintain control of the situation. Rather than risk the possibility of Reedcatcher's men escaping under cover of darkness, I decided on an offensive course of action. I deployed my men in a skirmish line around three sides of the seep, and at my command, we advanced as one on the Mohave position."

"And the Indians fought back?"

"Yes, sir, rather desperately."

"Yet you prevailed?"

"Yes, sir. I had good men under my command. They all performed splendidly. Ben Reedcatcher and several of his men were killed within the first fifteen minutes of the engagement. The others surrendered soon afterward."

"To what terms?"

"There were no terms, Major. The surrender was unconditional. One of my men and several of Reedcatcher's Mohaves received minor wounds during the confrontation. I had the injured men attended to and the dead buried immediately, because of the excessive heat. I ordered each grave marked with a piece of wood containing the deceased man's name, in case exhumation was ordered, and began my return to the Colorado River the following morning."

"On your return, did you encounter any sign of others in the area?"

"We spotted a party of surveyors on the Dutch Flats, but didn't question them."

"No evidence of road agents in the area?"

"No, sir, but it's a rather large area, with difficult terrain. Even with scouts, the presence of others could easily be overlooked."

"Very well. Thank you, Captain Reynolds. That will be all."

Session Ten

We pushed on through what remained of the day, and made a cold camp that night in the shelter of some mesquites growing at the mouth of a little side canyon. Our route had steepened sharply after leaving the rancho, winding higher and deeper into the rugged mountain range.

We rode single file because of the narrowness of the trail, and didn't speak again until we were in our blankets that night. Even then, we didn't have much to say. I think we were both aware of how vulnerable we were, and figured Trepan and his men had to know we were still following them. Our biggest advantage was that they probably didn't know about our Indian ponies, yet even so, we couldn't afford to relax our vigilance. John Trepan was no one's fool, and his men were as keen-eyed as hawks. They'd be watching, not only for us, but for those Mohaves.

We had the last of our leftover tortoise for breakfast the next morning—half-raw reptile ain't as tasty as you might expect—and saddled our ponies with subtle protests from our stomachs that didn't clear up for me until mid morning. I don't know how Claire fared after we got underway, but I could tell from the pinched expression on her face as we stepped into our rigs at dawn that she was suffering at least as much as I was.

After crossing a low divide shortly before noon, I pulled up and dismounted and loosened the gray's cinch. Claire did the same with her pinto. We could see the Colorado River way off in the distance, like a length of green ribbon dropped carelessly across a bolt of tan fabric, but we were more intent on trying to spot Trepan's gang somewhere below us, even if just a hint of dust, but the broken landscape revealed nothing. Only the tracks of the outlaws' horses in the flinty soil at our feet convinced us we were still on the right trail.

I'd left the tortoise shell back at the shallow cavern when I stripped my saddle from the sorrel's back, telling myself that it was too heavy and awkward to carry any farther, but I was soon wishing I hadn't tried to be so practical. We were down to half a canteen by the time I finished watering our horses from my leaking hat, and the Colorado a good way off yet.

There's no real need to relate our experiences for the rest of that day. It was basically just more of the same, although this time we did have a destination in sight, along with the promise of water, grass, and some pretty fair odds of finding something to eat along the river's banks. It was still hot, though, and we kept our horses to a walk all the way down out of the mountains, our eyes peeled for treachery. We were just coming out of the foothills when Claire pointed out a couple of columns of smoke way off to the northwest. I felt a budding excitement when I identified it as the billowing exhaust of a riverboat.

"The *Barbara Kay*?" Claire asked when I told her.

"If not the *Kay*, then another just as good. Headed down-river, too."

"Then we were right?" She sounded relieved, as if maybe she'd had her doubts, too.

"You were."

"We both were. If left to me, we'd be sitting our horses at Kingman's Siding today, wondering where Trepan and his men had vanished to."

Considering the angle of their trail, I didn't anticipate Trepan's gang reaching the river for several hours. Even then, they'd likely get there before the steamboat. I wasn't as sure about Claire and myself, but didn't want to push our horses too hard, in case Trepan veered off again before reaching the river, leaving us stranded on jaded mounts; the guy had me borderline paranoid by then, with all his switching back and forth, although you've got to admit his efforts had paid off. I doubt if there was a posse within a hundred miles of where we were at that moment.

Not long after spotting the riverboat, we left the mountains for a flat plain, and not long after that came to a corrugated trace carved through the sage and cactus, running at an angle from northeast to southwest. Trepan's trail turned onto a crude road, and so did Claire and I. It was nearly sundown when we spotted what I at first took for a small village, located within a stand of timber along the Colorado. When we got closer, I realized it wasn't really a town at all, but more like a trading post or a wood hawk's camp, even though I doubted the scattered groves of cottonwood and river elm that grew along that section of the river had ever been large enough to supply the half dozen or so steamboats that plied these waters over the years.

The twin stacks of the paddle wheeler were visible above the treetops, the thinning roils of smoke intimating that the craft was at idle, perhaps taking on wood. [*Editor's Note:* According to records from the Colorado River Steamship Company, located within the Arizona Historical Organization archives, wood to fuel the engines of the *Barbara Kay*—the corporation's only vessel—was hauled in from the piñon forests outside of Milkflake, Arizona, south of the lower bend of the Grand Canyon; Milkflake was abandoned in 1913, with only a few stone foundations remaining from the seventy or eighty residents who once lived there.]

Nudging Claire's pinto off the rutted trace, we rode into the trees about a mile above the trading post, where we dismounted to water our horses in the Colorado, then slake our own thirst. Although hungry, neither of us wanted to take time to hunt for food. We saw to our guns to make sure they were clean and functioning properly, then stepped into our saddles and reined south, following a narrow footpath along the Colorado's left bank.

You might think me negligent not to have insisted on Claire staying behind while I rode on into the settlement to apprehend the Trepan gang, but that would just show how little you know of the West, and of Western women in particular. As far as I was concerned, Claire had earned her right to be there, to exact whatever revenge she thought was deserved for the death of Charlie Red. Besides, who was going to try to stop her? She'd already loosened her pick and had it riding across the saddle in front of her, alongside the Parker.

We came to a small Indian village just north of the post, probably no more than a couple of dozen tiny, arrow weed–thatched wickiups strewn among the trees like wind-tossed tumbleweeds. A lot of them had racks of drying fish set up outside their low doors, and small reed rafts were pulled up on the shore behind them. Although there were several small fires burning in front of the lodges, I didn't see any Indians. I'd find out later that they'd spotted Claire and me coming in through the sage like we didn't want to be seen, and, with Trepan's gang already arrived, had decided to vacate their riverbank homes until whatever trouble we brought with us had moved on. Kind of like dodging a tornado, I suppose.

"Who are these people?" Claire asked, urging her paint horse alongside my gray.

I didn't have an answer for her, although I'd find out from the same individual who explained to me why they'd hightailed it into the brush that they were Cocopahs. The Cocopah Nation had a reservation down on the Gila River, but I suppose no one had told this bunch that that was where they were supposed to be. Rules were kind of lax in those days, and often overlooked if nobody was causing trouble.

Dusk lay heavy and damp across the bottomland when we finally came in sight of the trading post. Claire and I pulled up to study the little community in silence. The main building was made of adobe, with a warehouse and a sprawling corral out back, but there were also several smaller structures between the larger post and the river, including a blacksmith's shop and a small combination hotel, restaurant, and saloon. A sign hanging above the wide double doors of the trading post read: *Kwapa Post, Simon Williston, Mgr.* [*Editor's Note:* Kwapa is Yuman (*Yuman-Cochimí,* of the Colorado Delta region) for "The River People," which is how the Cocopah referred to themselves; Simon Williston ran the trading post from 1874 to 1886, when he sold the business to the Colorado River Steamship Company and returned to his native Scotland.]

Down close to the river was a low mountain of piñon wood, probably twenty feet wide, half again that high, and at least eighty yards long. At the far end, in the light of a freshly lit bonfire, a line of white, Negro, and Indian laborers were hauling cordwood aboard the *Barbara Kay,* stacking it close to the ship's boiler room.

Although there were hitching rails in front of several of the buildings, there weren't any horses in sight, and the corral behind the main trade room was made of the same adobe as the post, six feet high and impossible to see over from where we sat our mounts. I could feel Claire watching me, waiting for direction, but, not knowing where Trepan and his men might be holed up, or if they were even there, I wasn't sure what our next move should be.

I was still considering our options when an ear-crushing blast of released steam from the *Barbara Kay*'s engine room exploded across the levee. My Indian pony tucked its rump close to the ground and took off like a kicked dog, and I only barely managed to keep from being tossed from the saddle. I was still fighting the half-pitching gray when Claire's pinto bolted past me like a streak of rust, the McClellan's flapping stirrups urging the little horse on with every stride. Claire lay on the ground beside the narrow footpath with a stunned expression, and I swore in alarm and jumped to the ground. As I did, the gray jerked free and took off in the opposite direction of the pinto, its head high and to the side to avoid the reins snapping at its knees.

I reached for Claire, but she slapped my hand away and scrambled up on her own. Her cheeks were cherry red under her tan, her eyes flashing.

"Are you all right?" I asked.

"Yes, but that wicked little shit got away from me." Then her eyes widened and she touched her lips with the tips of her fingers. "Oh . . ."

I couldn't help grinning, even if it did cause my chapped lips to split a little wider. "Apologize later," I told her, ignoring the warm, salty taste of fresh blood on my tongue. Lord but we were a mess, and if things hadn't been quite so desperate, I might have laughed aloud at our situation. But there wasn't time for levity at the moment, and I nodded toward the ground at Claire's feet. "Grab the shotgun and your pick, if you're still set on using it, and let's get out of sight."

The gray was gone, taking the Marlin with it. Drawing the Smith and Wesson, I ducked into the foliage next to the path, Claire on my heels. I didn't say anything, but I regretted her pinto escaping toward the settlement. Around livestock, there's nothing like a loose animal to catch a person's attention. Even today, if someone yells that a horse is loose, I'll be out of my chair in a flash, and not even think about my creaking knees until we've got the animal corralled again. I was certain that pinto was going to draw someone's attention. I just hoped it wasn't Trepan or one of his men.

It was growing darker by the minute, which, along with the racket the wood hawks were making down by the *Barbara Kay*, was working to our advantage. Claire and I crept steadily closer to the trading post, dropping to our knees when we reached the edge of the clearing surrounding the settlement.

"Tom," Claire said after a bit.

"Yeah?" My reply was distracted, my gaze roaming.

"I want you to take this."

I looked around to where she was holding the Parker toward me. Pushing it back with my forearm, I said: "I've got my revolver. You keep that. You might need it."

"I don't want it. If you don't take it, I'm going to leave it here. I'll need both hands for my pick."

That made me mad, but I tried to keep my voice calm. "Damnit, Claire, keep the shotgun. When this is all over, and if we're still alive, you can go around and use that pick on whoever you want, but we've got to catch them first, and the odds are already against us."

"They won't give up without a fight, and I won't drive a pick into a dead man. I discovered that yesterday, with Bowers. Take the shotgun or leave it behind, Tom, the choice is yours." She placed the weapon on the ground at my side, then edged back as if washing her hands of the matter.

Although I swore softly at her stubbornness, I knew she wouldn't be swayed. Holstering the Smith, I pulled the shotgun close, and to tell you the truth, it felt kind of good to have it back in my grasp.

Hefting her pick in both hands, Claire said: "What do we do now?"

"We need to get closer. Stay behind me, and be ready to run

if someone starts shooting."

She nodded grimly, and we shoved out into the open like ships to sea. I was up front with the Parker's twin hammers rocked all the way back, Claire hard on my heels, her pickax at the ready. It was dark enough by then that we didn't have to sneak, but we kept our pace slow and our eyes darting, and when we paused outside the trade room's big open doors to peer inside, it was from a distance, well back in the shadows. The post appeared deserted, not even a clerk behind the counter, which seemed unusual. Leaning close, Claire whispered: "Where are they?"

"I don't know. Let's go around back and check the corrals."

We made our way cautiously to the rear of the building. There was a chest-high gate made of mesquite, and I eased the latch out of its socket so that we could slip inside. Claire was so close behind me at that point that I could feel her breath against the back of my neck.

Studying the corral's tall adobe walls from a distance, I'd assumed it was a single, large enclosure, so I was surprised when I found myself standing at the head of a labyrinth of smaller pens—some made from mesquite poles hauled in from the mountains, others of adobe, like the outer walls. Brush ramadas, individual stalls, and open-faced sheds added to the snarl—a maze without rhyme nor reason that I could detect.

The smell of livestock was strong inside the larger compound—horses and cattle for sure, plus goats, if my nostrils weren't deceiving me. At first I thought the voices I heard were coming from the woodyard, but as we started down the nearest alleyway, I realized they were closer. Somewhere near the center of the complex, perhaps.

"It's them," Claire breathed.

"Are you sure?"

"It's Miller," she replied gravely. "I'm very certain of that."

She was leaning into my shoulder, as if eager to press on.

"Take it easy," I said, pushing back. "Let's not walk into a trap after coming this far."

We edged deeper into the web of pens and passageways, our route dictated more by dead-end alcoves, tied-off gates, and the snorty attention of the livestock we passed than our preferred destination. If not for the light from the bonfire, I might have lost all sense of direction. As it was, I had not only a compass point to focus on, but the light of the blaze itself, reflected off the underside of the trees, to guide me. The voice grew steadily more distinct, until Claire and I came to a halt at the mouth of a lean-to, less than a dozen paces away.

"I'm tellin' ya, Brownie, it's one of them Mohave ponies. I recognize the saddle, too. It's her."

"It ain't her," another scoffed. "Them two's still hoofin' it over them stony mountains. They won't wander in here till sundown tomorrow, if they make it a'tall."

"Besides, those Mohaves took their horses with them," said a third, and my grip tightened on the Parker. I knew that voice. It belonged to Henry Brown, who'd ridden the coach out of Ehrenberg with John Trepan, Dan Garrett, and the Rhodes family.

"Not all of them, they didn't," the first voice insisted. "The way they turned tail, you know they left a few ponies behind somewhere."

"Well, you tell John what you're thinking when he gets back," Henry said, then chuckled. "I'd be real interested in hearing what he says."

"Where the hell'd he get to, anyway?" the second voice grumbled.

Claire slid her hand over my forearm, her fingers digging into the flesh. "That's Sam Miller," she breathed into my ear.

"The other's Henry Brown. I don't know the third man?"

"If Trepan's not with them, it has to be George Anders."

I nodded, then motioned toward the rear of the lean-to. "Let's slip in there a while and see what they're up to. Maybe Trepan'll show up while we're waiting."

We crept into the lean-to until we came to a gap in the slab-wood planks that offered a view of the area behind the shed. Brown, Miller, and Anders were sitting on crates hauled out of a brush-topped ramada. Their horses were crowded into a small corral to one side. Claire's little pinto was with them, the McClellan still cinched to its back.

This was my first close-up view of Miller and Anders, and I've got to say the figures weren't that impressive. Miller was the shortest of the bunch, a stocky man with ruddy cheeks and a mustache like a well-worn dust broom. Anders was taller and slimmer, with light-colored hair and a face scarred by smallpox. All three were toting revolvers, and keeping their long guns close.

They might have been sitting, but I noticed none of them looked overly relaxed. I believe a snapped twig might have sent all three surging straight up like bottle rockets. Claire eased alongside of me, sliding her free hand over the top of the plank. Her knuckles tightened when she spotted Miller, but that was all I noticed. The outlaws were still talking about Trepan, their voices low but urgent, Miller's and Anders's tinged with distrust.

"He runs off with that money, Brownie, and it's your hide I'm gonna pin to the wall," Anders said forcefully.

"Don't you worry about that money, Georgie. You'll get your share, and live free to spend it, too."

Miller chuckled low in his throat. "I think when I get mine, I'm gonna head on back to that orchard woman's place, have us a little fandango. I think she was growin' kinda sweet on me."

"You forget that woman. You done her enough harm."

"You mind your own reins, Brownie. I ain't about to forget about her." He laughed and made a crude remark, and Claire's knuckles paled on the slabwood board, like tiny tombstones lined up side by side. I put a hand on her shoulder to calm her, but it didn't do much good. Her entire body trembled with an eager rage.

"You see the look on her face when Trepan shot that red rooster of hers," Miller gloated. "I thought she was gonna . . ."

Claire gasped sharply, like she'd been punched in a kidney, and the three outlaws abruptly shut up.

Anders said: "What the hell was . . ."

Then Claire screamed her fury into the night, and lunged away from my side before I even knew what she was up to. I reached to stop her, but I was too slow. She burst out of the lean-to and spun around the corner so fast it's a wonder I could keep up at all. I'm convinced she would have charged all three of them with just her pick if I hadn't shoved her hard enough to send her stumbling into an empty stall across the alley. I heard a shout from one of the outlaws, then a gunshot bellowed from the ramada, roaring down the passageway like an enraged bull. I fired the Parker's right-hand barrel one-handed, and damn near tore my thumb off in the process.

Scooping the shotgun off the ground with my left hand, I started backpedaling fast. Gunfire lanced the alley, illuminating the lattice of corrals and pens in a series of quick, photoflash-like bursts. Bullets whistled past both cheeks, one of them slamming into a post just inches from my shoulder. I dove for the skimpy shelter of the lean-to, hitting the ground hard enough to jolt a grunt from my lungs. I could see running feet through the corral rails, and dropped to my belly just in time to empty the Parker's left-hand barrel at a pair of badly scuffed boots. The man in them yelled and staggered, then vanished from sight in an open stall.

Staying low and breathing hard, I crawled deeper into the shelter of the lean-to. Bullets splintered the thin slabwood, probing for a target. Acting instinctively, I broke open the shotgun with my left hand, using my right to fumble live rounds from my pockets, only to come up with a fistful of rifle cartridges for the Marlin instead. The 12-gauge shells I needed were with Claire, in a small leather pouch tied to her belt.

Jackknifing into a sitting position with my back to the wall, I tossed the Parker aside and palmed my Smith and Wesson. Then I just sat there and listened. Silence enveloped the corrals. There wasn't a peep anywhere, not even from the woodyard, although the writhing flames of the bonfire continued to cast its primitive glow over the scene. Despite feeling half sick with worry for Claire, I didn't dare risk giving away my position by calling to her. Or have Claire give away hers by answering.

The quiet seemed smothering and I itched to move, to jump up and take off and get it over with. But I'd learned over the years that impatience could get a man killed just as quick as a smart mouth or a cocky attitude, and held my position with my revolver ready, my ears straining for any telltale sound. It was several minutes before I was rewarded by the soft scrape of leather on wood, coming from the opposite side of the shed.

I curled my thumb over the Smith's hammer and waited. Claire was somewhere behind me, and I was hoping she'd stay put and not let her temper get the better of her again. Mostly, though, I was hoping she hadn't caught a bullet in the flurry of gunfire that followed her initial charge, and that the reason she was being so quiet was because, like me, she was waiting for one of Trepan's men to make the first move.

That night on the Colorado wasn't the first time I've gone up against armed men, and it was no different, either. My throat was tight and dry, my nerves humming. In looking back, I've sometimes wondered if I was really cut out for that line of work, but was maybe too proud to admit it. I will say I liked riding messenger. It was only those occasions when I was getting shot at that bothered me.

A pole creaked from behind the lean-to, and I started sweating. I didn't know whether it was one of Trepan's men crawling over a fence, or a horse or ox leaning into the rails. Moving slow, I pushed up on my knees, then rose to a crouch. As I did, the night seemed to explode behind me, the interior of the lean-to lighting up as if a bomb had been set off. I felt a gentle push from behind that was the percussion of a revolver fired from less than twenty feet away.

Trepan's crew were deadly shots. They had to be in their line of work, but whoever took that shot missed me clean. Not by much, mind you. I know because the next day I found a neat little bullet hole poked through the hem of my vest, the area around it smudged with powder burn. But close is as good as a mile in a situation like that, and I whirled real fast and snapped off two quick rounds that tore through the lean-to's planks into the body of the man standing on the other side. Later on I'd find Henry Brown lying dead behind a crate under the ramada where he and the others had been waiting for Trepan's return. I always kind of figured he was the one who'd taken that shot at me, although I never knew for sure.

The echo of the Smith's twin reports were still slamming through the maze of corrals when a commotion from the alley brought me around quick and low. I fired instinctively just as a bullet from George Anders's revolver sheared off a piece of planking at my side. I fired again, and Anders yelped and darted into an empty stall. I started after him, but he popped back out almost instantly and fired from less than thirty feet away, the heavy slug making an odd hissing noise as it streamed past my jaw. I fired twice more, and my second shot hit him square. Anders stumbled backward with a startled expression. Then one knee bent, and he dropped in a slow turn that left him lying face up with his arms outspread, his silver-plated revolver half buried in the dust at his side.

A brutish scream pierced the night, and my scalp started frantically crawling as I came on around and dropped to one knee, thrusting the Smith and Wesson before me. Sam Miller took a halting step forward and I pulled the trigger, but my hammer fell on an empty chamber, my gun shot dry.

I remember the sinking sensation I got, staring up at the outlaw and knowing in my heart that this was it, that I'd run my string. My gun was empty, and Miller hadn't fired a single round. He looked at me with his Colt leveled on the vee of my brows, and it was like staring into the dead eye of a Cyclops. I should have been dead by then, but as it turned out, Miller was. His Colt slipped from his fingers and he fell forward off his toes without having uttered a word, the handle of Claire's pickax jutting at an angle from his back.

I raised my eyes to hers, and neither of us spoke. Then John Trepan stepped out of the shadows and slid one arm around her neck, jabbing the muzzle of his revolver hard against her ribs. His lips peeled back in a mocking grin, and his eyes seemed to glow devilishly in the pulsating light. Laughing, he said: "Damnit, Slade, I ought to cut you in for a share. I figured I'd have to find a way to eliminate these boys myself, but damned if you haven't done it for me." He gave Claire's head a quick, upward pull, raising her to her toes. "You and the gal here."

Real easy, I allowed the hand holding my revolver to sag toward the ground, wondering if Trepan knew it was empty, and if there was any way I could turn that to my advantage. Not knowing why, I said: "Bowers thinks it was you who shot him in the back."

"Bowers is a smart boy."

I glanced at Claire. She was still on tiptoe, both hands hanging onto Trepan's arm around her neck. Her eyes were wide, her mouth open as if in a scream only she could hear.

"Drop the pistol, Slade."

I hesitated only a moment, then tossed it aside. "Are you going to kill us here, Trepan, with everyone watching?"

"Ain't no one watching, and no one would give a good goddamn even if they were. I can drill you both and walk out of here, and those boys down on the levee wouldn't say a word."

My mind raced as I tried to think of a way out of this, if not for me, then for Claire, but there was nothing left to say, no move that I could make that Trepan wouldn't be able to stop. He had us cold—and he couldn't afford to let us live. Having nothing left, I said: "I hope you rot in hell, Trepan."

He laughed. "Oh, I will, son, but I intend to live like a king before I get there." He cocked his revolver, and his voice dropped, as if in regret. "You should have gone back, Slade. You should have taken the woman with you, and let this one go."

"Hulce."

The voice came soft out of the night, and Trepan whirled, yanking Claire with him. He thumbed his revolver's hammer back and fired in as fluid a motion as I've ever seen, just as a brilliant flash of yellow blossomed from the passageway behind him. Claire grunted hard and sagged, and Trepan let her go. He fired into the alley again, then turned as if to run, but I was already racing to cut him off. The night exploded a second time, the roar of it like uncontrolled rage, and Trepan was flung toward me.

I braced to meet him, not noticing his finger tightening on the trigger until the revolver bucked in his hand, its blast hot against my face, pressing my shirt tight to my chest. Then his body slammed into mine and drove me back. Over his shoulder I saw Claire sprawled in the dirt of the alley, her bodice slick with blood, her expression slack. Then the back of my skull rammed into something hard and sharp, and my world turned black.

SESSION ELEVEN

That was kind of embarrassing. I didn't expect to choke up like that, and seldom do—except when I remember Claire, sprawled there limp as a rag doll in that odd light from the wood hawks' fire, her eyes open but unseeing—and all that blood. Jesus, all that blood.

Anyway, I'd rapped my head pretty good, and didn't wake up until dawn the following morning, when I found myself tucked into a cot in a small room with adobe walls and exposed ceiling beams, still fully dressed save for my boots. My head was throbbing so hard it hurt the backs of my eyes, and for a few minutes I had to squint just to have a look around.

There wasn't much in the way of furniture, just the bunk and a small table with a pitcher and bowl. A single sconce drilled into the wall held a hand-dipped candle, crooked as a broken finger and smelling strongly of animal fat. I was relieved to see my Parker leaning in the corner, the Smith and Wesson in its holster curled up on the floor beside it like a sleeping dog.

There was a small window above the cot, but no glass. Through it came the sounds of the levee, of wood hawks and deckhands and life starting afresh. Smells flowed in, too—the corrals and the river and the acrid stink of the *Barbara Kay*'s stacks, blowing black smoke into the gray sky. Gripped by a sense of urgency, I pushed my blankets away and cautiously swung my legs out of the bed. My boots sat on the floor beside me, my hat resting on top of them like a storm-battered roof,

213

likely placed there to keep the whiptails out. I pulled the boots on first, careful not to bend over too far or tug too hard. My hat was another matter, but by pushing it back on my forehead, I was able to avoid the lump at the stern of my skull where I'd popped it so hard the night before.

The world swayed a little when I stood up, then slowly steadied. I buckled the Smith around my waist and picked up the shotgun. Neither was loaded, but I remedied that quick enough.

Armed and as ready as I was likely to be for a while, I exited the room and made my way down a narrow hall until I came to a small lobby where a bald Mexican in a white shirt and plaid jacket sat on a stool behind the counter. He looked surprised by my presence, and immediately called into the other room, where the aroma of bacon and bread emanated like a sniff of heaven.

Giving me an apologetic look, the clerk said: "We did not think you would awaken so soon, *señor.*"

I didn't have an answer for that, and didn't try very hard to come up with one. A few seconds later, a tall man in a clean black suit appeared in the door that separated the hotel lobby from the restaurant, his gray ascot and gold stickpin standing out in the cool morning light.

You remember me talking about Harlan Price, don't you? The Coltrane messenger who had the *Barbara Kay*'s run from Yuma to the head of the Colorado's navigation. Ira and I had accepted the mine payrolls from Harlan in Ehrenberg, and although I hadn't considered the possibility of him being aboard the *Barbara Kay* so far north, I should have. There were some good-paying mines up around Eldorado Canyon and on into Nevada, and Coltrane contracted with several of them.

"Slade," the lanky messenger greeted me in his stony voice.

"Hello, Harlan," I replied, and, after a moment, added: "Was that you in the corrals last night?"

He nodded with more remorse than I would have expected from such a cold-eyed son of a bitch.

"I didn't know he had the woman," Harlan said, bringing back the image of Claire lying in the dirt, covered in blood. The pain in my head suddenly intensified, and the room took a little dip. I grabbed the hotel counter and briefly closed my eyes.

"I'm sorry, Slade. Was she . . . close?"

I nodded, even though I wasn't sure that was an honest answer. "Where is she?"

"They've got her at the trading post. Williston thought his woman could take better care of her there than anyone here could."

That stumped me for a minute. "What do you mean, better care?"

"Tend to her wounds."

"She's not . . . ?"

"Dead? Hell, Slade, I thought you knew. No, she ain't dead, but she's got a chest full of buckshot, and is hurting bad . . . hey!"

Harlan Price might as well have been whistling into the wind if he thought I was going to stop or go back to hear whatever else he had to say. I didn't run—I'd have fallen flat on my face if I tried, as wobbly as I was—but I sure didn't dally, either. I remembered the manager's name on the sign above the trading post's double doors from the night before—Simon Williston—and when I got over there I found out his woman was a Cocopah called Betsy, a heavyset gal of middling years and a gentle compassion in the way she spoke to me, and looked after her charge.

Claire was conscious, but so doped up on laudanum her focus kept wandering whenever I attempted a conversation.

"She hurts," Betsy explained, when Claire's voice drifted off and her glassy eyes slid closed. "The medicine makes her better, but makes her sleep, too. Sleep is good, makes her pain not so bad."

"How bad is her wound?"

"Not good, but she live, I think." She ran her fingers lightly over her own chest, clad in a light cotton blouse decorated with brightly colored ribbons. "Two times this, but less one," she added, flashing the fingers of her right hand before my eyes. I translated that into nine pellets, all but one of them dug out the night before, she assured me. "The other comes out in time, I think. Makes its own way."

I nodded understanding; like a splinter, the lead pellet would eventually work its way to the surface, where it could be plucked with tweezers. I asked her about the blood and she agreed that it had been a lot, but not too much.

"She live, I think. Not buckshot, that's good. Smaller pellets. You give her time, don't go bother her so much, she be all right." She made a shooing motion with her hands, indicating I was to leave.

I didn't argue, and walked back into the main trade room where Williston was talking to an Indian in white cotton trousers and shirt, reed sandals on his feet, and a straw hat on his head. A machete-like knife was sheathed at the Indian's waist, but he was otherwise unarmed. Williston stood behind the counter, leaning over it with his elbows propped on the scarred wood. They both looked up when I entered.

"She gonna live?" the trader asked.

"Seems like."

"Betsy's a good woman. Knows her medicines, too. Was I laid up, I'd rather have her looking after me than some book-trained sawbones."

"She seems in good hands," I agreed, walking over to the counter. The images of Claire—both from the night before and that morning, lying in her bed as pale as a ghost—were boring into my brain like steel bits, refusing me any relief. She was lucky Harlan hadn't been using buckshot. I've seen what double-ought can do, and it isn't pretty at close range.

"No offense, friend, but you look like hell warmed over," Williston said.

"I could use a drink."

"I don't serve it here. I'd lose my license to trade with the tribes if word got out I had whiskey on the premises, but they could likely fix you up at the hotel bar."

I was quiet a moment, thinking. Then I pushed away from the counter. "Let me know what the charges are for the woman."

Williston nodded. "Will do, but let's see how she does first."

I walked out into the growing light. I could hear the *Barbara Kay*'s engine building up to steam as her crew added more wood to the fireboxes. The massive paddle at the rear of the craft was already beginning its slow rotation, slapping rhythmically at the muddy water to counter the current. She would be pulling out soon, heading downriver with full racks of wood and plenty of power. Before she did, I wanted to talk to her skipper.

Jared Sanders was standing at the head of the gangplank when I got down to the river. He was consulting with his first mate and a brawny black man I took to be associated with the woodyard, since I'd never seen him aboard the ship before. I stopped at the foot of the plank and hailed the captain. Sanders gave me a dismissive glance, spoke again to the dark stranger, then motioned the first mate to follow the African back to shore.

"Get it settled, Gabe," Sanders called after his second-in-command. "We'll be throwing the lines as soon as we've got a full head." [*Editor's Note:* Captain Jared Sanders was skipper of the *Barbara Kay* during her entire run on the Colorado River, from 1877 until 1902, when the craft struck a sawyer above Fort Mohave and sank; a "full head" probably refers to a full head of steam for the ship's engine, while "throwing the lines" means casting off the heavy docking ropes and hauling them onboard.]

When the two men were gone, Sanders motioned me up the gangplank.

"Slade, isn't it?"

"Tom Slade. I'm the Coltrane messenger between . . ."

"Yes, Ehrenberg and Prescott." His gaze narrowed. "I hear you had quite a night of it."

"Six men held up the C and P stagecoach at Desert Wells. I tracked them here."

"Killed them, too."

"I killed three of them. They were trying to kill me." I was beginning to grow impatient with the captain's intrusive questions, not to mention the faint hint of disdain I heard in his voice. "My guess is that they intended to book passage on the *Barbara Kay*. Do you know if they did?"

"They didn't."

"How about just one of them, a man named John Trepan, although he might have used an alias." I gave him a brief description of the man, but Sanders was already shaking his head.

"No one booked passage on the *Barbara Kay* last night or this morning, and the only men allowed onboard were the laborers Stillwell hired to bring on wood." He nodded briefly toward shore, and I assumed he was talking about the Negro I'd seen his first mate leave with. "As soon as Gabe settles his bill, we'll be shoving off . . . without any extra passengers."

I hesitated only a moment. "Are you sure? Maybe your first mate . . ."

"My first mate knows better than to bring a man onboard without my permission, Slade, as does the rest of my crew. They'd find themselves set ashore as soon as the breach of protocol was discovered, and I wouldn't waste time steering toward dry land to displace them, either. If they couldn't swim, they could damned well drown, and they know I mean it, too."

I was growing angrier by the minute, but I had too many other possibilities to check out before I could accuse one of Sanders's men of colluding with outlaws.

"If you don't have any more questions, Slade, I need to ready the vessel for sailing."

"No, I don't suppose I do," I replied.

Sanders continued to stare, until I finally turned and made my way back to shore along the springy gangplank. I never had liked Jared Sanders, but I'd always been able to tolerate him in the past. Something had changed since Ehrenberg, though, and I found myself visualizing going back up the gangplank and kicking the arrogant bastard's ass off his own ship.

I went back to the hotel instead and talked to the desk clerk. I asked him about Trepan and his men, and when the clerk insisted he hadn't seen any of them until they'd been laid out before burial that morning, I was inclined to believe him. I checked the restaurant as well, and received the same denial.

"Try the corrals," the waiter grumbled. "Maybe someone over there saw 'em."

The corrals were going to be my next stop anyway, but I had no better luck there than I'd had with the hotel clerk or waiter. I was heading back to the trading post to talk with Simon Williston again when I noticed Gabe, the *Barbara Kay*'s first mate, and the black wood hawk called Stillwell, sitting at a table under a brush ramada, sharing a bottle of what looked like whiskey. I walked over, and Gabe greeted me by name.

"We were just talking about you," he said. "You made a hell of an impression on folks last night."

"I did what I had to do, but I'm not finished yet." I glanced at the black man, tall and broad through the shoulders, his already perspiring forehead glistening like polished coal. "Your name Stillwell?"

"Who's asking?" he replied in a slow drawl.

I told him who I was and who I worked for, and why I'd followed the Trepan gang all the way from Desert Wells to Kwapa Post. He listened without interruption, his lids heavy, his posture relaxed. When I finished, he said: "Yeah, I saw them."

"Did you see where they went after they got here?"

"I didn't pay any attention to where they went, or much give a damn. I'd have put them to work if they were looking for it. That damned Sanders wants his wood loaded about twice as fast as any normal crew can do it, and him not going anywhere until the next day, anyway."

Gabe chuckled and pushed back from the table. "I can't hear this, Stillwell. The captain would skin me down the middle for listening to that kind of talk and not putting a stop to it."

"He'd call it treason," Stillwell replied with a smile.

"He'd likely call it mutiny, and dock me a month's pay." The first mate tipped his hat to the wood hawk, nodded good-bye to me, and walked away.

Pushing the bottle closer, Stillwell said: "You want a drink, Slade?"

I shook my head. I was recalling something Claire had said back in the desert, when she accused Sam Miller of taking her rifle and ax and shovel. I hadn't thought about it at the time, but what if they'd buried the mine payrolls somewhere behind us? Somewhere way out in that blazing wasteland where the sun had already returned the recently overturned soil back to its original color. I felt oddly depleted with the thought, knowing that if they had, the odds of me or anyone else ever finding it were next to nil.

"You look like you just took a bite of rotten meat, Slade."

I shook my head and pushed to my feet. I suddenly felt exhausted, as if I'd been dragged through hell and back behind a lame ox. "You didn't see them talking to anyone?" I persisted.

"Nope, not a soul." He scowled. "Wait a minute. Yeah, maybe I did."

My pulse quickened as I stepped back to the table. "Do you know who it was?"

"Hell, I'm not even sure it was the man you shot. But I thought it was, when I saw him. It was dark, so I don't really know why I thought it was him." He shrugged. "Maybe it wasn't, but I know most of the men around here, and I thought it was a stranger. That's all I can say."

"What about the man he was talking to?"

"I didn't get a good look at him, either. Like I said, it was dark, and Sanders was riding my ass to get my wood on board."

"This was down by the river?"

"Yeah, near the *Barbara Kay*'s stern."

"Was there a second gangplank down?"

"Not that I noticed."

"This second man, was he short, tall, fat, skinny?"

Stillwell laughed. "He was just a man, Slade, a shadow under the trees. That's all I can tell you."

"All right," I said reluctantly. "Thanks, Stillwell."

"Hey, Slade, you ever need a job, come look me up. I could use a good man." Then he laughed again, and spread his arms wide to indicate the open-sided ramada. "My office is always open."

I forced a smile and told him I would, then headed for the trading post. I'd hoped to talk to Harlan Price again before the *Barbara Kay* pulled out, but I could already hear the ship's big paddle picking up speed, her engine thumping. They'd be casting off any minute now, with Harlan on board and Sanders too damned bullheaded to allow anyone on his ship that didn't belong.

On my way toward the adobe post, my thoughts kept returning to the *Barbara Kay*, and the men Stillwell had seen near the ship's stern the night before. He'd seemed fairly certain one of them had been Trepan, but who could the other one have been? And why meet so close to the riverboat, unless the vessel somehow played a part in the men's escape?

Or if not the men, then at least the money.

My pace slowed as I replayed Trepan's final moments from the night before, remembering the look of surprise on his face when he'd turned to confront the man in the shadows.

". . . *his real name's Hulce*," Bowers had said of Trepan, back at the little rancho right before he slipped away, and the muscles across my shoulders drew taut, my stride lengthening as I veered toward the *Barbara Kay*. I was still carrying the Parker, and brought it up across my chest as I broke into a run. I could see several deckhands struggling with the gangplank and shouted for them to hold up, but although one of them glanced my way, they didn't stop. I didn't figure they would. Sanders ran a tight ship, and his men would take their orders from him or one of the vessel's officers, not some Coltrane messenger with bleeding lips and a blistered nose.

I ran faster as the *Barbara Kay*'s whistle cleaved the muggy riverfront air. The ship's second mate was Jim Jacobs. He met me at the foot of the gangplank as I approached, throwing a hand up to halt my advance.

"We're getting ready to shove off, Slade," he said, trying to be amicable. "I'm afraid you'll have to catch the next boat downriver."

"I'm not looking for accommodations, Jim, but I need to see a man before you get started."

The ship's officer stood firm, his tone strengthening. "I'm afraid not. The ship's closed to land traffic. Captain's orders."

Jacobs had a couple of crewmen behind him, awaiting orders to haul the heavy plank onto the lower deck. He still had his hand out as I drew close, and started to lean forward as if to place it against my chest. It was a foolish move on his part, and I took full advantage of it. Grabbing his wrist, I yanked him forward, bringing my own body partway around to slam my shoulder into his side. Jacobs gave a startled squawk as he was thrown from the gangplank into the river, but I didn't wait to see if he could swim. The two deckhands had started forward as soon as I grabbed the second mate's arm, but backed off quick enough when I swung the Parker's muzzle up in greeting.

"Back off, boys," I snapped, and they scurried to comply. I went on past, hurrying up the ladder to the hurricane deck while Jacobs's sputtering cries sounded the alert behind me.

I reached the top deck as the door to the forward cabin was jerked open. Harlan Price stepped out, his perpetual scowl deepening when he saw me.

"You knew his name," I said, my pace slowing warily.

"What are you talking about?"

"Last night, in the corrals. You called him Hulce."

"I called who Hulce?"

I stopped about thirty yards away. "John Trepan. You called him Hulce."

"Don't be preposterous, Slade. I didn't call anyone anything."

My grip grew firm on the Parker's wrist, and my pulse quickened. I hadn't been a hundred percent certain until that moment, but Harlan's denial clenched it for me. "You knew his name, Price. His real name. There's only one way you could have."

I thought for a moment he might try to continue his charade, but then his expression turned to stone, and the muscles across the back of my neck snapped tight. The Parker's right-hand hammer was drawn to full cock and I had my finger on the trigger, but the muzzle was still pointed toward the deck. Price's shotgun was uncocked, but he was holding it in both hands, ready to swing instantly into motion.

"I didn't remember that until a few minutes ago," I went on. "Then it just all came together."

"Why don't you get off while you have the chance, Slade? Save the crew from having to clean up the mess."

"It didn't make sense that they'd bury the payroll in the desert. Claire and I were pushing them too hard." A frown creased my brow—so many questions unanswered, but time was already running out. If Price didn't react first, Sanders would show up at any minute with a bunch of crew members to forcibly remove me from his ship. Finally I asked: "You were going to take the money and meet Trepan . . . Hulce . . . later, weren't you? After he took care of the rest of his gang. Or I guess it was your gang all along, wasn't it? You were the one who knew when we'd be shipping several big payrolls at once. You had to be the one who recruited Trepan, who set up their elaborate escape. Were you behind the Mohaves jumping the reservation, too?"

"Shut up, Slade." Price's voice was low but hard, his eyes narrowed to slits. He wanted to bring that shotgun up so bad, but knew I had the advantage, however slight, by having one of my barrels already cocked. Then a muscle in his cheek twitched, and I threw myself against the side of the cabin nearest me, even as I brought the Parker's muzzles up level with the deck.

If I was faster than Harlan, it wasn't by much. I sucked my breath in sharply as shot from his scattergun pierced my arm and tore the Parker from my grasp.

"Son of a bitch," I grated, watching my shotgun slide under the railing to the deck below, but there was no one to hear my cry. Price had already fled.

Although my right arm burned like hell's own fire from shoulder to elbow, I still managed to drag the Smith and Wesson from its holster. With the revolver gripped firmly in front of me with both hands, I hurried down the deck, then around the front of the pilothouse. My gaze shifted briefly to the helmsman, standing wide-eyed but silent at the wheel. Then I eased along the front of the glass-enclosed wheelhouse and around the far corner.

Price was lurching swiftly down the hurricane deck's passageway toward the stern, but he was also keeping an eye on whomever might be following. As soon as I stepped into the clear, he turned and fired. I instinctively ducked back in front of the pilothouse, although I don't think the gunman's shot came anywhere near where I stood.

After that one wild shot, Price continued toward the *Barbara Kay's* stern. His right leg dragged awkwardly along the deck, leaving behind a trail of blood my eyes could follow from the bow. Coltrane insisted its messengers use double-ought buck in their shotguns, which is why my round had done so much damage. But for some reason, Price wasn't using heavy buckshot. If he had, Claire would have been dead and likely already buried, and I'd be lying on the shore side of the vessel with my arm shredded and useless.

Bless the Heavens for small miracles, is what my grandpappy would have said. Well, probably he'd tell me to let the son of a bitch run, but I wasn't going to do that.

"Price!" I shouted above the rumble of the steamboat's idling engine.

I don't think he heard me, being so near the ship's stern and the slowly rotating paddle that was keeping the vessel even with the river's current. But he still stopped and turned. He started to bring his shotgun up, then must have remembered that he'd already fired both barrels. Tossing the gun to the deck, he drew his Colt.

A revolver is a moderately accurate firearm, even at distances that can challenge an average shooter's ability with a rifle, but you have to know what you're doing. More importantly, you have to remain calm. I suspect that under less stressful circumstances, Harlan Price was a fine shot, but his skills were deteriorating rapidly under the pressure of pursuit, not to mention the buckshot deep in his leg and loss of blood. It's a wonder the man was still standing.

Price fired twice, and if the ship's cabins hadn't been there, I bet his second shot wouldn't have missed me by more than a few inches, rather than plowing into a door frame halfway down the length of the deck.

I held no illusions regarding my own skills as a pistoleer. Instead of trying to hit a swaying target at close to seventy yards with a one-handed shot, I leaned into the side of the pilothouse and took careful aim with the Smith still clutched in both hands—this all before Price got his second shot off. In fact, splinters were still flying from the cabin's wall when I squeezed off my first round.

Way down at the far end of the riverboat, Price yelled in pain and surprise, stumbling backward from the bullet's impact. I could hardly credit my shot, but what happened next stunned me even more. Price must have lost his balance. Or maybe it was his leg finally giving out. Whatever the cause, he tipped slowly backward over the stern's railing, seemed to hang there a moment, then spun almost lazily into the *Barbara Kay*'s turning wheel.

I uttered a startled curse, then started down the passageway at a cautious run. I don't know why I was so hesitant. Maybe I was expecting him to pop back up again and start shooting. If that was the case, then I sure would have handled it poorly, because he did reappear. Only Price didn't come up shooting. He came back plastered tight against one of the sternwheeler's slowly revolving blades. Even from halfway down the deck, I could see his blank expression, the limp way his arms flopped as the big paddle dropped from sight. I'd reached the far end of the ship by the time he came up again, his black broadcloth coat tangled in one of the wheel's iron spokes, hooked on a bolt the size of a man's wrist. I spoke his name as he passed, but Harlan Price was beyond answering. When the big wheel made its third revolution, he was no longer there.

I could hear Sanders at the bow, bellowing orders for his pilot to disengage the big drivers, and for the deckhands to re-attach the massive hawsers used to secure the *Barbara Kay* to shore. Turning away from the stern railing, I put my back against a cabin wall and just kind of slid down until I was sitting on the deck with my head tipped back, my legs splayed before me. The world seemed to be spinning in time to the *Barbara Kay*'s massive paddle, although more horizontal than vertical. Then the pain in my arm surged and I closed my eyes, paying no mind at all to Jared Sanders when he came striding up like some feudal overlord, demanding to know what the hell I thought I was doing aboard his ship without permission, shooting up the hurricane deck and gunning down a paying passenger. He asked why he shouldn't hang me on the spot for murder and destruction of personal property, and a lot of other crap I didn't have an answer for. After a while his words quit making sense, and his voice became distant and unimportant, making it easier to slide on into unconsciousness.

SESSION TWELVE

You want to know what happened afterward, huh? That's not going to be easy, because a *lot* of stuff happened afterward, just about all of it connected in one way or another, and a lot of it overlapping, too, until it gets so tangled it's hard to know where to even start. But I'll try.

After securing the *Barbara Kay*, Sanders sent a number of his crew to the lower deck to look for Price's body, while men and boys and dogs took up the search along the Colorado's muddy shores; they even got some Cocopahs out there with their reed rafts to float the river, but Price had vanished.

Although I came to after a few minutes and crawled back to my feet, I didn't take part in the hunt for Harlan's corpse. I had other things on my mind, and as soon as I was able, made my way back to the cabin that Coltrane Brothers Limited kept booked for its messengers. I found the stolen mine payrolls locked inside a common Coltrane strongbox, tucked under Price's bunk, and doubt if there's a soul anywhere in all of Arizona who would have suspected anything amiss if I'd stayed back at Desert Wells like I was supposed to.

It was an elaborate plan, but it was also a good one. With all of the C&P stock run off from the Desert Wells and Tyson's Well stations, and only Pete Driscoll's worn-out team on hand, Price and Trepan—I still call him Trepan, since no one was ever able to determine if Hulce was his real moniker, or just another alias—must have expected me to wait for the next stage from

Prescott to take me back to Ehrenberg and report the theft. My commandeering Pete's off-side leader, that jenny I rode as far as the Colorado, had been the fly in the ointment that ultimately wrecked their plans. A posse wouldn't have gotten into the field for at least another couple of days, and I'm guessing their pursuit would have ended at the Colorado, assuming—as I very nearly had—that the bandits had escaped by boat.

Even if the law did figure it out, they would have been too far behind to stop the transfer of the money from Trepan to Price, and probably never would have suspected Price of being an accomplice. I don't think it's bragging to make the claim that if I hadn't stuck to the outlaws' trail like a burr in their britches, Price would have carried that money out of Arizona slick as snake oil, and no one the wiser.

A man named Lawrence Kelly was who finally curried it all out. He was Coltrane's district manager at Yuma, in charge of the company's lines from San Diego to El Paso along the Southern Pacific railroad, and including its numerous arteries, of which the Colorado River was one of the biggest. Kelly was already in Ehrenberg when I got there aboard the *Barbara Kay,* and in the weeks following the robbery, he was all up and down that route, ferreting out and sorting through.

They say he talked to people all the way from the Pacific coast to the muddy levee at Kwapa Post before he was satisfied that all the participants in the robbery had been accounted for.

In Kelly's official report to Marty Coltrane, which I got to see a copy of, he'd come to the conclusion that from the little trading post on the Colorado, Price was to smuggle the money downstream to Yuma, then west to San Diego aboard the Southern Pacific. Trepan, meanwhile, would cross the California desert along the Old Spanish Trail, then travel south to San Diego, where he and Price would split the money before going their separate ways—although there was quite a bit of conjecture at the time that John Trepan never would have lived long enough to see his share of the loot.

Kelly agreed with my speculation that Trepan intended to do away with the rest of the gang at some point after the money was turned over to Price, probably on their way across California, although he also said he didn't think Price had any ill intentions toward Trepan.

"Price and Trepan served in the same outfit during the war," Kelly told me several weeks later, when I talked to him in Yuma. "They were a pretty cold-blooded pair, but loyal to one another."

I will say that of everyone I talked to about the Desert Wells robbery, Kelly was the only one who didn't believe Price would double-cross Trepan in San Diego. Even Marty Coltrane believed Price had turned bad to the core. Me? I guess I won't ever be able to shake the image of Price cutting Trepan down there in the corrals at Kwapa Post, but I don't know if it was a planned betrayal, or if it was as Kelly thought, a necessary murder to protect his own culpability?

Cold-blooded? I hope to tell you.

Harlan Price's body eventually did turn up. According to a report filed by the commanding officer at Fort Mohave, the corpse was found five days later by a couple of Mohave boys spearfishing in the Colorado, half a mile below where he'd gone into the river. Although the autopsy revealed wounds caused by both buckshot and a bullet from a .45-caliber Schofield, the official cause of death was listed as "blunt trauma to the body, resulting in the fracturing of over ninety percent of the victim's skeleton."

It wasn't me who killed Harlan Price, it was the *Barbara Kay*.

Claire lived, although it was touch and go for a while. In hindsight, I probably shouldn't have been in such a rush to take her away from the trading post, and the good care of that Coco-pah woman called Betsy. I just figured that with the *Barbara*

Kay already tied up and ready to push off, the smart thing to do was get her downstream to a real doctor.

Sanders about had a conniption when I ordered him to keep the *Barbara Kay* moored at Kwapa Post until we could get the woman settled in one of the empty cabins. He was still upset about my boarding his ship without permission, and against his second mate's orders, not to mention the damage Price and I did to his vessel with our guns. But he also knew how important his company's contract was with Coltrane, not to mention how others along the river might perceive his abandoning an injured woman on the banks of the Colorado with only an Indian to look after her. Besides, it only cost him a couple of hours, time he more than made up for by pumping the steam to the *Barbara Kay*'s big twin-cylinder engine all the way south.

We didn't take Claire off at Ehrenberg, since the town didn't have a doctor. Sanders took her on into Yuma, where she was placed under the care of a physician named Owen Foster. I didn't go with her, although I wanted to. Betsy had treated my wounds back at Kwapa Post, and they were healing nicely by the time we reached Ehrenberg. With Lawrence Kelly already sniffing around town like a bloodhound, Ira decided I'd better stay. He pulled me and the payroll money off at Ehrenberg, then sent the money on to Prescott under special courier, that being Antonio Robles handling the lines on the company wagon and five heavily armed guards. The payroll arrived safely two days later.

It was in Ehrenberg that I found out I'd been fired from Coltrane Brothers Limited. I guess after my disappearing for over a week following the robbery, Marty Coltrane decided I had to be involved. Even after he learned the truth, he didn't want to rehire me. In a telegram to Ira, Marty tried to lay the blame for the theft on what he called my "lax vigilance" for losing the money in the first place, but Ira wouldn't have it. He fired a missive right back to Coltrane's office in San Francisco, declaring me "one of the best messengers riding the lines," and reminding the man that the money might never have been recovered without my "due diligence."

It was some pretty fancy writing for a man of Ira's impatient temperament, but even when the job was offered, I almost didn't go back. If Ira hadn't put his own neck on the block with Marty Coltrane, I'd have likely told the whole outfit how deep to shove it. But my beef wasn't with Ira, and after he bought me a couple of drinks down at Molly Herriman's Saloon, I went back to messengering that Ehrenberg-to-Prescott run.

I worked for the Coltrane boys another seven years, until the Colorado and Prescott Stagecoach Company went under due to competition from the railroad and other staging companies. Coltrane transferred several of its agents and messengers to other, more remote locations, but Marty made it a point to let Ira and me go—still harboring ill feelings for the Desert Wells fiasco, is what I heard. A few years after C&P went under, Wells Fargo bought out Coltrane for a reported $600,000, a figure few men or women could get their heads around in those days.

You might be interested to know that I was called to a military inquiry at Fort Yuma some weeks after my return to Ehrenberg to testify about what I knew of the Mohave uprising, which we got a taste of at that little rancho east of Kwapa Post. Mostly, the army wanted to know about the arrows collected at Tyson's Well, and what our opinion was about them. Pete and I both testified, and pretty much corroborated one another's views that the Tyson's Well raid had been staged by white men, not Indians. In the end, the military decided the Mohaves had never ventured below the Bill Williams River, and deemed the insurrection a personal infraction between Reedcatcher's bunch and Trepan's crew, rather than a full-scale outbreak.

I got down to Yuma to see Claire a couple of times during

her recovery at the Fosters, and was giving some serious consideration toward courtship when her health improved. Then on my last visit to Foster's office, the doctor informed me that Claire had bought a ticket out of the territory aboard the Southern Pacific, and had expressly asked that he not divulge her destination to anyone—including me. Although Foster claimed to believe Claire was running more from the Mormons than she was from me, I had a hard time swallowing that. Not after our conversation that night in the desert, when she told me how her husband's other wives—his sister wives—really felt toward her. But hell, maybe he was right. Maybe I was just too close to it all for an honest perspective.

Well, I figured that was that, and it made me mad, to tell you the truth, but even though I swore I didn't care, I guess somewhere deep down I really did. About two months after being told that she'd left Arizona for parts unknown, I was back in Yuma on business and decided to talk to Dr. Foster one more time. It was a Sunday, and I had to go to the doc's house to find him. He recognized me as soon as he opened the door, but I asked anyway.

"Yeah, I remember you," he said warily.

"Then you know why I'm here?"

"Claire?"

I nodded. "I know she said she never wanted to see me again, but I'm not ready to give up just yet. Not until I hear it from her personally. If I went down to the station and bought a train ticket, could you at least give me a hint of what city I'd want to go to."

He got a funny look on his face. "I wouldn't buy a ticket anywhere," he said. "Claire told me that if anyone asked, I was to tell them she didn't want to be found. Then she said something I found puzzling. She said that if you came back a second time, I was to tell you where to find her."

I reared back and blinked. "Where?"

"Right here in Yuma. She's a cook at the Crowing Cock Café. I eat there maybe once or twice a week, and as far as I'm concerned, they've got the best fried chicken in the territory."

I stood there a moment, taking it all in. Then I laughed real loud and shook my head. "That beats all, doesn't it?" I asked, grinning like an electric billboard.

"Mister Slade, I don't mean to insult you or Claire, but she's been here a couple of times now to ask if you've come around, and she seems, well, kind of quirky, if you ask me."

I laughed at that, too. Quirky? Hell, yes. That's why I married her.

End Transcript

Excerpt from:
Pioneer Passings for: 1948
Number 16—Thomas R. Slade

Thomas R. Slade, of Phoenix, passed away peacefully in his sleep this year. Born on September 19, 1856, he died on December 8, 1948. He was ninety-two.

Thomas was the son of Randolph and Mildred (Mead) Slade, of Tucson, the oldest of three siblings, and a lifelong Arizona resident. His education was rudimentary, but common for the era. He attended six years of public education in Tucson, where he graduated in 1868. His earliest known employment was with the Huntington Wagon Works, of Tucson. In 1875, he went to work for Pantano Staging and Freight, first as a hostler, then as a messenger, riding shotgun from Tucson to Nogales.

In 1878, Slade took employment with the Colorado and Prescott Stagecoach Company, where he remained until 1889. [*Editor's Note:* As noted within the Slade transcripts, Thomas Slade was actually employed by Coltrane Brothers Limited, of San Francisco; as a Coltrane employee, he was a messenger for the C&P.] After the demise of the Colorado and Prescott Stagecoach Company in 1889, Slade went to work for the Bullock Brewing Company of Phoenix, where he was promoted to plant manager in 1892.

Thomas married Claire Adams in 1883. They had six children, Randolph, Peter, Sally, Harold, Edith, and James. Thomas retired from Bullock Brewing in September of 1921, and with his wife and five of their six children, returned to his hometown of Tucson.

Following Claire Slade's death in 1926, Thomas returned to Phoenix, where he took employment with Bullock Brewing Company again in October of that year as a night watchman. He quit a second time in March of 1927. In June of 1927, he went to work for the Starr West Meat Packing Plant as a janitor, and retired for the last time in June of 1932.

Thomas Slade is buried next to his wife at the Pioneer Cemetery in Phoenix. He was a true son of the frontier.

R.I.P., Old Friend

ABOUT THE AUTHOR

Michael Zimmer grew up on a small Colorado horse ranch, and began to break and train horses for spending money while still in high school. An American history enthusiast from a very early age, he has done extensive research on the Old West. Zimmer is the author of several previous novels. His work has been praised by *Library Journal, Booklist,* and *Publishers Weekly* among others. Zimmer's *City of Rocks* (Five Star, 2012) was chosen by *Booklist* as one of the top ten Western novels of 2012. His recent publication of *The Poacher's Daughter* (Five Star, 2014) received a starred *Booklist* review that stated "all westerns should be this good" and was selected as the winner of the National Cowboy & Western Heritage Museum Western Heritage Wrangler Award for Outstanding Western Novel (2015). Zimmer now resides in Utah with his wife Vanessa, and two dogs. Learn more by visiting his Web site at www.michael-zimmer.com. Watch for his next Five Star Western novels, *The Rusted Sun* and *Billy Pinto's War.*